The Courtship of Edward Gardiner

A Pride and Prejudice Prequel

Alix James

Blog and newsletter: https://nicoleclarkston.com/

Facebook: https://www.facebook.com/NicoleClarkstonAuthor

Twitter: https://twitter.com/N_Clarkston

Amazon: https://www.amazon.com/Nicole-Clarkston

Austen Variations: http://austenvariations.com/

Contents

Dedication   V

1. Prologue   1

2. Chapter 1   4

3. Chapter 2   10

4. Chapter 3   16

5. Chapter 4   22

6. Chapter 5   28

7. Chapter 6   35

8. Chapter 7   40

9. Chapter 8   46

10. Chapter 9   52

11. Chapter 10   58

12. Chapter 11   65

13. Chapter 12   71

14. Chapter 13   79

15. Chapter 14   89

16. Chapter 15   94

17. Chapter 16   104

18. Chapter 17   113

19. Chapter 18   120

20. Chapter 19   126

21. Chapter 20   135

22. Chapter 21   142

23. Chapter 22   149

24. Chapter 23   155

25. Chapter 24   161

26. Chapter 25   168

27. Chapter 26   176

28. Chapter 27   184

29. Chapter 28   191

30. Chapter 29   199

31. Chapter 30   206

32. Chapter 31   213

33. Chapter 32   220

34. Epilogue   232

35. From Alix   241

36. No Such Thing as Luck   243

37. Love and Other Machines   264

Acknowledgments   272

To my people, of every shape and size. Thank you for all of your love and support.
Many of you will never read this book, but your friendship has meant worlds to me.

Prologue

"It is a truth universally acknowledged, that a single man in possession of a good fortune must be in want of a wife."
—*Jane Austen, Pride & Prejudice*

London

May 1800

"I AM SORRY, SIR, but I cannot marry you." Mae Rutherford, the golden-haired daughter of London's most successful silk merchant, proudly arched her lovely neck as she gazed out of the window.

"Miss Rutherford," the gentleman protested, his face quite pale, "I do not understand! We have kept company all season—indeed, everyone has been speaking of our engagement as a certainty!"

"You are not the only gentleman to solicit my attentions, sir. Do you not remember that I have danced more with Mr Ryan than with you this season?" The young lady lifted her chin yet more, but her back remained resolutely turned.

"My humblest regrets," he answered bitterly. "My presence was required in Meryton when my father died, as you must remember. I returned to your side as soon as was humanly possible, Miss Rutherford."

"My father and I," she turned at last, her voice flat and devoid of feeling, "believe that it would be better that I should instead accept Mr Ryan's offer."

He gazed at her in some astonishment. "I was not aware that such an offer had been made."

Miss Rutherford blinked quickly, and for the barest second, she drew her lips between her teeth to still their quivering. "My father expects...." Her voice broke and she closed her luminous eyes.

"Mae," Edward Gardiner stepped toward the woman he admired, taking her hand in his. He waited for her to look up once more in response to his soft, intimate tones. "I love you, and I know you hold me in your tender regards. I beg you—please accept me! I will prove myself to your father!"

A small sob sounded in the young lady's breast, but she bravely stifled it. "I cannot, Edward," she whispered, daring at last to use his name. "My father insists. Mr Ryan's prospects are...."

"I know what they are!" he cried in anguish. "Have I not sufficiently proven my devotion to you? Does your father doubt my ability to care for a wife? I have the means now to purchase a house for us! You know I secured a new warehouse this spring, and my yearlys are...."

"I am sorry, Edward," the young lady interrupted firmly. "My father has just entered a partnership with Mr Ryan's tobacco import company. They have high hopes for the future."

He stepped back, his eyes hardening. "You would sell yourself to seal your father's business dealings? I had thought better of you than that, Miss Rutherford."

"Edward!" she sobbed, reaching for his hand once more but finding it withheld. "Please do not say such things! I cannot bear for you to think ill of me. Please, can we not remain friends, as we have been? I do treasure our time together!"

His face pinched in heartbreak. "You know the answer as well as I, Mae. If you insist upon accepting Mr Ryan, I must disappear from your life. Are you quite certain of this course?"

Her beautiful face lowered, hiding it from his penetrating gaze. In a voice so soft he could barely hear, she murmured, "Please, Edward, you must understand."

Edward Gardiner swallowed hard. "I do understand. Goodbye, Miss Rutherford."

Chapter 1

Two Months Later

"U NCLE GAR'NER, UNCLE GAR'NER!"

Edward looked up from the paper spread upon his desk at the youthful voices. "Janey! Lizzy!" He jumped from his chair just in time to brace himself before two little girls piled into his arms. "Good afternoon, my dears!"

"Papa said you would take us to the Square!" demanded Lizzy pertly. "Can we go now, Uncle Gar'ner?"

"Lizzy," admonished her very slightly older sister. "Papa said we mustn't ask! We have to let him offer first!"

He laughed, giving each girl a peck on the cheek and setting their feet upon the floor. "We will go, I promise. Thomas!" he extended his hand toward his chuckling brother-in-law. "It is good to see you. I thought I was to journey to you on the morrow!"

"Mrs Bennet found herself unwell," Thomas winked. "We thought it best for you to avoid Hertfordshire altogether."

Gardiner smirked. "Ah, so you found an earlier departure was more strategic? Yes, I understand. I assume my sister has commissioned you with a heavy shopping list?"

"One would expect no less," Bennet grinned, drawing a long fluttering scrap of paper from his pocket and waving it before his brother-in-law's eyes. "I will need some assistance, I imagine."

Gardiner took the list. "I will send my clerk, and have it billed to my account. We can settle it later."

"Thank you, Edward," Bennet sighed in relief. "Though I had looked forward to a few hours in the lace shop."

"Pretty!" Lizzy cried in glee. Her sister promptly shushed her.

"Girls," Gardiner returned to his desk to draw two lovely, sweet treats from it. "I found these hidden in my drawer only this morning. Do you happen to know anyone who might like them?"

Two pairs of eyes—one sky blue, the other deep chocolate brown—gazed up at him in polite wonder. Both girls were gasping and nodding. "Please, Uncle?" begged Lizzy in her very most hesitant voice. Jane smiled shyly.

"First you must forgive your old Uncle for forgetting your birthdays. Let me see, now Janey, you must be twelve, and Lizzy, you must be fourteen. Is that right?"

"Uncle!" came the girlish squeals. "Jane is the oldest! She is eight now, and I am seven!" Lizzy puffed her little chest proudly. Jane giggled, allowing Lizzy to speak for her.

"My mistake. A gentleman ought never to assume a lady's age," he laughed, handing them the treats. The girls scampered away to a window seat to enjoy their sweets. Gardiner sighed. Seeing his innocent nieces was the first real pleasure he had experienced in some while.

"I believe this is my first time in your new warehouse." Bennet cast an appreciative gaze about. "Very fine, indeed! 'Tis a pity you had not purchased that house you spoke of; I imagine the girls would have admired it excessively."

Edward clenched his eyes and strayed a bit closer to his nieces so he might enjoy their chatter. He offered no comments, refusing to rise to the dangled bait, but Thomas Bennet needed no one's participation to seek his amusement. He wandered over to the desk. "This is a very interesting edition of the Times," Bennet noted, a sly edge to his voice. He turned the page over, observing the date. "A week old already, I see."

Gardiner turned back to his brother, his shoulders sagging. "I have read it."

Bennet picked up the paper, reading aloud. "Miss Mae Rutherford, daughter of Warner Rutherford of Cheapside, to Mr David Ryan...."

"Please, I beg you, Thomas!" Gardiner snatched the paper from Bennet's hands and crumpled it into a twisted knot, then threw it haphazardly in the direction of his wastebasket.

Bennet's face, for once, softened with sympathy. "Cheer up, Edward. The greatest days of a man's life are those heady days of courtship, where one's love blossoms sweet and fragrant. You partook of such delights yet have been spared the mundane drudgery of marriage."

"You are blasted little comfort, Thomas." He pressed his fingers into his eyes, longing to quell the pounding in his head and heart.

"No, perhaps not. I am afraid I do not paint the marital estate as prettily as some, but no matter. I am sure that in time, some other young thing will catch your eye, and you will once more have the pleasure of spending your time in such a pursuit."

Gardiner sank heavily into his chair. "It was not the thrill of the pursuit which I had anticipated, but the comfort of companionship."

Bennet made a wry face. "If it is a steady and reasonable companion you seek, perhaps you ought to rent a room out to your clerk. I doubt, sir, that you will find such an amiable and sensible relationship with a woman. That has not been my experience, at any rate, and I've six of them in my family."

Gardiner exhaled slowly. "Not all women are as flighty as my sister. I did warn you, you know."

"And that warning I took with as much gravity as any young man, dazzled by a pair of fine eyes. You will do no less when your time comes, mark my words."

"I had hoped…" Gardiner propped his elbows on his desk and covered his mouth as his chin sank into his hands. "Well, never mind. It is done, and we have a journey to Sheffield for a diversion. I am much obliged to you for suggesting it. I have long wished to travel beyond Hertfordshire to the north."

Bennet scowled. "Yes, well, I tell you, it was not wholly undertaken for your benefit, though I might like to claim the credit of such thoughtfulness. My younger brother Thaddeus is ailing, as I think I wrote you. He claims I must come at once. I know not why he settled in such a god-forsaken territory!"

"I am grateful to you for inviting me, nonetheless. I am still in awe, however, that you managed to leave Fanny behind! Even unwell, as you say, I cannot believe she would permit herself to be left at home with adventure afoot."

Bennet waved a hand in careless dismissal. "She thinks little enough of business travel and wants nothing to do with my brother—he still stands to inherit the estate, you know, and she cannot forgive him that. I promised her that I would have Hill bring her to Town to meet us upon our return. She thought that a suitable compromise."

"And how are the littler ones? Mary must be nearly five now, is that right?"

"I imagine your memory might be better than mine," Bennet answered drily, though his eyes twinkled. "She is nearly as tall as Lizzy now, but she developed the very slightest cough last night, and Mrs Bennet insisted that she remain in bed with the others. She was outraged that I would bring Jane and Lizzy along. I am determined to prove my dear wife's concerns unfounded when I return with both girls safe and sound."

"Ah, things become clearer now!" grinned Edward. "Thomas," his voice changed as he looked his brother-in-law seriously in the eye. "I know you are doing this to distract me from my troubles, but a tour of either pleasure or business with a moping brother and two tender children is not normally the sort of journey to interest you. Truly, if you would prefer to call it off, I should not be offended. I can engage a nurse to look after them. You would be more than welcome to leave the girls here in London during your travels."

"I find that a perfectly agreeable proposal, and no doubt Jane would as well, but I leave it to you to inform Lizzy of the change in plans. I do not relish it."

"I would not wish to disappoint her," Gardiner laughed.

"In addition," Bennet continued, beginning to pull down a ledger from the shelf, "your natural gratitude for my company and that of my very charming daughters will, of course, compel you to offer to pay for your fair share of the traveling expenses. I've no doubt as well that we will be far more comfortable traveling in your carriage than by post." Bennet lifted a sage brow, his eyes twinkling in that peculiar way of his, which Gardiner knew to mean that the man was only half joking.

"Naturally," Gardiner returned evenly, shaking his head in wonder. Of all the men he knew, only Bennet could be so blunt and yet not give offence.

"Well, now, I see you have some new books in inventory. I thought I might borrow a few for the journey. I may read in as much peace in a coach as in my own library, may I not? Ah, here..." he traced down the sheet of book orders with his finger, his brows jumping in interest at each new title.

Gardiner chuckled. "It is fortunate for me, then, that I began recently to carry books. I see now why you detoured so far out of your way before beginning the journey."

"Indeed," Bennet mused without looking up.

Chapter 2

MADELINE FAIRBANKS EASED OFF her stool with a sigh of relief, dragging the heavy portfolio from the desk as she did so. Another barley season's numbers were tallied and committed to paper, most of the spring wool from the local flocks had gone to market, and she might now look forward to a few weeks of relative peace. With an air of finality, she slid the thick accounting book into its place on the shelf.

Her father's soft tread caused her to turn with a smile at his arrival. "Ah," he beamed in pleasure. "I am glad to see you not working."

"I have finished, Papa," she replied with satisfaction.

His weathered brow wrinkled as he came forward. Lifting her hand with his own, he turned it over to inspect the ink smudges upon the lower part of her palm. "So you have. It is not right that you should take on so much of the bookkeeping, my dear. You ought to be out with the other young girls—looking at bonnets, enjoying an occasional picnic...."

"And which young girls might those be?" she teased. "Miss Mayweather married last month, and Miss Simmons has gone to Bath, as a companion to her aunt."

"You were always such friends with Miss Tuttle and Miss Perry," her father protested. "I scarcely hear a word these days of you spending time with them."

"Oh, had you not heard, Papa? Why, it is the most splendid news! Miss Perry is engaged to a gentleman from Leicester, and they are to wed next month. Miss Tuttle had to take on a position as a nurse. You know how she dreaded it, but she has found the most wonderful position at Pemberley. She cannot often leave her post of course, but she writes notes, and says that the little Darcy child is *such* a darling. I do think it a perfect place for her, and she is still quite near enough to visit her mother when she has a holiday."

Mr Fairbanks nodded thoughtfully. "The Darcys will treat her kindly, I daresay. Such a pity about the poor Mistress! I do hope our Miss Tuttle can be of some comfort to the dear child."

"I am certain she shall," Madeline asserted confidently. "Someday I should like to walk the grounds. She tells me they are perfectly delicious!"

"Madeline," her father frowned, "I do not care for such florid speech. Choose simple words with meaning, my daughter."

"Yes, Papa," she sobered. "Shall I make you some tea?"

Mr Fairbanks sighed and glanced about the room. "You are certain that the corn totals were accurate for Mr Baker? He has bid for a contract with the Jenks' poultry farm, and he wished his last season's numbers to be reviewed."

"I checked them twice, Papa. Also, I went over Mr Williams' ledgers and found where he had made an error in his market estimates. I corrected it and sent a copy already."

Mr Fairbanks brushed a weary hand over his forehead. "I think it is time I retired, my dear. You have done more of my own work than I have these past months. Next year, I will hire a clerk."

"What could a clerk do that I cannot?" she soothed, looping an arm through her father's. "I enjoy assisting you, Papa, and if we can spare the expense, that is all the more we can save for Robert's schooling."

"It is not the work of a young lady to fund her brother's education," her father admonished. "You ought to marry, Madeline."

"And someday I shall, Papa," she agreed cheerfully. "If only Mr Lawrence had not such a dreadful habit of drink!"

"It is no laughing matter, my dear! A young lady simply cannot take over her father's bookkeeping firm, and though Robert is bound to do far better than I, he must look to his own future. I must see you well settled, Madeline. You would not wish to become a nanny yourself, would you?"

"Come, Papa," she laughed lightly, "it is not so dire as that! Here, rest by the fire and I shall bring you your tea."

"That would be lovely, my dear." He sank gratefully into his worn chair and gazed lovingly after the retreating form of his eldest child. He had to squint his eyes a deal more these days to do so. Before she had gone many paces at all, he could not have made her out from the rest of the furnishings, save for the soft melody she hummed as she moved about the house.

He rested his head against the wing of his chair. A new clerk might save his eyes a precious little, perhaps delaying his necessary retirement by a year or two, but the additional salary would mean all the less he could put away for his children. He chewed his cheeks thoughtfully, wondering if the expense might be recovered in time, or if it would prove folly. He truly had very little choice. Perhaps if he found a proper assistant, Madeline might be persuaded to spread her own wings.

"Uncle, puh-lease, hurry!" begged the plaintive voice of a very impatient seven-year-old. "Papa, you said we were going to feed the geese!" The dark-haired little maid, ringlets bouncing, hopped and wrung her hands with the very agony of waiting at the front door.

"Lizzy, what have I taught you?" replied the indifferent tones of Mr Bennet.

The girl blew a distraught huff of air through her lower lip, causing the brown curls over her eyes to feather and fall into disarray. "Ūnus, duo, trēs, quattuor, quīnque, sex, septem, octō, novem, decem, now may we go to the park?" she rambled, without once pausing for breath.

Gardiner, who had begun an excessively leisurely search for his hat—he really did enjoy watching her simmer—raised a brow. "You are teaching your daughters Latin?"

"Anything to keep them occupied," groaned the beleaguered father. "Jane gives me little enough trouble, but Lizzy is forever invading my library!"

Gardiner chuckled, then extended his hand to his eldest niece. Jane, he thought, was a treasure often overlooked by her father simply by virtue of her even disposition. She was easily the beauty of the two, and the envy of every mother with her cherubic face and her habit of keeping her clothing to its freshly starched perfection.

It was the second child, however, who seemed to demand her father's attention. Where Jane might be likened to a garden rose—deliciously fragrant, soft, and perfectly formed—Lizzy was more like a wild spray of pungent lavender. She was clearly the greater challenge to parent, but complete opposites that the girls were, they were thoroughly devoted to one another.

It was going to be interesting, he reflected, to watch these two little flowers grow to maturity. Both promised to be lovely in their own way. In another ten or fifteen years, Jane would likely be the sweetheart of the county, and it would be a lucky man who won her hand. Lizzy, however... he shook his head. She would need a husband with an iron will! Whoever the man should be, Gardiner decided, he had best win the girl's respect early, for Lizzy would not be apt to grant him a second chance.

Today, though, the last thoughts he wanted to linger on were those of marriage. He very much looked forward to the afternoon's walk to the park, despite the deliberate delays he had made to torment his niece. It was an innocent diversion. The weather was pleasant, and his companions amiable. What could possibly weigh his heart down today?

A quarter of an hour later, he found out. Approaching the paved walkway, he glimpsed the figure he had thought never to see again. "Is that not...?" Bennet began to ask, then thought better of it.

Gardiner swallowed hard and began to turn his steps in another direction when the lady and her companion saw him. "Gardiner!" boomed the cheerful voice of the gentleman.

His fingers clenched nervously until Jane began to squirm, her hand in discomfort. "Ryan," he smiled tightly as the others approached. "It is a pleasure to see you and Mrs Ryan again," he lied.

"Likewise. I was sorry to hear you could not come to the wedding. I hope your sister has recovered?" Ryan slid his gaze between the other two men, a knowing hint to his smile.

"She... why, yes, I should say...."

"My wife is recovering well, I thank you," Bennet interjected, cocking a sly eyebrow at his brother-in-law. "We were most fortunate that my brother could come to us for the fortnight. He was of very great service."

"I would imagine so," Ryan answered slowly.

The new Mrs Ryan kept her eyes low, raising them only when her husband tipped his hat. "Good day, Gardiner," he grinned. At this, she met the tortured gaze of her former admirer with an expression full of regret. She said not a word and turned away, following her husband's lead.

Gardiner let out a long sigh, closing his eyes. He opened them at the clap of his brother's hand on his shoulder. "Come, girls," Bennet was saying, "I see the duck pond just this way!"

Jane followed her father happily, but Lizzy remained, staring at her uncle. "May I help you, my dear?" he asked hesitantly. There was no telling what the precocious child had perceived.

"She should have married you," the girl asserted.

"I beg your pardon?" he laughed in surprise.

"Mama says she was greedy. I think she was afraid. She is sorry now."

"I must ask you not to speak of this further, Elizabeth," he commanded firmly. "These are not matters of concern to little girls."

She tossed her dark curls carelessly, apparently deciding to obey—for now. "She is not nice enough, Uncle," she added flippantly as she placed her hand in his. "And not pretty enough, either."

Gardiner rolled his eyes and decided in that moment that if he ever had a daughter of his own, he would take more care to check her tongue.

Chapter 3

THE PARTY OF TRAVELERS departed from London early the next morning. They were to journey slowly and stop frequently because of the tender ages of the children, but Gardiner could not have objected. Indeed, he began to appreciate his brother's wily genius. Their wonder at the scenery about them caused the girls to chatter constantly, providing him the benign distraction his wounded heart required. Bennet, on the other hand, was able to bury himself in a book and allow his vivacious daughters to entertain their uncle. He spent the better part of that day in peaceful oblivion, while Gardiner and his nieces shared their perspectives on the view.

"Where are we stopping tonight, Uncle?"

Jane, who had taken the seat next to him, peered around him at a particularly beautiful field rolling by the window. It was the second day of their journey, and already Gardiner felt some of his cares easing. "Northampton, I believe, my dear," he chucked her chin affectionately. "In a few days we shall be traveling through the Peaks district. Have you heard of it?"

"No," she shook her head innocently, crystal blue eyes wide in curiosity.

"I have, Uncle!" Elizabeth, her attention torn between her book, the scenery, and the conversation, had nearly missed an opportunity to impress her uncle with her knowledge of geography. "It is to the north of Leicester, and the mountains are so big, and the rocks...."

"Yes, yes, Lizzy," he quieted her. "I think you will like it very much, Jane," he assured his elder niece. "I have heard the area is one of the most beautiful in all of the kingdom. I am looking forward to discovering it for myself!"

Jane nodded silently, her eyes smiling back her pleasure, and lapsed into peaceful enjoyment of the countryside. Gardiner, too, trained his gaze on the rolling green landscape. Yes, this was precisely the escape he had needed! The more distance he gained from London, the better his perspective became.

It is perhaps only human nature to begin to search that which has been irretrievably lost for some reason to no longer regret it. So it was with the jilted suitor, who had only weeks ago thought to find all of his earthly happiness in the being of a certain blonde maiden. Having now no means of recapturing his visions of domestic felicity with the young lady in question, he began to examine his feelings more critically.

As a very young man, when the dream of having a wife and family of his own were yet unattainable, he had formed some expectations of the sort of wife he would prefer. She ought to be clever, he decided—that much was not negotiable. Though it was not the proper fashion, he wished for the kind of woman who could help him with some of the more puzzling decisions with which a man of business must wrestle. If all a wife could do was to lend a sympathetic and intelligent ear, he would ask it of the woman who would one day share his home.

He frowned as a humiliating conviction dawned. Mae did not suffer for any lack of intelligence, but she had never shown any interest in cultivating her mind. Even less desire had she for listening to his business matters. That, she had always told him, was not a thing with which young ladies ought to trouble themselves. Young Edward Gardiner, starry-eyed and infatuated, had assumed that she was correct. After all, he had never met *any* young woman who would care to hear him unburden his concerns to her. It had seemed likely that it was he who had formed unrealistic expectations.

He had now, he thought, an opportunity to test that presumption. Did there exist somewhere in the kingdom a respectable and genteel young woman who possessed the sharp mind and keen interest he desired to help him think through his dilemmas? Could she be the sort of woman who would sit patiently and companionably at his side in the evening after a long day, or were they all after the pattern of his fidgety sister? There was yet the most staggering question of all; if such a rare creature in fact lived, would she have him?

A jostling at his side returned his attention to the more angelic of his two nieces as she shifted for a better view. His thoughts now forming to a conclusion, he fixed his gaze upon the girl. What he would give to find a woman like Jane might be someday! Such a woman would possess the sweetness and gentility he longed for to ease his cares, and the wisdom to shepherd his household in the ways of grace.

"Papa!" cried the lesser saint among the two cherubs in the coach.

Grimacing, Edward Gardiner shifted his gaze. Elizabeth was thrusting her book before her father's face. *Is Bennet ever going to control his daughters?* he thought ungenerously.

"Lizzy, do calm yourself!" groused the father, annoyed at the interruption to his own book.

"But Papa, I found out how far it is to Sheffield! Look! We started this morning from Leighton, and we traveled thirty miles yesterday. Tomorrow we will stay in Leicester, and the day after that, Nottingham—just like Robin Hood! Or shall we stay in Derby? I think it is the more direct...."

"Lizzy," her father interrupted. "Do have mercy on my poor head. Read your book quietly, like a good girl. That's the way," he encouraged. The lass shifted back to her own side of the coach and, looking a little hurt, took back her book.

Gardiner smiled as a new idea struck him. No, the ideal woman for him would not be an older version of Jane, sweet as she was. She would be a mixture of the two. She would be graceful and serene, yet vivacious when called for. She ought to possess that same spark of eager intelligence which Elizabeth so regularly displayed—but not too much! A very little of Elizabeth's brand of energy went a long way.

THE THIRD DAY PASSED in much the same manner. Acres upon acres of glorious countryside rolled by the carriage windows, punctuated by coaching stations and small towns. Leicester proved to be a much larger affair than Gardiner had imagined. They stopped early in the afternoon, and he reflected with a smile that Bennet was certainly in no hurry to arrive at his brother's side, else they could have traveled much farther each day.

He had wondered at first what would have inspired Bennet to bring his two daughters on such a journey, but Bennet was nothing if not cunning. The man may have disliked direct confrontation, but he was not above employing any means at his disposal to frustrate whoever might be perceived as an annoyance. Perhaps Bennet doubted that his brother was truly faring so poorly and merely looked to this trip as a chance to escape his cares at home for a time. Rarely was the man able to find so many hours together to simply enjoy his book.

Whatever the case, the girls did not seem to mind that they were but an excuse to allow their father the delay he desired. Elizabeth relished every moment of their travels, while Jane appeared to be as contented in the open-windowed carriage as she might have been anywhere else. This afternoon, however, as Gardiner helped her down from the carriage, he thought Jane looked more weary than she usually did. He quickly dismissed it as the natural effect of the journey contrasted against her sister's bubbling energy.

He briefly strolled with the girls through the streets as Bennet secured their lodgings for the evening. By the time they returned to the coach, he had begun to think himself right about little Jane. Her steps were coming heavier now and her eyelids drooped, but she refused to complain. "Janey," he spoke soothingly to the child, "Why don't you and Lizzy go on up to your room for a little rest? Your papa will come for you in a while."

Jane agreed, seeming relieved. By the evening meal, she appeared much recuperated, and the travelers made plans for an early morning departure. The next day would take them into some of the most breathtaking scenery on their journey, and while Bennet cared little enough for that, the others most certainly wished to explore Derbyshire upon their arrival. Gardiner had long desired to try his hand at trout fishing, and he nursed a rather unrealistic hope that this one evening in the region might be his opportunity.

"Uncle," Elizabeth yawned as she was sent off to bed, "will we be able to climb the peaks?"

"Of course, my dear!" he teased. "Right to the very top of the tallest mountain. Shall we make it a race?"

"Uncle," she crossed her arms and looked up at him with all the practical seriousness of a seven-year-old. "That is not fair. Your legs are longer."

"Perhaps," he agreed with equal gravity. "I shall give you a head start, then. Come, Lizzy, off to bed with Jane."

She yawned again and threw her short little arms around his neck, hugging him tightly. "G'night Uncle Gar'ner," she sighed into his cheek.

Warmed, he returned the child's embrace. *This*, he thought to himself, *easily makes up for all the headaches!* Lizzy's heartfelt abandon wholly eclipsed Jane's placid affection. Though he felt certain that the two girls both held him in equal devotion, it was Lizzy's care-free expression which brought him the most joy. As he watched her scamper away, he straightened and mentally added another quality which he would seek in a woman. She ought to openly demonstrate her feelings... but modestly, of course.

Chapter 4

"MISS FAIRBANKS, HOW DO you do today?"

Madeline paused only fractionally as she recognized the voice. "Good day, Mr Lawrence," she answered politely as she continued her walk through the town.

The gentleman was not eager to be left behind. "I was on my way to call upon your father! It has been too long since I have had the pleasure of your company, Miss Fairbanks."

"Indeed, Mr Lawrence," she nodded, stopping fully. "He is at home now; I am certain he would be gratified to see you as well." She wrinkled her nose. She never had cared for the smell of ale, and it accompanied Mr Lawrence's person with unusual potency today.

"May I see you home, Miss Fairbanks?" Lawrence removed his hat, revealing his thinning sandy pate, and proffered his arm. "It would be my pleasure!" he assured her.

"I thank you, Mr Lawrence, but I have other business." She started away again, but he caught up to her.

"Might I ask to accompany you, then?"

She turned rather firmly. "I am afraid my business is of a personal nature, Mr Lawrence. Good day, sir." She turned abruptly to open the door to the nearest establishment, which happened to be the Lion's Head Inn. Allowing the door to swing closed behind herself, she drew a deep sigh. It made her uncomfortable to behave so abruptly with anyone, but there was little else a woman of good manners could do to discourage an unwelcome suitor. She would not sully herself by rudely declaring to the man what she thought of him, nor would she quietly endure much time in his company.

"Ah, Madeline! Good morning. What can I do for you?" The innkeeper's wife materialized instantly at the jingling of the door, her welcoming smile even brighter than her freshly starched apron.

"I only stopped by to wish you a good morning, Mrs Porter." Madeline forced herself into an easier posture, almost believing her own words. Mrs Porter was, after all, one of the kindest, most motherly women in all of Lambton, and Madeline had developed a special affection for the woman after she had lost her own mother.

Mrs Porter leaned slightly to her right, peering over Madeline's shoulder through the window. "Mr Lawrence?"

Madeline winced. "I am afraid so."

Mrs Porter chuckled. "Come, then, as you will not be wishing to leave straight away, I've some fresh drapes to hang. You can lend me a hand, dear."

The two puttered amiably about—Madeline helping with odd jobs at the inn until long after Mr Lawrence was sure to have gone. She liked spending spare time here, but it had been some while since she had done so. Her father's business typically kept her otherwise engaged. After a short while of checking the candles, dusting off the mantelpiece, and refilling the cream and sugar dishes in the main dining area, the two settled into Mrs Porter's kitchen for a mid-morning repast.

"Madeline," Mrs Porter began, her voice lightly scolding, "Why have you not found some nice man to marry?"

"You do not think Mr Lawrence nice?" Madeline inquired, her eyes wide in mock astonishment.

"He is a nice customer in the tavern. I would not recommend his company to a young lady," scoffed the older woman. "A terrible reputation he has! Why, I heard that last month, he was before the magistrate for breaking into Jenks' poultry barn. He frightened those hens so badly they did not lay for days!" She shook her head, tsking between her teeth. "There is no making sense of a man who drinks."

"I have no intention of trying. It is a pity you had only the one son," Madeline winked.

"There are others," protested Mrs Porter. "What of that cotton miller who travels through every fortnight... let me see... Davis, is that his name?"

Madeline raised her eyebrows. "I had no idea that the local selection of gentlemen had grown so thin, Mrs Porter, that you would be suggesting a man twice my age to me."

"He has a steady income, my dear," frowned the older woman. "But you are quite right, a young lady of your looks and character ought to do better." She pressed her lips together as her eyes glazed over in thought. "I think that Mr Williams chap who is to come in a fortnight about purchasing the inn may be single... but I am not certain of it."

"Would you suggest that I ensnare myself a soldier of the regiment when next we have some in town?"

"Not at all! A soldier, my love, can barely feed himself."

"Oh, but they are so very handsome!" Madeline teased. "I do love those red coats; they always look so distinguished!"

"Handsome or plain, my dear, you must have something to live on. No, do not set your eye on any soldier. Perhaps you ought to have gone to London for the Season."

"Mrs Porter, I cannot leave my father. I am quite convinced that if I am but patient enough, my path will be made clear."

"That path," admonished the older woman, "may well be spinster-hood! You are already two and twenty, my dear."

"And what if it is?" she answered with more cheer than she felt. "I would not be the first, nor shall I be the last. I would prefer many things to life with a man I could not respect."

Mrs Porter clucked, shaking her head. "I admire your faith, Madeline. I only hope you shall not meet with disappointment. A spinster's life can be a very lonely one."

Madeline sighed. "I know, Mrs Porter, but I shall not be persuaded to matrimony merely for the sake of convenience or company. I hope to find love, the very deepest kind. I believe that one day I shall."

The innkeeper's wife drained her teacup with a very faint roll of her eyes. "Fanciful notions do not give you a home, my dear. You have always been too choosy. Be careful that you do not reject what Providence sends your way!"

As the rolling terrain gradually gave way to the rugged beauty of the mountains, the occupants of the carriage looked on in rapturous silence. All, that is, except for Mr Bennet. He glanced up frequently, when a gasp from one of his daughters heralded a stunning new vista, but always his eyes returned to his book. A scene did not change so quickly, after all, that he might not be able to enjoy his book for a time before another new sight could capture his fancy.

The roads were somewhat less frequented now, and more than once, the carriage startled wildlife along their route. The girls, though no strangers to the countryside themselves, always rushed to the windows in delight. As the day wore on, however, Gardiner's sharp eyes watched Jane's enthusiasm ebb and fade. By the middle of the afternoon, she lay her head listlessly back against the squabs and only followed the scenery with her eyes.

"Janey?" He put a hand on her little shoulder at length. "Are you well?"

She blinked languidly. "I am tired, Uncle. Will we be stopping soon?"

"A few hours more, I think," he frowned. He glanced in annoyance at his brother-in-law, who had scarcely seen fit to raise his eyes from his book. *Fool!* he could have spat. Bennet's desire for delay and distraction had thoroughly worn the girl nearly to the point of illness. She ought to have been left at home with her mother and... *oh*.

He sighed with realization. Jane had apparently carried with her the trifling cold which had troubled her younger siblings at home. Though it might not have caused her much concern there, as she was older, now she was weary from travel and more vulnerable.

He looked up to survey Elizabeth, seated across the carriage from him. She was as bright and undiminished as ever, her sparkling eyes devouring everything they touched upon. She had always had the hardiest constitution of any child he had ever known, but even she might be struck low under the circumstances. Jane would certainly be in no condition to travel many more days, and Elizabeth ought to be protected while she yet could be.

At the next coaching station, Gardiner pulled his brother-in-law aside to discuss his concerns. Bennet, oblivious as ever to the nuances of his family, glanced back at his daughter in surprise. Jane leaned quietly against a beam of the coaching inn, watching but not participating in Elizabeth's spinning pursuit of a passing butterfly.

"She looks well enough to me," Bennet shrugged. "She is not as lively as Lizzy, you know, and we are all fatigued."

"Thomas," he spoke lowly, "Look at her cheeks, how flushed they have grown this afternoon. I fear Jane ought not to continue as far as Sheffield. You could greatly endanger her health if she is not allowed to rest."

"We cannot return to London any more quickly than pressing on toward Sheffield. Once there, we will no doubt be detained some days, and she can recover there. Come, I see the horses have been changed, and we only delay our arrival in Derby this evening."

Gardiner pressed his lips thinly. One day, he thought grimly to himself, Bennet's careless disregard for the keeping of his daughters would cost the family dearly. But there, his brother was correct, and their best option at the moment was to once again mount the carriage and continue on toward Derby.

Chapter 5

THE UNUSUALLY LOUD BANGING of doors without raised the lad's eyes from his book with an expression of faint disapproval. Such outbursts were never tolerated in this house, but he felt reasonably certain that he understood the cause. There was a dedicated staff member whose sole duty it was to quiet the creator of the disturbance... but in this case, no one would be scolding harshly.

Before dropping again to his book, his gaze caught the sparkling green of the fields beckoning to him through the windows. His young body quivered in anticipation. *One hour longer*, he promised himself, and he would have finished his studies for the day and could enjoy the glorious early summer sunshine. Doggedly, he returned his attention to the pages before him.

Not half a minute later, the door to the library was next to fall victim to the pillager without. At the very first twitch of some unseen hand on the outer latch, the boy's deep brown eyes fixed patiently upon it. It fluttered hesitantly at first, and then with a great jerk, as though some small figure had to leap for it, the handle was thrust downward. The door swung open with a rush. Standing there, like a miniature plundering raider, was a starched and primped little girl in pink ribbons.

Her great round eyes searched the room, squinting against the sun from the window, until she found the figure she sought. "Will!" She scurried over to the boy as quickly as her short little legs could carry her. Not caring that she caused him to drop his expensive book, she dove into his arms.

The boy sighed, embracing his little sister. "Sweetling, did you run from Nurse again?"

She shook her head vehemently, her face burrowed into his chest.

"Look at me, Georgie," he commanded, but his youthful voice lacked the force of authority he tried to affect. His sister did not respond.

"Father will be very angry," he warned. This had the effect he desired. She sat back upon his lap but fisted her little hands over her eyes. She continued rubbing them a long while, doing her best to avoid looking at him.

"Georgie," he spoke gently, "you must not make things hard for Miss Tuttle. She is here to look out for you."

"I don't like her," the child pouted, dropping one hand to peek at him.

"Why not, sweetling? Is she unkind to you?"

"She makes me eat awful things."

The boy laughed softly. "What is it this time? Peas? Or is it carrots today? You cannot grow strong and beautiful on pastries, little love."

The small girl at last dropped both hands, but her lips quivered. "Mama never made me eat peas," she sniffled.

There was no surer thing she could have said to win her brother's sympathy. His heart broke anew and his eyes pricked with unbidden tears. "I know, Georgie," he choked, pulling her close.

It was in this tender embrace that the harried nanny at last found them. She rushed into the library and skittered to a halt when she discovered the identity of the person comforting her young charge. "Forgive me, Master Fitzwilliam! I was..."

"Do not be concerned," he assured the woman, doing his best to adopt his father's confident manner. "Please allow her to remain with me a while."

Miss Tuttle curtseyed and left them, perhaps feeling relieved that it was the young Fitzwilliam who had discovered her error rather than Mr Darcy. The younger Darcy still possessed the gentle empathy his little sister required and would not be so likely to scold the failings of a new nanny.

The boy pressed his sister back by the shoulders to look at her tear-streaked little face. She blinked, then wiped her eyes on the sleeve of her dress.

"Georgie, you ought to use a handkerchief," he chided her softly.

She sighed and wiped her eyes again on the other sleeve. "Will, can you play with me?" she begged.

He looked again to the window which had called to him before and studied it in silence a moment. "How would you like to go for a ride with me, Georgie?" he suggested.

She brightened instantly. "Can I ride by myself?"

He laughed, rumpling the carefully arranged curls over her forehead. "Only if we stay in the yard. I thought you would prefer to roam a little farther. Come, let us ask Mrs Reynolds to pack us some cold meats."

"**T**HOMAS." GARDINER SAT HEAVILY down at the table of the Derby inn. "Jane is too ill to travel tomorrow. We must remain here a day or two so she may rest!"

Bennet gazed drowsily at the fire of the common room. "A night of good sleep is surely all she needs, Edward. Children often shake these little fevers quickly. You will see, tomorrow she will be right as rain."

"And what if it is more serious, Thomas? She is weary from travel and cannot recover properly in a bouncing, draughty carriage."

Bennet raised a brow, regarding his brother-in-law with a practiced casual air. "Then I expect she will die of this ailment and I may then send word to my brother that my arrival has been delayed, or perhaps prevented altogether."

Gardiner fairly snarled in disgust. "Come, Thomas, do be serious! We must decide how to proceed. Even a single day of rest may be all she needs, but it is unfair to ask her to continue in the morning. You ought not to have brought the girls at all!" he finished angrily.

"I thought you enjoyed their company," Bennet returned mildly. "Besides, what better way for them to learn their geography?"

Gardiner bit back an exasperated sigh. "You know I adore the girls, but this is not a leisure trip, Thomas. You have a destination you must reach, and though we are traveling gently, we are not at liberty to do as we please. We must think of what is best for the girls! What if you were to go on without us?"

Bennet gave a little snort. "Lizzy would be most disappointed," he mused wryly. "No, Edward, it is not possible. Why, it is not even proper for you to remain as their sole guardian!"

Gardiner grumbled. "You know I would look after them as though they were my own. We are not talking about young ladies with delicate reputations, but children, Thomas! They are old enough to care for their own personal needs, and surely, we can find a local woman in need of temporary employment to help them."

Bennet raised his eyes speculatively to the barmaid serving drinks across the room. Gardiner caught the direction of his gaze. "A *respectable* woman, Thomas!" he hissed.

Bennet shook his head and waved a dismissive hand. "I see little alternative but to continue on, Edward. We shall make certain that she is bundled properly and that every consideration is made for her comfort. We will be in Sheffield in two more days."

Gardiner leaned back in resignation. "Very well, Thomas."

THE PARTY PRESSED ON the following morning, after Gardiner insisted on an hour's delay for Jane's comfort. It was still clear to him that the girl was growing steadily more miserable. She drooped and very quickly fell asleep against the side of the carriage.

Gardiner, glaring daggers at his brother-in-law, tugged the child over to his own shoulder so that he might support her better. Brushing his hand over her forehead, he determined that, indeed, she had developed a marked fever. He had no experience in such matters, but he did not think it a dangerous fever... so long as she was able to rest!

Even little Lizzy, in her boundless energy and untiring zest for the scenery, had grown concerned for her sister. She watched silently as her uncle tried to offer some comfort to Jane and soon moved to sit on the other side of her sister. The two held her hands and cradled her head while Bennet observed them in stoic silence.

At the first coaching station, the concerned father finally overcame the detached lover of convenience. Bennet was the first to dismount the carriage, and stepping quickly, hailed the nearest groom. "Pardon me," Gardiner heard him say, "is there vacancy for a party requiring three rooms?"

"Aye, sir, but 'tis no' a fair place for the childer," came a gruff voice. "Best press on if yo' can."

"What is the name of the next stop on the road?"

"Lambton," the unseen man replied. "Not twelve miles on. Not much of a town, sir, mostly a farmin' village. There be two 'spectable inns and a decent place to sup, sir." Bennet acknowledged the man and then Gardiner heard his boots crunching the gravel as he went to learn more of the town.

Gardiner had chosen to remain behind in the carriage rather than unsettle Jane. In a few moments, his brother-in-law had returned. He waited stonily for the other to speak.

"Well," Bennet lifted his hat, rubbing his forehead thoughtfully. "I trust you will not object to remaining a day or two with the girls?"

"I suppose not," Gardiner answered evenly. "It seems we have little enough choice, do we not?"

Bennet sighed heavily, his eyes on his firstborn. She still slept on her uncle's shoulder, her angelic face thoroughly flushed and her little rosebud lips slightly swollen. "No," he replied slowly. "It seems we do not."

He entered the carriage once more and resumed his seat. "I have asked about the town. It sounds as though it will be comfortable enough. The Rose and Crown is said to have more spacious accommodations, but the Lion's Head is the more economical. I thought, since you would require little for only yourself and the girls need their own room, not to mention the hire of some attendant, if we can find her...."

"I am sure the Lion's Head will do nicely. If we have any qualms whatsoever upon seeing the place, we can alter that plan. Will you be staying, or proceeding on directly?"

Bennet was still gazing at his daughter, his face now showing faint symptoms of worry. "We shall see how she settles in, Edward, and what manner of help we may find. We shall see."

Chapter 6

MADELINE POKED A NEEDLE through the very last bit of the final knot. Finished! She snipped the thread and held her completed project up for inspection. It was an embroidered apron she had begun months ago for her dear friend, Mrs Porter. It had been originally intended to be a Christmas present, but the demands of the past year had forced her to prepare a smaller gift for that holiday. She had picked it up now and again, when she had a few spare moments. The other morning spent in her mentor's company had inspired her to finish it at last.

"Papa?" She rose from her seat, folding the apron as she walked toward the back of the house. "Papa?" She peered into his little study, but it was in the kitchen that she found him. "What are you doing in here, Papa?"

He glanced up. "The parlour is a little too warm today, and I find the light better to read by here."

She drew near, looking him over in concern. "Your eyes are troubling you again?"

"Again? Still, my dear." He pulled his nearly useless glasses from his face and squinted at them in frustration.

"Papa, I am going to call on Mrs Porter. Is there anything I can get you first, or do you need anything while I am out?"

"No, nothing," he waved her off. "Wait—stay a moment. Will you take the letter from my desk to be posted? It should be ready."

"Of course, Papa." She leaned over his shoulder and dropped a kiss on his cheek. "I shall return shortly."

Her father grunted a nondescript reply as she departed. She fetched her bonnet and spencer and lastly retrieved the letter for her father. The post office, she determined, would be her first stop, though it would cause her to step round the longer way when she went to the inn. No matter, for her spirits were high and the day was lovely. She might, in fact, have wished for a longer walk.

She delivered the letter and sucked in a delicious breath of the summer air as she stepped out of the office door. She loved this time of the year. Spring had spoken of its promises long enough, and the time had come to deliver them. Closing her eyes briefly as she strolled down the street, she relished the fragrance of the growing hay fields near the village. So enraptured was she by the vibrancy of everything touching her senses, she tipped her chin yet higher and claimed another refreshing breath. It seemed the whole world was warm and alive!

Without warning, something else warm and very much alive assaulted her about the knees. Madeline nearly stumbled in shock. She opened her eyes and put her hands protectively forward, fearful of either falling or dropping her precious parcel. "B-beg your pardon!" tumbled automatically from her lips.

There, splayed on her bottom in the dust of the road, was a young girl in a light green traveling smock. She was turning her indignant little face slowly upward to survey her attacker. Her brow puckered and her dark eyes sparkled curiously.

Madeline gave a start. She shifted her parcel at once to help the little girl to her feet. "I am so sorry! Did I hurt you?" she inquired gently.

The child looked back thoughtfully for about two seconds, then her face lit with good humour. She began to laugh merrily and accepted Madeline's offered hand. "No!" she answered brightly. "I am not hurt! It is such a lovely town, and there was a bird just there that I was watching and... oh, I think I am also to ask if I hurt you. Did I?"

Madeline chuckled at this extraordinary child. "Not at all. Where do you come from, my little bird-watching friend?"

The child's eyes became at once suspicious. "Papa told me when we set out that I was not to speak to strangers."

"Oh, of course he is quite right," Madeline agreed seriously. "A lady can never be too careful."

The child grinned happily again. "I suppose it is all right, if you are a lady, too. You *look* like a lady—oh, my, your dress is such a pretty colour! I so love lavender. My mama does not like me to wear that colour because she says I stain it so in the grass, and green hides it better, but when I am old enough to wear my hair up, I will wear lavender every day."

Madeline was, by now, biting back a peal of laughter. What an unusual and interesting child this was! She dipped a slow, exaggerated curtsey. "Well, *I* am not forbidden to speak to strangers, my young friend, and I would very much like to make your acquaintance. My name is Madeline Fairbanks."

The girl made an answering curtsey, her radiant smile now allowing Madeline to count her missing teeth and make an approximate guess at her age. "Pleased to make your aqu—acquain-tance, Miss Fairbanks," she answered in the scripted way of a child using words she did not fully understand. "My name is...."

"Lizzy! Where did you go off to?" A young man now turned the corner of the building from where, Madeline guessed, the child had just come. He was striding quickly, his manner intimidating and agitated. He was peering right and left until his eyes lit on the girl and his face set into a look of great annoyance. "Lizzy!" he repeated as he drew closer, his voice growing more threatening. "I told you to stay with the coach and not to wander."

Madeline's protective instincts flared, and she stepped a little nearer to the child, perhaps intending to shield her from a less than amiable parent. The child, whose name apparently was Lizzy, looked up to him with complete unconcern.

"I did not *wander*, Uncle. I was *following* something. I think it was a robin, but I do not see it now. I have not gone far, Uncle—you see, the inn is just there."

"Elizabeth—" the man clearly fought back his temper to keep his words civil—"your father may allow you to speak back to him in such a way, but I will not while you are under my care. Come, your sister is resting now. We must go."

Madeline made a soft noise. Perhaps it was understandable that the man was flustered by his precocious and lively young charge, but it was more than a little mortifying that he had yet to even *notice* her standing three feet away. She had not thought herself so invisible as that.

The man looked up to her quickly and blanched in horror. "Forgive me, Miss... er, I hope my niece did not trouble you."

"Not at all," she answered coolly. "I sometimes find children more amiable than their elders."

The man grimaced, obviously understanding her meaning. He tugged his hat from his head and offered her a much-belated bow in greeting. "Edward Gardiner at your service, Miss. My apologies again for just now. I was... well, in truth, I have no excuse."

She lifted one expressive brow and the edge of her mouth tipped very slightly. "You are quite forgiven, Mr Gardiner. I have had occasion to learn before that the most sensible of people can appear quite unreasonable when trying to manage a child."

A slow, hesitant smile began to grow on his face—and a rather pleasant face, it was. At last, he gave a light chuckle. "I see you have gotten to know my niece rather well already. Might... might I have the pleasure of your name, Miss...?"

"Fairbanks, Uncle!" Elizabeth spoke up pertly, happy to be of service. "Her name is Madeline Fairbanks, and is she not just lovely?"

Both parties reddened profusely. Madeline's fingertips flew to her mouth and her eyes widened in embarrassment.

Mr Gardiner cleared his throat. Clearly, he had little choice but to agree with his niece, so he smiled, nodded uncomfortably, and answered, "Yes, of course... I mean, it is very lovely to make your acquaintance, Miss Fairbanks. I am afraid we must be going, however. My brother-in-law is waiting for us."

She drew an uncertain breath. "If you are going into that inn just there," she nodded toward the back of the building, "that is my destination, as well."

The man brightened in interest. His eyes revealed, far more than the words his niece had coerced from him ever could have, what his first impression of her truly was. He flushed shyly, perhaps wishing to escort her, but little Lizzy spared him the trouble of asking.

"We can walk you there, Miss Fairbanks!" she bubbled. Madeline found a small, somewhat sticky palm thrust into her own, and she had little choice but to fall into step with the pert young girl and her uncle.

Chapter 7

M R GARDINER HAD, AT first, appeared to be thinking of drawing away his niece and offering her his own arm, but in the
end, they settled for flanking the curly-headed child. Mrs Porter waved
her over as soon as they walked into the inn. "Madeline," she huffed,
beaming a smile, "you are just the person I was wishing to find! I sent
someone to your house not five minutes ago."

Madeline gave a polite nod to Mr Gardiner and his niece as she
stepped away from them. "What is the matter, Mrs Porter?"

"This family here—" she indicated the people Madeline had already
met. "The father of these two girls is traveling on to Sheffield, and the
older sister has fallen ill. She needs to stay over and recover a few days,
and they are hoping one of our own Lambton ladies might be..." Here
she blinked sweetly to her young friend, "*prevailed* upon to lend the
girls some assistance."

"Oh! Why, the poor dear! Is she very ill?"

"She is very miserable; I will say that. It doesn't look serious to me,
but the poor child is already asleep upstairs. Ah, here comes her father
down. Mr Bennet—" Mrs Porter caught that gentleman's attention
as he gained the lower floor of the inn, "I have just the young lady I
was telling you of. Madeline Fairbanks, this is Mr Bennet. She will take
wonderful care of your daughters, sir."

"What... Mrs Porter!" she cried in confusion. "What is this about?"

Mr Bennet's eyes twinkled as he looked her up and down. He was at least ten or fifteen years older than herself, his temples already turning silver. He was of medium stature, a wiry man with quick eyes and a mischievous air to his bearing. Madeline could instantly recognize the resemblance to the dark-haired minx behind her.

"I must beg your pardon, Miss Fairbanks," he spoke at last, "but my eldest daughter has taken such a fancy to the neighborhood that she has determined to stay for perhaps an indefinite period of time."

Madeline's eyes narrowed at the quirky gentleman. "I am afraid I do not understand," she answered carefully.

Mrs Porter excused the two of them from her guest, tugging at Madeline's elbow. Mr Bennet pardoned them with a mercurial smile, wandering over to where his younger daughter and her uncle stood.

"Madeline," she whispered excitedly, "I need you to look after these girls while they remain in town."

"Why me?" she asked in utter bafflement. "I am no nurse. I know nothing of children or their illnesses!"

"You are *perfect*," insisted Mrs Porter. "They only want a little assistance, you know, for propriety's sake. The apothecary will be called if the girl's illness is very serious, but that should not be necessary. That gentleman over there is their uncle, and he will be staying with them while their father travels on."

"Yes, I met the gentleman, but I still do not understand why you are insisting that it must be I? Surely there are any number of women of all work who would be only too glad of the pay. What about Widow Tuttle?"

"Did you say you met the gentleman?" Mrs Porter grinned wickedly. "Then you ought to know why it must be you!"

Madeline's mouth dropped open in astonishment. "Mrs Porter!"

The woman gave her no further opportunity to object. She hooked her hand through Madeline's elbow and dragged her back toward the small party gathered in the dining area. "Miss Fairbanks will be delighted, Mr Bennet and Mr Gardiner. Now, if you gentlemen will excuse me, I will see to fresh linens for you. Mr Bennet, I shall also pack you a cold luncheon for the road." She bustled off, giving Madeline a cheery pat on the shoulder as she abandoned her with the virtual strangers.

Madeline paled, staring back at them. All three were smiling—Bennet with that peculiar spark in his eye which caused her to wonder precisely what he was thinking. Little Elizabeth grinned broadly up at her, and Mr Gardiner looked rather bashful, but immensely pleased. "I..." she faltered, her gaze flitting about the trio. Swallowing, she decided that she felt most comfortable speaking to the child. Girding up her courage, she did just that, pretending that the two gentlemen were *not* staring at her with open curiosity. "I understand we are to spend a few days together, Miss Bennet," she smiled kindly.

"It will be such fun! Oh, how you will love Jane, she is..." Elizabeth stopped herself, her forehead wrinkled in thought. "But she is ill just now. Papa said we would be finding her a nurse. Are you a nurse, Miss Fairbanks?"

"No," she admitted, "I am not."

"I didn't *think* you were. You are a *real* lady," Elizabeth asserted in satisfaction.

"Well..." Madeline draped one hand uncomfortably over the other—distantly noting that in the confusion, somewhere she had misplaced the all-important parcel which had brought her here in the first place. "I am not a gentleman's daughter, as I think you mean. My father is a bookkeeper. I help him some. I truly do not know why Mrs Porter recommended me to you."

"Elizabeth likes you," Mr Gardiner interjected warmly. "That is high enough commendation, Miss Fairbanks. It is a relief to find someone who has a way with children." He seemed to catch himself after this pronouncement, drawing in his breath and sealing his lips as though afraid he had spoken too much.

"Thank you," she accepted the compliment shyly. "Mr Bennet, sir, I would expect that you might have some misgivings about leaving your children with a complete stranger! I understand your predicament, sir, but are you quite certain?"

Mr Bennet looked down to his daughter. "Miss Fairbanks, I ought instead to be asking *you* that question. Your friend Mrs Porter gave you little enough choice, I see, but if you can tolerate a rift with her, I think we might be able to find other arrangements—if that is your wish."

"No!" The objection crossed her lips before she could think better of it. "I would be most delighted to be of service to travelers in need, such as yourselves. It is only..." she darted her eyes self-consciously to Mr Gardiner, who was still smiling and, if she were not mistaken, blushing. "You know nothing of me, sir."

Mr Bennet tilted his head. "Have you any intention of selling my daughters to passing gypsies, Miss Fairbanks?"

She stared. "What... of course not, sir!" she retorted, flustered.

"And you do not use vulgar language, have the pox, or sip your tea from the wrong side of the cup?" Beside her father, Elizabeth started giggling. Gardiner rolled his eyes, shaking his head.

Madeline gazed back at him in speechless wonder.

"And I am also to assume, Miss Fairbanks," Mr Bennet continued, more reasonably now, "that you have no other commitments at present?"

This question she could understand. She pulled herself from her silent amazement at this singular gentleman to make reply. "I do help my father, sir, as I mentioned, but his business will be quiet for a few weeks—until the hay season, sir. I believe he can do without me during the day, but I shall, of course, need to look in on his meals."

"Agreed, Miss Fairbanks. My brother-in-law, whom I understand you have already met, shall have chief authority over the girls, but as you must understand, it would not be right for him to exclusively tend Jane while she is ill. I hope you have a sturdy constitution, Miss Fairbanks."

"I rarely fall ill, sir," she assured him.

Mr Bennet's eyebrows raised. "Oh, it was not that which concerned me, but that you would also have to keep up with Elizabeth. My best wishes to you, Miss Fairbanks." Mr Bennet smiled, then took his little girl by the hand to walk with him to his carriage. Madeline gazed blankly after them, her mouth very slightly agape.

Mr Gardiner cleared his throat gently. "Are you well, Miss Fairbanks?"

Her eyes shifted to focus on him. "I do not know what has just happened," she murmured hazily.

Gardiner chuckled. "I often feel that way after a conversation with my brother-in-law! Those daughters of his are no better, but Lizzy is by far the most bewildering, and you have weathered her well enough."

She shook her head in vague confusion. "What am I to do? Truly, Mr Gardiner, I am honoured to be of help, but I know nothing of children."

He smiled reassuringly. "Fear not, Miss Fairbanks. All we truly need is someone to look in on Jane and perhaps help to keep Lizzy occupied. Mrs Porter is too busy, I gather. I do apologize for imposing upon your time without warning, as we have done. Will your father be very displeased?"

"I do not think so. I think I must go explain to him at once, however."

"I had thought you might. Would you mind if I introduced you to our Jane first? After that, if it is agreeable to you, it seems only right that I also would speak to your father, to assure him of our intentions."

She tilted her head slightly, narrowing her eyes in an unspoken question.

He shifted his feet awkwardly. "If I had a daughter, Miss Fairbanks, who suddenly found herself required to attend to the relative of a strange man...."

Her eyes cleared with understanding. "I see. Of course, Mr Gardiner. Please, do introduce me to this other niece of yours before we go." She tensed slightly as she spoke the words, wondering what sort of obligation she had committed herself to.

"Do not worry," Gardiner winked, noticing her sudden flash of nervousness. "Jane is far sweeter than her sister."

Chapter 8

"JANEY?" MR GARDINER'S VOICE dropped to impossibly gentle tones as he tapped softly on the door. "Janey, are you awake?"

Madeline was watching the man in some curiosity. He was taller than his brother-in-law, as well as broader of shoulder, with rather non-descript brown hair and soft, expressive brown eyes. Perhaps he was not the most striking man she had ever encountered, but there was a congeniality about him which rendered his rather average features all the more agreeable. He glanced over his shoulder to catch her eye when there was a low response from within. She smiled back in acknowledgement that she, also, had heard.

He opened the door to the most beautiful child Madeline had ever seen. If the little sprite she had met before could be said to sparkle, this angelic creature shone. Her face could have been painted by Gainsborough, so perfect was the symmetry of her features. She lay quietly upon the pillow, her fair hair tousled and her eyes slitted open at her uncle's entry. Madeline could see plainly the effects of the fever spread over the girl's cheeks, but as her uncle approached, she made an effort to rise from her pillow.

"No, it is all right, Jane," he stopped her softly, holding out a hand. He spoke barely above a whisper, hoping to help her remain at peace. "This is Miss Fairbanks. She will be looking in on you now and then."

The child's listless eyes switched to Madeline and she attempted a smile in greeting. "Good morning, Miss Fairbanks," she murmured dutifully.

Madeline carefully reached to take the girl's hand, wondering how high her fever was. "Good morning, Jane. I am very pleased to meet you. Would you like some tea, or anything to eat?"

Jane's eyes rolled closed and she shook her head subtly. "No, thank you, Miss Fairbanks," she answered, but it was apparent that she was quite asleep again before the last word was out of her mouth.

Madeline's face and heart fairly melted. "Oh!" she gasped, her hand once more covering her mouth.

Mr Gardiner started. "What is it? Is her fever dangerous, then?"

"Oh, no! At least, I do not think so. It is only that she is so polite, even when she is so ill. She must be such a dear, Mr Gardiner."

His features relaxed somewhat. "Jane is a good girl, Miss Fairbanks. No one could dislike her. I do not know from where she inherited her generous nature, but I am very fond of her."

Madeline raised a finger to her lips. "We should let her rest," she whispered.

The tender expression wiped from his face, replaced by a more comfortable business-like manner. "Right, then. To your home, Miss Fairbanks." He followed her down the stairs, glancing about as they reached the bottom for his other niece. "Now where do you suppose...?"

Madeline tipped her head, smilingly, toward the common room. Mrs Porter was pushing a broom about and chattering away with her miniature assistant, who followed with the dustbin and a mouthful of questions. Gardiner laughed. "Well, I expect that will keep her occupied for a few moments."

FITZWILLIAM LIFTED THE FENDER flap of his saddle, tightening the girth one last time after leading his gelding from the stable. Saul was a crafty old horse; a seasoned veteran who never failed to flex his great heart-girth muscles when he was first saddled. He eyed the beast in annoyance as he discovered once again just how much slack the gelding's trickery had purchased. It was a good three more holes before the saddle was tight enough for him to mount.

That job finished, he flipped the leather straps back into place, ran down his irons, and gave one last cursory glance at the bit before preparing to swing aboard. Just as his boot touched the iron, the sound of his name arrested him.

"William!"

His face crumpled in frustrated disappointment. No one but his father used that name alone, and it was most decidedly his father's imperious tones which echoed to him now. He allowed his foot to fall to the ground and turned. "Yes, Father?"

George Darcy strode slowly to his son, exercising his parental authority just a little in forcing the boy to wait. The younger Darcy's fingers twitched and tightened on the rein in his hand. With the intuitive foreboding well known to all boys, he began to realize that he would not be riding today, after all. He swiftly categorized the possible reasons his father might have had to call for him and tried to calculate how serious this conversation might be.

Perhaps Father had heard about his little jaunt yesterday with Georgiana, and how he had ridden for more than two hours with a tender young girl before returning home. He could fully admit to his wrong there—he ought not to have taken his sister so far, but it had been the first time she had seemed happy since... well, since a long time. He deserved a harsh set-down for that infraction, though. He waited in agonized silence as his father closed the distance toward him.

"William, I have just spoken with Mr Wickham and he tells me you forbade George to enter the stables. May I ask what business it was of yours, and with which authority you spoke?"

Oh. The lad bowed his head. *That.* He took only the barest second to compose himself, then raised his eyes respectfully to his father's. "He was harassing a colt, sir. I told him to stop, but he would not. He kept pulling it away from its mother, tying the mare up and then chasing the colt about for fun when it tried to return to her. The colt slipped two or three times, sir, and I feared...."

"William," his father held up a finger, "the stables do not belong to you yet. You will let Mr Douglas handle all matters pertaining to the horses and refer any other issues directly to me."

Every youthful feeling of justice rebelled within the boy, but he was too well brought-up to voice his indignation. His teeth clenched, fire kindled in his dark eyes, but he answered simply, "Yes, Father."

The elder Darcy let out a sigh of regret. "I understand your anger, William. We must never allow one among us to abuse man or beast. It is against every principle we hold dear to needlessly trouble another creature. I am glad that you can defend a colt, but you must not overlook the man—or boy, in this case. George has not had your advantages, my son, and he does not understand—as you do—the full weight of a man's responsibility. It is our duty to show him as we can."

The boy's face had changed slowly during this speech, from hot anger to simmering resentment and finally to mere frustration. "Father, by your leave." He waited silently for his parent's permission to speak candidly. When his father merely lifted a brow, he continued. "George does not listen. I try to talk to him, to tell him the things you tell me, but he only laughs. How am I to lead by example when the person I am trying to lead will not follow?"

"In my experience, boys do not make good leaders for other boys, my son. You must simply do as you know is right and allow George's father or Mr Douglas to intervene when it is necessary. It is not for you to sit in judgement over him; the authority is not yours. If you were very much older than he, or if you were master of the estate, things would be different, but at present they are not."

The boy's shoulders dropped in defeat. "Yes, Father."

The Master of Pemberley clapped a hand over his son's back. "I know how it is, William. George has no true responsibility and behaves as a boy, with few consequences or expectations placed upon him. You have much responsibility and a great many expectations heaped upon you, and great are the consequences if you should fail. That is to be your lot in life, my son, and while I regret that it seems unfair now, I am proud of the man I am beginning to see. You will understand justice and righteousness, but you must recognize that you are not that man yet."

Fitzwilliam swallowed, meeting his father's eyes. It was the first time the man had commended him in a very long while, and it came as part of a life lesson. "You are saying—" he mulled his father's words over, mining them for nuggets of wisdom—"that even when I am in the right, it is not always for me to act?"

"Precisely. Well said, my boy. Sometimes the correction may come more effectively from one in better authority. There will be other times—" he leaned a little nearer, pinning his heir with a compelling gaze—"when *you* will be that one in a position of better authority, and it will be for *you* to set right a wrong in defence of another. It is a wise man who can discern the difference."

Young Fitzwilliam Darcy nodded eagerly, glad to have apparently understood his father rightly. The man smiled kindly, sliding his hand affectionately up to the back of his son's head. "Now, go enjoy your ride."

The boy's eyes flew wide in surprise. "You are not penalizing me?"

The father winked, the first time he had done so in some months. "Do your best by George, my son. That is penalty enough for one day."

His heart beat lightly and freely. He might go! Quickly, he spun back to his mount as his father began to walk away. The voice, however, interrupted him again.

"Do you not think—" George Darcy continued walking, facing away from him as he called back—"that Georgiana will be disappointed that you rode without her today?"

He gulped, his foot falling once again. He turned to look over his shoulder with a guilty conscience. His father merely continued walking—but he was whistling. Fitzwilliam smiled, looking back at his saddle. Perhaps he would have to take Georgie out again... tomorrow.

Chapter 9

MADELINE STOOD STIFFLY IN her own parlour, feeling as though she were the guest on display rather than the daughter and de facto mistress of the little home. She had assured the gentleman escorting her that the explanation to her father might come more easily from herself than from a stranger, and he had reluctantly agreed. "I still feel it rather ungallant," he had protested. "I do not like asking a lady to arbitrate my affairs for me, but if I try to consider your father's perspective, I quite understand."

"Papa," she blushed at her father's look of confusion when they entered the house together. She had never before brought a man to his notice, and she rushed to justify the situation before her father could leap to any conclusions. "This is Mr Edward Gardiner from London. He and his nieces are guests at the Lion's Head, and one of his nieces has fallen ill. Mrs Porter asked if I would be willing to assist the girl while they remain."

Mr Fairbanks, squinting and unconsciously adjusting his glasses, came forward to greet the stranger. "Mr Gardiner? From London, did you say? Your nieces are ill?" He surveyed the man in great perplexity.

Edward had opened his mouth to perform the customary niceties expected on such an occasion, but Fairbanks' questions caused him to alter what he might have said. "Yes, sir, from London. I was traveling with my brother-in-law and his two eldest daughters to Sheffield when we were required to stop over here. At present only one of my nieces is ill, and we are in hopes that she will soon recover. Her father had rather pressing business in Sheffield and has continued on, which, unfortunately, leaves me alone here with the two girls."

Something he had said caused Madeline to turn to him in mild surprise. "These are only the eldest? Are there more daughters?" she asked softly.

One side of Gardiner's mouth turned upward in a sheepish smile. "Three more. The youngest is only two."

"Three!" ejaculated Mr Fairbanks. "Five daughters?" He quickly raised a hand in apology for his outburst, leaving unsaid what most fathers of daughters would have quite naturally been thinking: a man with five daughters would bear a substantial burden caring for them and ensuring they might all be safely married off one day.

"I am sure they are all most lovely, Mr Gardiner," Madeline was declaring.

Gardiner cleared his throat uncomfortably. "Well... perhaps I am not a fair judge of children, being a bachelor, Miss, but... yes, I am certain they are lovely."

Madeline laughed. "Surely you have seen them, Mr Gardiner."

His eyes drifted to her father, sensing an immediate kinship with the man who also understood what had so far escaped his daughter. "Some might say that. I think I must know very little of bringing up children, Miss Fairbanks. I often... well, that is to say, I feel much more comfortable with the elder girls. They are a delight, and such a pair!"

His face had waxed sentimental, but in a moment, he recalled the true purpose of this visit. "Pardon me, sir, but I forget myself. I wished to ask your blessing to allow Miss Fairbanks to attend my niece, Jane. I assure you, sir, every propriety will naturally be observed. I cannot care for her myself, and Mrs Porter praises Miss Fairbanks very highly."

Fairbanks nervously removed his glasses, then replaced them again. "I suppose, if Madeline has no objections. Do you, my dear?"

"None, Papa. Mr Gardiner's nieces are charming girls, and Mrs Porter will be at hand if I should need anything. I was just going to pack a small bag for myself so that I may stay in the room with Jane. Will you fare well enough without me?"

He waved his hand. "Of course, of course. Mr Gardiner, may we offer you something while you wait?"

Madeline flew to her packing, not wishing for a long delay before she could assume her new task. When she returned with a light valise, it was to the sound of masculine laughter from the drawing room. She stepped into the room cautiously—experience having taught her that where men laughed and joked with one another, it was often not a conversation fit for a lady's ears. In this case, to her relief, she need not have worried.

Mr Gardiner was the first to notice her return. "Miss Fairbanks, allow me!" He nearly leapt to her side to relieve her of her bag.

"Thank you," she blushed once again. "I hope I did not interrupt anything?"

"Not at all!" Gardiner beamed. "Your father has much wisdom about trout fishing, and I find myself quite in awe. I am hoping that I will have an opportunity during my stay to learn a few things from him."

"Does that not depend on the speed of your niece's recovery?" she inquired slyly.

"Why yes... yes, it does." He frowned. To admit that he desired to remain several days in the area would be to sound as though he wished for Jane's illness to be of a more serious nature, and he had not the heart to voice that thought.

"I am sure," Madeline continued, her eyes twinkling uncannily like his brother-in-law's, "that you will want to be sure that she is very *well* recovered before you depart, and that little Elizabeth is not at risk. One cannot be too cautious, Mr Gardiner."

A wide grin split his cheerful face. "You are quite correct, Miss Fairbanks."

"**M**AY I ASK, MR Gardiner, have you always lived in London?" Madeline smiled up at the gentleman as he briskly moved to place himself between her and the street. She had known men who were more suave in their manners, but Mr Gardiner's charm was in his ready attentiveness to her. He was... sweet... if, indeed, one might apply such a word to a grown man in the prime of his strength.

"No, Miss Fairbanks," he answered. "I have lived in London only for the last ten years. I come from Meryton in Hertfordshire, a small town much like this one."

"That makes more sense." She tipped her face straight ahead once more, a slight lilt in her voice. No man could resist such a cryptic tease, and Edward Gardiner was no exception.

"It does?" he inquired with a grin. "How so?"

"You appear to suffer no distaste when surveying our town, Mr Gardiner. Many Londoners do, you know."

"Distaste? Why, not at all, Miss Fairbanks. I think Lambton everything lovely. It is your good fortune, indeed, to call home such a charming town full of good folk and nestled here at the very feet of the mountains."

"You enjoy our views of the peaks, sir?"

"Indeed, I do! I have long wished to tour this country, Miss Fairbanks. I have always enjoyed any escape from the city, but Hertfordshire is not nearly so wild as this district. Do not mistake me, Miss Fairbanks. I like London well enough. It is my life and livelihood, do you see? Have... have you ever been, Miss Fairbanks?"

"Once," she smiled mildly at the sudden hesitation in his voice. He appeared to have great interest in her impression of Town. "My father and I paid my brother a visit last November. He is studying to enter the legal profession."

"An honourable employment!" enthused her companion. "My father was an attorney in Meryton. He desired for me to follow in his footsteps, but while I was still young, my eldest sister married his assistant, a Mr Philips. When my father retired, Miss Fairbanks, Mr Philips made arrangements to purchase the business—with my blessing—and I sought my future in London."

"It is rather ill-bred of me, sir, but might I inquire what you do there?" She turned sparkling eyes up to him as she asked. If her judgement of this man was correct, he would be far from affronted at her interest.

"I do not think you ill-bred at all, Miss Fairbanks." He smiled candidly. "I distribute textiles and various goods and household items to the shops of London. I have trade agreements with manufacturers and suppliers from all over the kingdom, as well as France, Scotland, and I have recently made a contact in Belgium."

The lady's golden eyebrows arched. "That is a deal to accomplish in only ten years!" she exclaimed.

"Well," he smiled modestly, "I cannot take all the credit. I found employment with a Mr Wilson, a man nearing retirement age who had spent an entire career developing contacts and building the warehouse business to a state of prosperity. He took a fancy to me and trained me as his successor. Mr Philips' purchase of what was to have been my interest in my father's firm allowed me to supplement my own income. I lived economically, and within five years I had purchased the business outright."

"That must have required much dedication, sir."

"My father taught me to work with all my heart, Miss Fairbanks. Oh, dear, I am afraid this conversation has become rather indelicate. Do please forgive me for speaking of such dull matters! I ought instead to be telling you of the many fine walks and sights of London."

Madeline glanced up once more with a merry smile. "I do not find it indelicate, sir! Perhaps it is I who lack refinement, but I have always admired one who works faithfully and with a will. I have assisted my father for two years, sir, which is not at all a proper diversion for a daughter, I must confess. Most think it wholly unfitting and unladylike, but I cannot regret it as I likely ought to."

Edward stopped on the walk as they reached the door of the inn. He gazed thoughtfully down into the cheerful, kind face before him. "Miss Fairbanks," said he, "I do not believe it could be said that you lack any refinement. There are those who would value a woman of practicality far above one of manifold charms. You, Miss, have been blessed with both virtues."

Chapter 10

T HE REMAINDER OF THE day passed peacefully. After making certain—and checking in a few times, just to be absolutely sure—that Miss Fairbanks was comfortable in Jane's room, Edward had challenged Elizabeth to a game of chess in the common room. For a seven-year-old, she was surprisingly adept. It seemed that she was the only person at Longbourn willing to learn, and Mr Bennet had made good use of his second daughter's interest and active mind to teach her well. Elizabeth won two of their four games, though it would be only fair to state that her uncle had coached her somewhat.

After the last checkmate, Edward finally yielded to the fidgeting bundle of energy who had been required to sit too long in one attitude. "Lizzy," he suggested, "let me go look in on Jane once more, and then why don't we take a little walk?"

As though a great spring had been released, the child jumped from her seat. "I will get my bonnet!" she cried as she raced up the stairs.

Chuckling, he followed her. He felt scarcely less eager than Elizabeth, quite of a sudden, and he was certain that the reason for his impatience lay beyond Jane's door. *Miss Fairbanks.* Such a lovely name! His fingers tapped nervously along the stair railing as he climbed and sought the proper words to excuse this particular interruption. He had nearly exhausted his ideas. How many ways were there in the

English language to inquire after a child's health? There must be at least one more he had not yet tried.

Elizabeth naturally had the door open first and was softly tiptoeing behind Miss Fairbanks when Edward reached them. "Elizabeth," he heard Miss Fairbanks laugh, "there is no need for such stealth!"

He looked into the room to find Jane sitting up in her bed, drowsily awake and smiling faintly. Miss Fairbanks had been reading to her, and the book still rested open in her lap. Edward was warmed and somewhat impressed. He had not thought to bring her any reading material—much to his embarrassment—so apparently Miss Fairbanks had brought her own. He wished very much to know what it was. Instead, he smiled kindly at his niece.

"How are you feeling, Jane?"

Madeline, who had not yet noticed Edward's entry, turned in surprise at the masculine voice behind her. Edward's eyes flicked in interest to her face as she looked over her shoulder at him, but he quickly redirected his gaze to Jane.

"I am well, Uncle," Jane managed softly.

"You are not well at all, Janey, but you are brave to say so." He smiled, stepping near to stroke a wisp of hair from the child's forehead. "Is there anything I can bring you?"

"Mrs Porter is bringing her some soup," Miss Fairbanks informed him.

"Excellent." He chucked his niece on the chin. "Try to eat as much as you can, dear one. You need your strength. Is your room warm enough, and have you enough blankets?"

Jane nodded, though it appeared that the movement hurt her head. She closed her thick lashes over her round little cheeks. "My throat hurts, Uncle," she rasped.

"I know, Janey," he answered gently. He glanced up to Miss Fairbanks, who was watching them with a soft, warm expression. "Thank you for helping to keep her comfortable, Miss Fairbanks. Would it be any inconvenience to you if I took Elizabeth out for some air? Is there anything I may procure for you to make your time pass more pleasantly?"

She smiled, allowing him to admire the very small, delicate crease near her lips where her mouth already seemed quite acquainted with the sunny expression. His gaze fixed with satisfaction upon that well-exercised furrow in the lady's otherwise perfect skin. He liked a woman who smiled easily and often, and Miss Fairbanks was looking more interesting to him by the moment.

"No, thank you, Mr Gardiner," she replied, her eyes smiling quite as eloquently as her lips. "I am very comfortable. I expect that Jane will need to take a rest once she has supped, and I shall come below while she sleeps."

Gardiner nodded, grateful for this intelligence. He determined to keep his walk as short as Lizzy would tolerate. "I shall see you when you come down, then, Miss Fairbanks."

MADELINE'S LIGHT FINGERS STROKED over the counterpane, tucking and bundling the poor girl with a touch which could only be called motherly. Little Jane Bennet was fast asleep. The child's thick dark lashes, in contrast with the fair hair tousled over her brow, twitched against her fevered cheeks as she dreamt. Madeline smiled affectionately down at the child. She had known her only a few hours, but already she sensed a protective attachment growing within her bosom. What prodigious care, and what maternal pride must this girl's mother find in her child! The woman, Madeline was almost certain, had to be a wise, sensible creature to have borne such a beatific daughter.

After lingering one final moment to make certain that Jane was resting comfortably, Madeline left the room. She hesitated on the stair, her heart hammering deliriously. *He* was down there waiting for her—Mr Gardiner, with his bumbling, winsome ways and his gentlemanly bearing. He had sent her a message through Lizzy only a short while before that he had ordered a meal for the three of them, and that he most sincerely hoped she might be able to join them in the common room. She clenched her trembling fingers into a little knot at her stomach.

Why was she so nervous? The room was full of people—some travelers, some local bachelors and widowers who did not have a pleasant wife to cook for them at home. They would be just two more among a dozen such, taking their meal.

She wondered how often the genteel-looking Gardiner had been required to sit at a common board with farmers. In London he might not rank as the cream of society, but here in humble Lambton, an affluent businessman was nearly as far out of her reach as the Darcy family themselves. What might be such a man's opinion of her? Fleetingly, she wondered if the man were as wholly unattached as he appeared to her. Might he not have some fair maiden awaiting his return to Town?

Stop it! She at last ordered herself. All of this speculation was pointless and costing her a warm meal in agreeable company. Whether anything might be made of it was yet to be seen, but she would never know unless she went below.

L IZZY PUT AWAY HER meal with ravenous zest and commenced to fidget beside her uncle. The entire bench squeaked as she swung her little feet to and fro. Gardiner bit back an aggravated sigh, meeting Madeline's eyes. "Lizzy," he suggested at last, "if you are quite finished, you may take your geography book over there to the window ledge. Miss Fairbanks and I would like to finish our meal in peace." The girl complied brightly, only too eager to be set at some liberty.

Madeline kept her mouth pressed into a dignified expression, but she could not conceal the brilliant spark of her eyes. The child obviously discomposed her uncle, but he was too good to become truly cross. He was peeking cautiously up to her from his plate now, his colour somewhat heightened. Though they could scarcely be said to have been alone together in this crowded room, it was the most intimate setting they had yet found for quiet conversation. He seemed... nervous!

"I say, Miss Fairbanks," he began hesitantly, still toying somewhat with his fork, "I noticed that you had brought a book with you this morning. Are you fond of reading?"

"I am, sir, though I find few enough opportunities to do so."

"You must be kept very busy," he replied, with an intent to sound gallant, but such was not the effect.

Madeline's cheeks flushed, and she glanced down. She was no woman of leisure, as would be so many of the girls he probably knew in London. Even a modestly well-off tradesman's daughter might fancy herself something of a lady, but Madeline could claim no such luxury.

Recognizing his blunder, Edward groaned. "Forgive me, Miss Fairbanks!" he pleaded. "I only meant to say that you must be a great comfort to your father, and much of your time must, of course, be spent in help—er, caring for...." He finally stumbled to silence, his face bright red.

Madeline's eyes twinkled with mirth at his discomfiture. "You are making it worse, sir!" she laughed.

His face crunched into dismay. "I humbly beg your pardon, Miss Fairbanks. It is not often that I have an opportunity to converse so openly with such a lovel...." He stopped himself again, dropping his face to his palm in abject horror at himself. What on earth was the matter with him? He had never embarrassed himself so thoroughly in Mae's company! Had he, her mother surely would have seen fit to never receive him again!

Madeline's dainty fingers were curled near her mouth to disguise her amusement. She did not wish to mock him, but he was *so* endearing! His honest attempts at conversation all came out as some form of praise, whether socially correct or not, and she found his stumbling efforts far more pleasing to her taste than smooth flattery. At last, she could contain herself no longer, and a small squeak of laughter escaped her.

His teeth clenched in a mortified grimace, he dared to squintingly meet her eyes. "You must think me an utter boor, Miss Fairbanks!"

Her laugh grew heartier, and she shook her head. "Not at all, I assure you, Mr Gardiner! I am only relieved to find that I do not suffer alone in anxiety."

Concern replaced the humiliation in his expression. "Miss Fairbanks, it would trouble me greatly if you were distressed in my presence. I regret very much if you have been made to feel uncomfortable! Is there something I can do for your relief? Would you care for a glass of wine?"

Her smile deepening, she looked blushingly at the table and shook her head. A maiden was never encouraged to keep eye contact with a man, particularly not one she had known for only a day, and Madeline had been taught properly, after all. Very soon, however, she raised her searching eyes back to his face. He was quite too interesting for her own good! "I am well, Mr Gardiner," she assured him when his face still bore a look of apprehension. "I do not often converse with gentlemen, either."

He took a cleansing breath, willing his tension away. Here he was seated in a respectable inn, having a perfectly innocent conversation with the most appealing young lady he had yet encountered. He had no cause to be nervous, as though he were at some nefarious devilry! He ought instead to be at his most charming! How else was a man to win the favour of a young woman?

His eyes cast about quickly as he desperately sought some way of setting them both at ease and redeeming the conversation. At last, his expression cleared as he struck upon the perfect solution. "Miss Fairbanks, do you happen to play chess?"

Chapter 11

THE FOLLOWING MORNING DAWNED with the promise of a full day of cloudless splendour. Young Fitzwilliam rose early so that he might complete his self-appointed studies quickly. He had made plans with his little sister the night before, and he intended to keep them. Just before midday, he called for her, following through with his promise.

Mrs Reynolds had a small parcel of food prepared for them, and he had ordered a bag placed beneath his saddle for the day. He and Georgiana intended to enjoy a long ride and then a leisurely picnic at a particular meadow he had discovered some months earlier. The very same stream which cut through Pemberley wended its way along the edge, with a small stand of trees at one end. It was the perfect place for an hour or two's quiet reflection; a place where one could listen to the soft babbling of the stream and the majesty of the wind through the trees and be left entirely alone.

He had yet to show his little paradise to her, as it was a good hour's ride from the house at the pace he would be required to keep to with her aboard. Reason naturally dictated that a three-year-old girl was too fragile and easily tired for such a long journey. His recent ride with her had taught him otherwise. His little sister was hardy, and there was nothing which brought her more delight than a long amble on horseback in her brother's strong arms. He would ride Saul again, who was as good-natured as a horse could be, and also well-exercised from the day before. Little Georgie would be quite safe.

"Come, Georgie!" he called with enthusiasm once he had inspected his tack. "Are you ready, little love?"

"I was ready all morning, Will!" she giggled. "Pick me up!" She reached for his outstretched arms, and he lifted her gently to the front of his saddle.

He darted a glance over his shoulder to be sure he was not seen, then he adjusted her short little legs so that she was sitting astride the horse's neck. Unladylike though it might be, he did not care to rob her of stability in favour of propriety. There would come a day for that, but not yet.

"Hold his mane, Georgie, like I showed you. Do you have a good grip? Just one moment, and we shall be off." Carefully trying to hold his reins with the same hand she leaned upon, he performed the precarious task of mounting behind her. Once settled, he wrapped his right arm tightly around her, pulling her close, and they started out.

They spoke little, both being of a more reserved disposition. Though she was a full eleven years his junior, there were few people with whom he could be quite so at ease. They were alike. They shared the same quiet, thoughtful nature, and they shared the same sorrows.

It was a pity, he had often reflected, that Georgiana would little remember their lovely mother when she was older. Perhaps it was in truth a mercy, for she would also little remember the grief of losing her. In that alone, they were different. Young Fitzwilliam had been as enamoured with his angelic mother as any boy could be, and to lose her at an age when he was still very much in need of her gentle guidance and still so strongly desired the encouragement that a mother's budding respect might offer a young man... it would be a blow he would suffer for all of his life.

Father understood, of that he was certain, but George Darcy's heart had been rent in two when his love had left him alone. Fitzwilliam instinctively did not press his father for the comfort they both so deeply craved. It would not have been proper, and a Darcy was nothing if not proper.

He drew a long breath, closing down his heart's pain for a while and reveling instead in the glorious fragrance of fresh grass and blooming fruit trees. Georgie's head draped back over his chest as she, too, thoroughly relaxed in the beauty of their day together. He snuggled her just a little tighter. He was no longer naive enough to believe that he would never desire the love of a woman other than his mother, but for just now, his baby sister possessed his heart. For the hundredth time since their mother's death, he made a silent vow to protect her always.

"Lizzy," Miss Fairbanks sighed. "You must not jostle Jane's bed so!"

Elizabeth glanced up, pouting a little. She had taken a shine to the pretty lady from Lambton—at least, she was very interested in impressing her, since the lady seemed to bestow praise quite unreservedly. In addition, she was fascinating to talk to. When she read stories aloud, she performed different characterizations for each voice, which Lizzy had never heard done before. Best of all, she seemed to truly enjoy Elizabeth's company, a feat which only the most serene and engaging people of her acquaintance ever fully managed.

It appeared, however, that even the imperturbable Miss Fairbanks had her limits. After almost three hours together in Jane's cramped little sickroom, Elizabeth was very nearly climbing the walls, and Miss Fairbanks was quite close to digging her fingernails completely into her palms. "Lizzy," the lady repeated, "do stop swinging your feet!"

Elizabeth affected the melodramatic groan and whole-body flop backward, which has since been employed by countless bored children across the kingdom. "But Miss Fairbanks," she whined, "when will Jane wake up?"

Madeline Fairbanks was a generous sort, but not at all inclined to tolerate the rather haphazard manners which Elizabeth had been taught. She felt reasonably certain that the child's uncle would support her, so she at last determined to correct the wayward girl. "Elizabeth Bennet!" Madeline snapped in a cool, stern tone. "A lady never complains in such a crude, unmannerly fashion. Now, if you wish to remain, you must sit up straight and behave properly, as becomes the daughter of a gentleman!"

Chastised by the woman she so desired to please, Elizabeth mutely straightened in her chair. Her childish, mournful eyes fastened upon her dear Miss Fairbanks' face, watching for any flickers of approval as she strove to contain her impulse to fidget.

Madeline sighed, almost sorry now that she had scolded the girl. "Do you not wish to go below stairs? Perhaps Mrs Porter could use some help preparing the afternoon tea."

Elizabeth shook her head. "No... no, thank you," she glanced quickly to the lady's face again as she amended her speech. "Miss Fairbanks, when did Uncle say he would be back?"

"That I do not know, Elizabeth. He wished to explore the region and asked where he might hire a saddle horse for the day. Fear not, my dear, he will return soon. A gentleman does not sit all day in a child's sickroom, particularly not when the weather is so promising out of doors."

Elizabeth, forgetting once again the genteel deportment she was trying to mimic, propped her chin upon her hand and leaned forward on her elbow. "May we go downstairs together?"

"I cannot leave Jane, Lizzy," Madeline smiled with regret. "Her fever is a little worse today, and I am considering sending for the apothecary."

"Is she going to die?" breathed the wide-eyed little damsel.

Madeline patted her hand in reassurance. "I think not, but perhaps the apothecary has some remedies which may shorten her fever."

Elizabeth's little brow wrinkled. "Why have we not sent for him earlier, then? I know Jane would want to be up and well!"

The lady sighed. "Sometimes the best thing we can offer is rest and nourishment." She brightened in sudden inspiration. "Lizzy, would you like to help Jane rest even more soundly so that she may join you all the sooner?"

The child perked up, all attention. "Yes, Miss Fairbanks! What may I do?"

She squeezed the girl's hand and surveyed her with a steady, serious gaze. "Ask Mrs Porter if she has any red hogsbreath powder. Powdered, mind, not minced! She will know what I speak of. You must have it made into a strong tea for Jane, but you must be patient! It sometimes takes a very long time to brew."

Elizabeth nodded, awestruck at the wisdom of this pretty lady. "Yes, Miss Fairbanks!" She scampered from her chair and disappeared out of the door of the room with a loud bang.

Madeline sagged back into her seat, exhausted. She could not decide whether she was ashamed of deceiving the child, or proud of her clever little ruse. Either way, the girl needed to be out where she could move, not cramped in a dim room on a beautiful day. Let her go downstairs, where her fidgeting would not be a concern. The girl was a dear, but Madeline sincerely hoped that not *all* children bubbled and overflowed with as much energy as that particular little sprite!

Chapter 12

Edward crested the top of a small knoll and drew up his mount. Marvelous country, Derbyshire! He patted the rented sorrel in satisfaction, allowing the horse a breather after the gradual but steady climb out of the village. From here, he could see wild spires of rocky outcroppings in one direction and rolling, cultivated fields in another. This country was paradise itself!

He was glad he had finally convinced himself to some exercise. Though he was no expert horseman, and never would be with as much time as he spent at his business, there was something primal and virile about a good long gallop on horseback. It appealed to those untamed parts lurking in a man's heart; those hidden places in the soul of every man which compelled him to search out hardship and adventure, leaving behind him for a time the quiet, civilized life of a London businessman.

He studied the horizon for a time, and, quite naturally, his thoughts turned from the land itself to the good fruits it produced. Agricultural bounty lay before him, but perhaps it was not fruits of that nature which stirred his interest. *She* had grown up here. This rugged terrain, raw and simple, had shaped her mind and experiences from infancy. Some romantic notion caused him to hope that if he understood the land, it could help him to learn more of her.

Before very long at all, his gaze had dropped blankly to the pommel of his saddle, where his hand pressed against it to allow him to shift his protesting thigh muscles. His mind saw not leather and sweated horseflesh, but honeyed curls and clear, honest blue eyes. The truth was, if it were not for his notions of propriety, he would have kept watch with her at Jane's bedside rather than venturing out as he had done today. He wished to know her thoughts, to explore what she would say or do in response to any number of things he had imagined asking her. Oh, and he was naturally quite concerned for his niece as well. Of course.

He let go a long, reluctant breath. There was a reason, and a very good one too, that a proper courtship was such a slow process. Time must be invested to truly know someone, and it ought not be all lumped together into one twenty-four-hour period. He only hoped that in this case, he would have enough of it to at least curry the lady's favour before he would be required to return to London. It would be well worth a return trip if he thought she might welcome him!

He wondered what she thought of him thus far. He had sampled a good deal of his own shoe leather nearly every time he had spoken with her, but she seemed only to find amusement rather than offence. Did she laugh at him, or did she find his company agreeable?

His own opinion of her was clear; she was a remarkable young woman. He hesitated to so quickly become enamoured with any young lady, knowing his own feelings to be yet vulnerable, but... well, quite simply put, Madeline Fairbanks was everything that Mae Rutherford would never be. That much had taken only moments to discern once he had set foot into her home, and had seen the respectful, open way she related to her father. She was clever and gentle, humble and sincere. She was properly modest, but still she spoke what was on her mind much more forthrightly than Mae ever had. And she had beaten him at chess! Try as he might, she had captured his king... and quite possibly much more than that.

You have known her only one day, fool! he chided himself. His reason scolded him for giving rein to his fancy, but his heart retorted that when a man finds exactly what he has been seeking, it would be supreme idiocy not to attempt to win it.

His mount stirred, shifting its feet restlessly. Edward returned his attention to his surroundings to quiet his horse. The horse, however, had other ideas. It rooted for the bit, tossing its head and nearly causing Edward's hands to slip far back on the reins. "Who-ah," he called. "Steady, my good fellow!" In truth, he had not even checked to see if this horse was a "fellow" or not, but he doubted it mattered to the horse what he called it.

The horse stamped and shifted again, and Edward began to feel just a little nervous. He only ever rode sedate, well-trained mounts, and had never been required to school an unruly one. "What is the matter, my friend?" he soothed, stroking the horse's crest and squeezing just a little more tightly on the reins.

The tension building in the rider did little to calm the anxious horse. It swung its hindquarters to the side and lifted one foreleg as if to paw the ground. At last, deciding that walking forward might be easier than standing still, Edward gave a little slack on the reins. The horse shifted at once into a ground-eating stride, asking with a pull on the bit to move ever faster.

Edward glanced about himself in confusion. This horse had seemed perfectly tractable and content only a few moments ago. There was nothing present to startle the horse, no movement or sudden sound nearby. As a matter of fact... he stiffened.

There was no noise at all. The birds which had sung to him on his ascent up the hillside had gone still. He was no woodsman, but he had sense enough to experience a swell of foreboding.

With determination, he turned the homeward-bound horse about so that he could once more survey the landscape. From his new angle, he could pick out a flock of sheep down below, just over a ridge of the slope. He squinted, trying to decide if he was really seeing what he thought. The flock was being driven hard by two human figures, scampering for cover.

He shaded his eyes better with his hand to look more closely. What could be…? Looking about again, he finally noticed what he had missed. Rising over the mountain, in the middle of one of the most beautiful summer days he had ever seen, was a great, black cloud.

"WILL, LOOK!"

Fitzwilliam, who had been lying on his back with his eyes closed in a pillow of soft green grass, raised himself upon his elbow. Georgiana toddled near, her arms absolutely full of yellow dandelions. She beamed and struggled closer to him through the tall blades of grass.

"So pretty!" she enthused, dropping them in a heap at his feet.

He chuckled. "They are weeds, little love!"

She poked her fists into her waist and cocked her head knowingly. "Weeds aren't pretty, Will," she informed him.

"Oh, I suppose not," he smiled, corrected. "Did you eat enough luncheon, Georgie?"

"Yes, Will," she answered, distracted now as she tried to split one of the dandelion stems up the middle.

He leaned closer, curious. "What are you doing there?"

"Miss Tuttle showed me," she tilted her chin importantly, certain that she had the advantage of her brother in at least this one point. At last, making her awkward fingers perform her desire, she managed to loop the head of one dandelion through the split stem of the other.

"Ah, you are making a chain. Very clever, Georgie! May I help?"

She frowned, disappointed that he had so quickly seen her purpose, but handed him a pile of the sticky weeds. They worked until Georgiana had not only a tiara, but also a necklace and then a girdle with a long train dragging behind her.

"There," he laughed, settling one drooping flower back into her crown of mussed blonde curls. "You are the prettiest girl in the county!"

"As pretty as Mama?" she asked, her eyes suddenly wide and serious.

His smile faded. He gazed back into her face, sensing the reassurance she needed. He could not dare disappoint her, but he also knew that she had placed their mother on a pedestal of perfection and would bear no slights against her. "Prettier," he whispered at last. "But Mama was not a girl, she was a Mama. They are special."

Apparently, he had answered her rightly, because she threw her arms about his neck, squashing her wilting necklace in her abandon. "Oof! Georgie, I cannot breathe!" he gagged.

She giggled and tightened her arms even further, dissolving into peals of laughter when he dramatically choked for breath, then fainted dead away upon the grass. When he did not move again, she grew somewhat alarmed, standing over him in helpless surprise. It was not like her big brother to play-act. She could have truly killed him!

"Will!" she gasped, falling to her knees and shaking him. "Will, wake up!"

He lay still, his eyes closed, but his sister did not notice the smile twitching upon his lips until it was too late. He waited until she leaned her head against his chest to see if she could hear him breathing, and then wrapped her in a bear grip. "Ha! I have you now, Georgie!"

"No tickling, Will!" she squealed, writhing and kicking. "It's not fair!"

"The world is not fair, sweetling." He tormented her only a moment more, then sat up, placing her back on her feet so she might catch her breath. Releasing her, he gave a great stretch of his youthful frame, then leaned back upon his elbows. His affectionate gaze lingered on the child as she suddenly bent to examine an insect on a blade of grass.

Certainly, it would not do for them to always behave so informally, but just for now, before they were both grown too old for such enjoyments, he delighted in playing with her. She needed someone to indulge her, and though he could not replace Mother, he could give her the tender care that no hired nanny could provide. It was a pity that Father was always otherwise occupied, for he could have done much to encourage his daughter. Young Fitzwilliam feared that Georgiana's confidence might be forever shaken without the constant, loving hand of a parent to shepherd her. The Master of Pemberley, however, had many cares and worries, as well he knew.

He sighed, his own obligations returning to the fore of his consciousness. "Georgie," he called for her attention again, "I think we must return home." He rose, dusting the grass from his breeches, and turned to once more take in the peace of his favourite meadow. As he did so, he froze, his breath catching.

Where his back had been turned, a storm was approaching. It had not yet darkened the sun, but it was enormous and growing quickly. His pulse began to thud as he took half a moment to evaluate it. This would be no passing seasonal drizzle—this was a bona fide thunderhead of significant proportions.

"Georgie!" His adolescent voice cracked in fear. "We must leave, *now*!" Wholly ignoring the remains of their picnic, he grasped her hand. Soon, impatient with her short strides, he snatched her up as he fairly ran to the beech tree where he had tethered Saul.

Fool! he scolded himself. *How could I not have seen that coming?* His hands flew to his saddle and bridle, outfitting the placid old gelding more quickly than he had ever done before. He prayed he had not missed any details in his haste. He tossed his sister aboard like a grain sack and was instantly behind her, wheeling his mount for home.

At precisely that moment, the first thunderclap boomed across the landscape. Georgiana cried out in terror, and even Saul trembled at the shock of it. Fitzwilliam's hands were shaking on the reins. In only a few moments more, the soft leather would be slick with rainwater, and he would have a frightened horse to contend with. Glancing once more at the blackness creeping steadily overhead, he suspected that this was more than a simple thunderstorm. Those clouds looked to his Derbyshire-bred eyes like they carried hail.

Keeping Georgiana safe became the only thing he cared for. She was quivering and whimpering now in fright, clinging to his arm. They would never make home in time! Desperately, he spun his gaze about. The best shelter at hand was the trees. While they might afford some protection from rain or hail, he had seen enough trees struck down by lightning to know better than to seek shelter there.

"Georgie," he bent to speak as reassuringly in her ear as he could, "we must make our way to Lambton! We can be there in a quarter of an hour—less if you hold tightly enough for us to gallop."

"Will!" she sobbed, trying to turn her little face to his chest to hide from the storm. "I want to go home! I want Mama!"

He gritted his teeth. "Hold tight to me, Georgie. We will be home soon enough." Spurring the reluctant horse, who had every notion of returning to his familiar stable, he grimly forced the animal to change course. Lambton was their best hope for safety.

Chapter 13

Edward had begun his descent toward the village, taking a more direct route down the mountain than he had in climbing it. From this path he could continue to watch the movements of the shepherds in the fields below him. They knew the region far better than he, and their frantic body language informed him rather clearly that there was good cause for concern. The loud report of thunder overhead a moment later only confirmed that opinion.

His horse shied, but a shout from one of the shepherds—now not three hundred yards from him—alerted him to the fact that his horse was not the only frightened beast on that mountain. Several of the sheep peeled from their larger flock, scurrying off in a random direction. Edward watched as one of the shepherds parted from his companion to divert them back toward safety.

He reined in his horse, taking in the scene. The rain had yet to reach them, but he could see it coming, and it would be torrential when it struck. Those men, struggling to secure their terrified flock, would certainly be caught out in the storm. His brow puckered in thought for only a few seconds, then he clamped his legs against his mount's sides.

"Ho, there!" he called to the nearest man as he drew up. "May I help?"

The fellow turned round in confusion but was not above accepting his offer. He hesitated only briefly, then waved his hand after the strays. "Get 'head o' them!" he cried.

Edward nodded in acknowledgement, pushing his unwilling horse through the low brush and around two or three boulders. The horse held the advantage of longer legs and sure guidance by his rider, and very soon they had outdistanced the frightened creatures, cutting off their escape. *Just like my great uncle the army colonel!* he chuckled to himself, despite the situation.

Edward looked back at the man, the sheep now between them. The shepherd gestured, pointing him to a place where the rocks formed a natural bottleneck. If driven into it, the sheep would be forced to rejoin their group. He nodded and slowly, so as not to frighten them further, horseman and shepherd pushed the animals ahead of them. Thunder rumbled again, scattering the creatures, but this time the only way to go was in the direction their handlers desired.

He heard the rain long before he felt it. It swept toward them like a wave, as though a row of washing women had all emptied their buckets simultaneously. He cringed and hunched his shoulders, knowing his thin riding coat would offer little to no protection.

"Sir!" The shepherd he had spoken to was now beckoning to him. The sheep had rejoined the flock, and just ahead he could see their destination. The sheep, now seeking shelter themselves, fled into a series of natural caves against the hillside which looked as though they had been used for that purpose before. "Yo'll n'a make the village, sir!" he cried. "Best come t' the cave!"

Edward nodded wordlessly, cowering his head just as the downpour struck. He would be grateful to wait out the worst of this weather almost anywhere dry—even if it did smell like sheep.

"Miss Bennet, you are smudging my clean windows!" clucked Mrs Porter. She bustled about the common room, her hands constantly busy as more people came from out of doors to seek shelter somewhere warm and dry.

Elizabeth's eyes were round as saucers, absorbing the ferocity of the Derbyshire thunderstorm. The rain had only just begun, but she had been hearing the echoing thunder and watching the sky light up for nearly ten minutes already. She had never before witnessed such raw power, such terrifying savagery from the skies. She pressed her face to the window, fogging it and wiping it repeatedly. This was by far the most magnificent thing she had ever seen!

She remained there, thoroughly enraptured, until Mrs Porter tramped up to stand behind her. "'T'will be a bad one!" she tsked, shaking her head.

Elizabeth turned to face her. "Does it always storm like this in Derbyshire?" she asked breathlessly.

"No, lass," Mrs Porter answered, her eyes still fixed out the window. "And a good thing, too. This will make a pinch for the wheat crops this year!"

Elizabeth took a moment to think about that, then spun back to the window. She did not wish to miss a second! Guilt quickly overcame her, however. "Mrs Porter," she asked without turning back around, "is Jane's tea *ever* going to be done brewing? Miss Fairbanks said she needed it."

Mrs Porter chuckled, patting her on the shoulder. "Soon, Miss Bennet. Very soon. You stay here while it finishes brewing. I'll not forget you."

"Yes, Mrs Porter," she answered dutifully as the woman walked away. She was not disappointed to wait. The window in Jane's room was small and faced entirely the wrong direction to watch the storm. It was only a pity that there was no one here with whom to share her enjoyment! A quick glance about the room revealed only adults—some labourers, some travelers—all of whom appeared occupied enough with the business of getting dry. The storm had taken everyone by surprise, and a number of people had been caught in town, far from their homes.

Elizabeth was musing over her disappointment when the door opened again to admit more wet residents. This time it was a tall boy, quite a few years older than herself and obviously a gentleman's son. He was carrying a little girl of about Kitty's age. They were both bedraggled mops, and the girl had her face buried in the boy's coat. It looked like she was crying.

Her interest piqued, Elizabeth hopped down from her window seat. The boy had stopped upon entering the room, his eyes roving nervously about the tables. Some of the men gathered round the private alcoves reserved for the gentry were staring back at him in recognition. One even started forward to welcome the boy with his sister, but the tall boy brusquely turned aside. Why he would not simply join them, Elizabeth could not understand, but the friendly stranger withdrew, rebuffed. All others remained still, at a watchful and respectful distance.

She held no such trepidation. She marched up to them and spoke directly to the little girl. "Good day! I have a very comfortable seat at the window. Do you like watching thunderstorms? I do hope you will join me."

The girl shyly picked her head up from the boy's sodden chest, peering at Elizabeth through a single blue eye. She promptly hid her face once more. Undeterred, Elizabeth tried again. "Mrs Porter is making me a special tea that is for resting—you know, there is nothing like a hot cup of tea for real comfort. It shall be very nice and warm, and I would be pleased to share it with you!"

The girl dared to peek up once more, but again, only briefly. Elizabeth puckered her little lips and looked up... and up... to the boy's face. Why, he was nearly as tall as Uncle Gardiner already! He was glowering back at her in annoyance, tightening his grip upon the girl.

"Your sister is all wet," Elizabeth informed him.

"I had not noticed," he retorted obtusely. He gave her one last disdainful look, as though she were a filthy dog to be avoided lest one acquire muddy paw prints over one's person. He shifted the girl in his arms and walked over toward Mrs Porter.

Elizabeth glared after him. Of all the prideful, vain, unfriendly people! She crossed her arms in frustration and fumed for about three seconds. Then another thunderclap diverted her attention back to her main source of entertainment for the afternoon. She rushed back to the window, the disagreeable boy and his inarticulate sister temporarily forgotten.

A moment later, there was a tap at her elbow. Mrs Porter was there, glancing with wide eyes over her shoulder at the boy and girl. "Miss Bennet," she hissed lowly, "you are a friendly sort. Can you help ease this poor child? She has had the wits frightened out of her! I am afraid she is quite terrified by me as well, but you are closer in age...."

Elizabeth tipped her chin up primly. "I already tried, Mrs Porter, but they are not at all nice."

Mrs Porter shushed her promptly, glancing again over her shoulder to see if Elizabeth's saucy words had been overhead. "They are from one of the most prominent families in all of Derbyshire! Of course, they are above this present company! The young master does not seem to desire to take the private parlour, though I am certain those gentlemen there would gladly give it up if he wished. Nor does it seem fitting that they should remain with the common folk by the fire, though they are wet to the bone, the poor dears! I think they would prefer to share your quiet place by the window here while I fetch some dry things. I have told the young master you are a gentleman's daughter, so it would be no disgrace to allow the dear child to visit with you. Now, do yourself credit as a young lady, and use your very best manners! I am bringing you all some tea."

"Tea?" Elizabeth perked up. "Oh, is it Jane's special tea?"

"It will be very special," Mrs Porter promised with a whimsical smile. "I have already taken some very nice tea up to Miss Fairbanks. Do not fret about your sister. Now be a good little lass and watch your tongue!"

Elizabeth sighed glumly. Though she had longed for company to enjoy the storm with, she did not relish sharing her window seat with silent and unfriendly companions. Why, she might not even get to enjoy her glorious storm if she had to constantly worry over whether they were comfortable.

Pouting just a little, she eased off her bench and presented herself once more to the tall boy with the dripping brown hair. She bobbed a proper curtsey—imitating Miss Fairbanks rather than her mother, because she thought Miss Fairbanks was the most elegant lady she had ever seen. "Pleased to make your acquaint-ance," she managed, smiling at her more successful pronunciation of the long word.

The boy still stared at her in something akin to scandalized fascination. "I do not think we have been properly introduced."

She wrinkled her brow. "Did not Mrs Porter tell you my name? She told me who *you* are." She stretched the truth only a little. She knew they must be wealthy, but she had not caught their names. Nor, thought she, did she care to really know more of them.

"Apparently it escaped her," he returned drily. He glanced down at his sister, who was hugging his leg and still trying to hide her face. He leaned to murmur some reassurance as the thunder rolled once more, causing her to clutch him even more tightly.

Elizabeth sighed in irritation. She started to turn back to the window to watch her storm but felt a tug of pity for the littler girl. She did, after all, have younger sisters with no nanny, and she and Jane both knew a thing or two about comforting them. A stern glance from Mrs Porter across the common room assured her that it was most certainly in her best interest to be kind to the little one.

Casting about for some item of interest, her eyes fell upon her geography book, nestled where she had been sitting before. She retrieved it quickly, causing the boy to tilt his head and gaze after her in astonishment. Such abrupt manners he had never before witnessed!

Elizabeth returned to the little girl, who hid her face all the more determinedly in her brother's embrace at her approach. "Would you like to look at my book?" Elizabeth asked brightly. The child peeked suspiciously at her, but turned her face away again. The brother's gaze had shifted up over her head to take in the sheets of rain falling against the window, and Elizabeth felt quite invisible to this haughty boy and his unsociable sister.

She frowned, then her natural will prevailed, and she decided to try again. One way or another, she *would* make this girl like her! She flipped open her book and dropped to her knees before the child, causing the eyes of both to fix upon her in amazement. "Look here, this is Hertfordshire, where I come from."

The girl—whose eyes matched Jane's nearly to perfection—gazed carefully back. "Hertf…" she attempted hesitantly.

"Good!" Elizabeth encouraged. "Hert-ford-shire. You can say it!"

The boy shook his head, scowling. "Let her alone, please." He turned to pick his sister up once more.

Elizabeth jumped indignantly to her feet. "I am only trying to be nice! You ought to as well."

The boy narrowed his eyes, glaring at her. "She prefers only my company. It would be a kindness to leave her be and not to trouble her with your presence."

"Then I shall!" Elizabeth flew back to her window in a great huff, crossing her arms and sulking in the window seat. The very insolence of that boy! She supposed the very wealthy were all like that, caring only for their own pride and the dignity of their position. At least, she had read something like that somewhere, and it looked to her to be true. She sulkily tucked herself into her little nook, back turned to the other children, as she pressed her face once more to the window.

Lightning clapped several times in succession, and a moment later the very building shook with the power of roll after roll of thunder. Elizabeth gasped in awe and trembled a little herself at the unbridled fury of the elements. A mild-very mild—sensation of guilt pricked her when she heard a wail rising from the terrified little girl, but it was quickly stifled. Elizabeth did not turn round to find out how.

"Here you are!" Mrs Porter's cheerful, calming voice added another layer of conviction. Elizabeth looked up to see the matronly woman arriving with a steaming tea tray and a stack of dry linens. "Will the young Miss be comfortable with only these, sir?"

Elizabeth observed him narrowly. Mrs Porter must hold this boy's family in some high regard, to be calling a lad of fourteen 'sir'." It seemed he was not well used to such address, either. He flushed and awkwardly accepted the woman's kindness. He quickly wrapped the little girl in a blanket, using it to dab her hair and face where she would let him. He never once made a move toward his own comfort—his attention and care were all given to the child. That—along with an-other firm sideways glance from Mrs Porter as she left them—sealed Elizabeth's contrition.

She slid down from her seat once more and addressed herself to the tea tray. It was a very *nice* tea service, once more confirming the status of this family—at least in Mrs Porter's eyes. None of the inns they had visited thus far had graced the Bennet party with such a setting. Goodness, who *were* these people?

Glancing up, Elizabeth saw that the disagreeable boy was not paying her any mind. Well, she would not allow *that* to trouble her. She hefted the pot with both hands and carefully poured a cup of tea, just as she had been taught at home. Her little tongue tipped her lips as she slowly measured out the hot liquid, spilling only a couple of drops. She lowered the pot proudly. She was getting better at this! One day, she might be as elegant as Miss Fairbanks.

She tilted her head and considered the young child buried in the blankets, as though she could determine by looking at her how she took her tea. At last, she simply made it the way she did Mary and Kitty's, with generous quantities of both cream and sugar. Gingerly, she picked up the delicate saucer, and with silent little cat paws, walked as gently as she could to offer the beverage.

Ignoring the boy—who, she had to admit, seemed kind enough to his sister, though he cared little for anyone else—she spoke to the girl. "Here is that special tea I told you about. Would you like to try it?"

The child's head popped curiously out of the blankets. Elizabeth extended the cup and saucer enticingly, then set them down on a little round table next to her window seat. She retreated away quickly, just as she did at home when she tried to feed the bashful squirrels.

Eyes wide, the girl slowly eased herself out of her brother's embrace and toddled toward the little table. Elizabeth, by now, was pouring a second cup, and a moment later she returned with it. With satisfaction, she saw the little girl inspecting the cup, touching her fingers daintily to the side to test the temperature.

The boy, however, was scrutinizing her like an insect under a magnifying glass. Elizabeth did not care to be treated as a spectacle, though it did happen so often. She lifted her little chin, staring right back.

"I... I must thank you," he fumbled as she came near. He extended his hand to accept the second cup and saucer, but Elizabeth did not offer it. Instead, she turned toward the table with the girl.

"You may join us if you like," she shrugged airily as she walked past. "There is still another cup."

Chapter 14

E DWARD HAD HUNCHED HIS shoulders down inside his coat, but it was little use. The garment was light, made for summer wear, and thoroughly drenched. He found more comfort in removing it and warming himself by the modest little fire the shepherds had made in the mouth of the cave to dry their clothing. Crouching low near it, he held out his hands as though he could absorb more of the fire's heat through his palms. The others were doing the same, and he wished to prove himself not so very different from they. So far, both were still regarding him with some unease.

He cleared his throat. "I say," he began somewhat nervously, "it was right good of you to share your shelter with me."

They blinked at each other, then the elder of the two nodded. "We're 'bliged for your 'elp, sir. We might still've been searchin' for the missin' ewes."

"Think nothing of it," he replied cheerfully. "I would not have gained the shelter of town soon enough, in any case. I am afraid I wandered too far today! Egad, but this is beautiful country you have here."

The younger of the two, the one he had spoken to first, promptly agreed. "'Tis, sir. Spent a year in the city, I did, and 'tis right glad I were to come back, sir, though I did make better wages there."

Edward regarded him with new interest. "May I ask which city?"

"Manchester, sir. 'Ad to take fact'ry work to feed my wife and boy. We 'ad a bad year, two year back. Lost 'alf the flock in a storm like this."

The other man grunted his concurrence and Edward looked back out at the rain in some puzzlement. "Like this? Forgive me, it did not seem to me so very bad. It is only a little rain, is it not? I would have expected it to pass quickly."

"'Tis not the rain, sir," the elder of the two shepherds spoke up. "'Tis the 'ail. The flock were all shorn, 'ad no fleece."

Edward glanced at the animals crowded behind him, realizing the truth of the man's words. They gleamed with fresh downy softness, evidence of a recent shearing. He then cocked an eye conversationally toward the weather. "You think it will hail?"

As though he had pressed some invisible trigger with his words, a gale of tumbling ice chips fell upon the mouth of their cave. Edward's eyes widened in enlightenment. "I see," he murmured, but his words were lost in the clamor of the elements. The rocks falling from the heavens began as small little diamonds, but rapidly grew in size. Some were nearly as big as the end of his thumb, and he imagined that in their multiplied power, they could do a deal of harm.

Conversation had been difficult before, but it was now impossible over the noise of the hail. As the three men watched helplessly, the hail continued to increase in size. Stones as large as their palms were not uncommon, and the ground was very quickly covered in pebbles of ice.

Edward began to appreciate yet another problem for the shepherds. Once the storm was over, it would be some hours before the ice had melted enough for the flock to roam safely over the slopes. Water and feed for the ewes and lambs would be a challenge until then, and the tender, valuable young animals would be distressed. Even after the ice had melted, there was no telling what damage might be done to their forage.

He swallowed hard, shaking his head. He was glad he had not been born into a farming family.

MADELINE HAD ABANDONED HER post at Jane's bedside to gaze in horror out of the small window. She knew, perhaps as well as anyone, the full magnitude of the damage such a storm would inflict. She had assisted her father for the past two years and had seen the financial impact on the livelihoods of the local farmers.

She crossed her arms, shaking her head in pity. All of those animals caught out in the storm! And the wheat, and the hay! The young wheat would be nearly a total loss. Some of the first hay cutting might be salvageable if allowed to dry properly, but not without compounded labour for a much poorer crop. She sighed, gazing out upon the white streets. This was bad timing indeed for such a storm!

Suddenly, she blinked, and her stomach clenched. Edward Gardiner was out there still! As the storm continued to grow in power and vehemence, she blanched in utter fear. He would not have known where to find shelter! A man could be killed by a single hailstone as large as those even now falling on the street.

She hoped against hope that he had cut his ride short and might have already returned in safety. She glanced furtively at Jane Bennet, still resting comfortably in her bed, before she rushed out of the room. Flying down the stairs, she at once sought Mrs Porter.

"Have you heard from Mr Gardiner?" she asked her friend breathlessly.

"Nay, I've heard naught," she shook her head as she poured a fresh kettle of hot water. "Benjamin!" she called to her husband. "The fire needs tending, and the gentlemen in the private parlour asked for fresh tobacco!" She bustled off, leaving Madeline helpless and worried behind her.

She glanced about until she spied young Lizzy with another little girl at the front window of the inn, the one facing the street. "Lizzy!" she hurried close. "Have you seen your uncle?"

The child shook her head, her dark eyes suddenly growing wide. "No, Miss Fairbanks. Maybe he is at the stable?"

Madeline bit her lip and fisted her white hands, completely powerless. "I do hope so, Lizzy!" She sighed, trying to blink away her worry. He was such a *nice* man! She truly hoped he was safe. Unfortunately, there was nothing she could do but wait and pray that he had found shelter. Well, that was not entirely true. She could see to the man's nieces, as she had promised she would.

"Lizzy, are you well?" she forced herself to ask, though the answer seemed plain enough. "You are not frightened by the storm?"

"Oh, no, Miss Fairbanks! It is wonderful!" She leaned close in a confidential whisper. "The *little* girl is scared, and I suppose I might be too, if I were little, like she."

Madeline suppressed a chuckle. "It is a good thing, then, that you are no longer little. I trust you can help comfort her."

Elizabeth nodded solemnly. "Her brother is not nice at all, but she likes me," she whispered. "I think I shall read her a story when we have finished our tea."

Madeline glanced up to the window once more, for the first time noticing the back of a tall youth. Where most others in the room had removed their wet outer clothes, this lad still wore his sopping riding garments. He did not turn around—his gaze was fixed out of the window. More travelers, she guessed, and by the look of the boy's jacket, rather well-heeled ones.

"Lizzy," she murmured low to the child, "do take care to watch your tongue around these people."

The little imp tilted her chin upward to look Madeline in the eye. "That is exactly what Mrs Porter told me. I wonder why?"

Madeline shook her head. "Just be polite," she advised. "It would not do to frighten your young friend further, now, would it?"

"No, Miss Fairbanks," the child sighed. "May I see Jane?"

"She is resting, my dear. I think you can do more good here," she winked, glancing once more at the round-eyed little girl watching Elizabeth.

"Yes, Miss Fairbanks," the girl replied with apparent reluctance. A second later, however, Elizabeth had turned back to the little girl with her and brightly engaged her once more. Had Madeline not been consumed with worry for the gentleman, she would have found amusement at the quick spirits of his niece.

She glanced over the room once more. There seemed little more she could do here, so she resolved to watch over Jane Bennet as diligently as before. Certainly, Edward Gardiner was safe somewhere. She hoped, at least.

Chapter 15

THE HAIL CONTINUED TO pelt the little town for over a quarter of an hour. It fell in fits and starts, sometimes lightening and looking as though it might cease altogether, but then picking up force once again. While Gardiner was taking shelter in the cave and thinking in gratitude on the relative safety of his nieces, another man was pacing the floor of his opulent home and fretting over the welfare of his children.

As soon as there appeared a short moment of relief, George Darcy ran to the stables himself, clutching his hat down over his ears to prevent it from flying away. "Douglas!" he bellowed as soon as he had gained the door.

His head groom was already waiting for the master, touching a hand to his cap in respect. He was well acquainted with the Master of Pemberley and required no questioning from his employer to be ready with a response. "The young master is still out, sir. He said he was going in the direction of the eastern meadow, on the edge of the creek, and that he and the young mistress would be some hours. It was long before the weather turned, sir, and we'd no cause to caution him."

George Darcy glared hard at his trusted stable man, knowing that the man spoke in full truth, but furious at himself for having let Fitzwilliam go. He had that morning thought the air had felt a bit ominous, but had not warned his son, thinking the lad would not be harmed by a good wetting if it came to it. It was with some horror that he had witnessed the torrent of hail, and suddenly accounted for Georgiana's absence. Only yesterday he had tacitly encouraged the boy to take little Georgie, for he too had sensed that the time spent with her older brother would be a comfort to her—but on today, of all days....

"Sir, I have already sent two of the grooms out in search of them," Douglas assured the master. "I shall have more once this hail clears and I can alert my men."

Mr Darcy's gaze had fallen from his head groom to the empty stall where Fitzwilliam's horse ought to have been standing. "How long ago did you send them?"

"I had them saddle as soon as that cloud came up, sir. They'll be well-nigh halfway to that meadow now."

Mr Darcy turned, surveying the ruined field behind him. "Not in this. They would have had to take shelter," he mused.

"With respect, sir," Douglas spoke a little stiffly, "I had them take oilskins and thick rugs for the horses. My men would not retire to shelter until the young master and mistress are found."

Darcy turned back to his man. "I do not doubt their faithfulness, Douglas, but in such conditions, the horses cannot even walk without collecting ice balls in their hooves." He stared pensively again at the empty stall. "Fitzwilliam would have seen to his sister's protection. I have confidence in him, Douglas." The last statement was spoken softly, as though the man himself had only just come to believe his own words.

George Darcy paused another moment, his pained eyes turned up to the heavens as if he could pinpoint the last icy stone which would mark the end of the storm. It would not come for a while, he realized with a sinking stomach. A shift in the wind caused another slight break in the onslaught, and Darcy prepared to run back toward the house.

Just before he did so, however, he turned back to his groom with a final instruction. "Fitzwilliam may have sought shelter in Lambton, if he had enough start. Hitch up the carriage and have it ready immediately the hail ceases. I shall send Mr Wickham to search there for them and to settle with any debts they may have incurred while taking shelter."

Douglas touched his cap smartly. "Yes, Mr Darcy."

E LIZABETH CLOSED THE BOOK she had held before herself, revealing once more the rounded, expressive eyes of the little girl. "Did you like it?" she chirped gleefully.

The girl—whose name Elizabeth had yet to catch—nodded and smiled shyly. "Eugenia sounds nice," she whispered. "Like my mama, but mama was pretty."

Elizabeth glanced down at her book in some dismay. "It is not Eugenia you are supposed to like, but Camilla."

A sliver of flint appeared in the child's eyes, and the striking resemblance to Jane's sweetness, which Elizabeth had noted, suddenly disappeared. Indeed, the face looking up to her now bore an expression very like Elizabeth's own mirror. "I like Eugenia!" she maintained, sticking her lower jaw out in the manner of an obtuse little tot.

"Well," Elizabeth dropped the book, deciding that she, at age seven, was possessed of far too much dignity to argue with a three-year-old. "Perhaps you may read the rest of it some day and come to understand it better." It was not without some degree of condescension that she spoke. She was not insensitive to the fact that the novel was one that fashionable young ladies read and was therefore not at all a children's book. How fortunate was she that her father permitted her to read whatever she liked!

They had been left in merciful peace for some while, as the ill-natured older brother had taken himself to the livery stable down the street to see to his horse as soon as the hail had passed. It had been with a surly glare that he had allowed his little sister to remain with Elizabeth, but he had little choice if he did not wish to expose the child to the rain once more. It happened to be that he had just returned, once more dripping wet and glowering his disapproval as he stood behind the oblivious Elizabeth.

"Do you mean, child, that you have been reading to my sister from a *novel*?" he sneered in disgust. "I ought to have known."

She turned to him with all the salt and pluck she possessed. "Yes, you ought, for novels and the people who read them are *interesting*, while you are not!"

Stunned, William's mouth nearly came unhinged as he gaped at this outrageous child. What horrendous manners! And where the devil was her parent? "Georgie!" he snapped, "Come with me at once!" He snatched his little sister's hand and attempted to drag her away from her abominable companion. What would his father say if he knew the daughter of Pemberley had been seen with such a beastly little scamp? Feeling he had twice failed to protect his sister in one day, he forgot to consider poor Georgiana's tender feelings from earlier and moved to dispatch the budding acquaintance with celerity.

"No, Will!" Georgiana allowed her hand to go slack and wormed it from his tight embrace, even as he tried to secure his grip. "I want to stay!"

Fitzwilliam Darcy, the future Master of Pemberley and a strapping, educated lad in his own right, was left to stand helpless and embarrassed before the two pint-sized females. It was, he would eventually discover, an experience which would one day become all too familiar. In this moment, however, he only paused in horror at this regrettable turn in his sister's sentiments. "Georgie!" he cried in betrayal. "Come wait with me over by the table."

Little Georgiana crossed her arms, the first flicker of defiance she had ever shown to him. "Lizzy is my friend," she declared with childish determination. "Lizzy," whoever she was, somehow managed an expression which appeared both pert and serene at the same time. She tipped a puckish little smile up to him, smug in her victory in the battle over Georgiana's loyalties.

Never before had the carefully schooled would-be gentleman been tempted to wring the neck of any human—except for George Wickham—but just then, he would have given a great deal to wipe that saucy look out of the child's eyes. Whoever had the management of this wicked girl had done her a great disservice, indeed!

Oh, to be sure, she was clearly the daughter of a gentleman. Her dress, her concise speech, her level of education—all pointed to a gently reared child who had the opportunity to garner accomplishments. He doubted rather strenuously, however, that such an impertinent youngster had been given the proper guidance for such an undertaking. Never had he known any young girl of his own sphere to be permitted to behave so outrageously!

Speaking more from the furious thoughts tumbling round his mind than the failed attempt to secure his sister, he growled lowly. "It is not meet, girl, that a child should think herself a young lady before she has taken the trouble to improve her manners!"

The odious little creature stared right back at him, but rather than taking his constructive advice to heart, she burst into laughter—laughter so merry, it grated on his ears and made his fists curl. She squealed in delight, and even Georgie saw fit to join in.

Fitzwilliam blanched in horror. To be defied by a child of half his age and less than half his station in life was mortifying enough. To have her openly mock him and holding sway over his own sister... *Think!* he ordered himself. *A Darcy does not tolerate the ridicule of an urchin such as this!*

The girl was pointing at him now, still giggling. "'*Not meet*'," you say! Papa read me that phrase from one of his big books, and we did laugh so. Do you really talk like that?"

His ears turning red, Fitzwilliam made another grasp for his sister. "Come, Georgie!" he demanded—not very gently. "We shall be going home soon enough!" He trapped the squirming child beneath his arm and carried her away from the window seat to another, much smaller window. Scowling darkly, he turned his back to the room and forced Georgiana to do the same.

There was no sniffling, no sound of heartbreak or remorse behind him. If that dreadful little girl were disturbed at losing her companion, she gave no sign. As staring out of the window upon the abandoned street was not the most diverting of pastimes, he cocked a curious look over his shoulder... just to see if she happened to be watching.

She was not. She had wandered over to a chessboard, apparently quite unmoved by his disdain. Intrigued, he watched her a moment, expecting her to bump the board and send the pieces flying like any other child would have. Rather than fulfill his expectations, however, the girl pulled a chair up to the board, and began a careful inspection of the arrayed battle which some other patrons had begun.

He could not stop watching her. Apparently, someone had taken the time to instruct her, for she began playing both sides of the board. His interest in the child sharpened as he amused himself by watching her strategies. Short little fingers hovered over the knight and he tensed, knowing before she made the move that it would leave her queen vulnerable. Not that it mattered, of course. He did not care, naturally! And besides, she likely did not either, as she had no opponent.

The girl's brow was puckered in thought, and her fingers moved away from the knight to make an entirely different move. Fitzwilliam was impressed, to put it mildly. He clenched his teeth, turning back to the window. Georgiana, beside him, had dropped off to sleep in her seat. He tucked a blanket more snugly about her, but his ears listened behind him for the soft taps of wooden chess pieces on the board.

His lips sealed in frustration. Was it ungentlemanly to refuse to make amends with a child of lower station, and a girl at that? It certainly *was* impolite to leave her to play chess all by herself while he sulked in the corner. His stomach twisted in conviction. She was not such a bad girl, really—and she *was* the daughter of a gentleman, placing her more firmly within his own sphere than he had originally wished to confess.

She had been attentive and kind to Georgiana since the first moment he had stumbled through the door with her and had asked nothing of him but basic civility. He clenched his eyes. *He*, Fitzwilliam Darcy, the darling of the region and the most well-brought-up young man for fifty miles around, had acted so disgracefully he was ashamed to even confess his own name.

What would George Darcy think of the figure his son had cut this day? A fool and a blackguard! A vain and selfish boy who had arrogantly assumed the care of his sister, failed to properly safeguard her, then lashed out in wounded pride at the first being to cross his path! That little girl deserved better... why, his own dignity and the honor of his name deserved better from him! His conscience continued to niggle at him until at last he growled in reluctant surrender. Perhaps she might prove generous enough to allow him an opportunity to better acquit himself.

Lizzy—that was her name, if he remembered correctly—looked up in astonishment when his large, brown hand moved the bishop from the other side. "Would you like an opponent?" he asked, suddenly shy.

She tilted her curly head and studied him in childish gravity. "Very well," she shrugged. "But you must play this side."

He frowned, and his gaze swept the board. "That seems unfair. This side is currently losing the match. I should take it."

"No," she grinned—a sparkling, joyful expression which he liked better than he cared to admit. "I should, because if I lose to you, I may then claim that I began with the disadvantage."

Stunned, he gaped as she serenely pirouetted into the position she had claimed for herself, leaving him to assume the other. Then, Fitzwilliam Darcy did something he had not done in a very, very long time, except with Georgiana.

He laughed.

"**M**Y GOOD FELLOWS." EDWARD extended his hand to each of the two shepherds in the frank custom of the region. "I am much obliged to you."

The two men shook hands cheerfully, wishing him well. "Ar' yo' sure, sir, that yo' wish t' ride out now?" the elder of them asked dubiously.

"You said yourself that you would not expect any more hail," Gardiner reasoned. "Yes, I think it for the best. Look, see, the clouds are already lifting in that direction. It shall be a wet ride, but I think not a cold one, and I have my nieces to see to. I do hope you lost none of your flock in this!"

"Not so many as we might, sir, thanks t' yo'. Taik care, sir."

Edward swung up on the rented sorrel and pointed the horse back toward Lambton. His thoughts had not wandered far from his nieces—likely frightened out of their wits they were! He also chafed at losing the opportunity to enjoy a quiet luncheon with Miss Fairbanks. Amiable as these rough fellows were, he was quite sure that he would have preferred to comfort the lady during the storm.

Seven miles away, and from another direction, another man was setting out in the rain for a similar reason. James Wickham, steward of Pemberley, strode briskly from the house after receiving his instructions from the master. His caped coat and broad hat would keep him moderately comfortable for the journey to the carriage, where he would be entirely dry for the duration of his travels. It was a privilege he did not dismiss lightly, for his driver and horses had no such luxury. He mounted the coach, with a simple, "Lambton, please, Foster."

As he began to seat himself, his son's voice over his shoulder called back his attention. "Father, may I come?"

Mr Wickham checked himself. "Had you not ought to be working with Mr Douglas in the stables this afternoon, as Mr Darcy instructed?" he asked his son firmly. "I believe you had a considerable list of chores to complete."

"I have done so, Father," the boy answered—almost truthfully. "I wish to help you search for Master Fitzwilliam."

His father eyed him cynically. "I am not sweeping the countryside as the riders are but going directly to Lambton. There are only two possible places to look there. I think you had better stay."

The lad raised imploring eyes to his parent—that same expression copied from his mother, to be quite truthful—and James Wickham had never yet learnt to deny it. "Fitzwilliam is my only friend, Father," he sighed with aggrieved resignation.

Mr Wickham frowned. That boy of his could bamboozle almost anyone, and he, intelligent manager though he was, was nearly powerless to refuse George's wishes. His only hope was that time spent alongside himself in worthy pursuits, and the unflinching expectations of his wise and honourable employer, might in the end guide the boy along the paths of rectitude. "Come ahead, then," he relented.

Chapter 16

"**Y**OU CANNOT DO THAT!" The girl's fine brown eyes flashed in indignation.

"I just did. Look here, the move was perfectly legal!" Fitzwilliam replaced the pawn he had claimed and recreated the move. "Do you see, you advanced two squares, and I immediately moved forward here..." He repeated the sequence a few times, demonstrating to her young understanding the best he could. "It is called the *en passant*, and you should have employed it on me earlier. You might have had a chance to turn the game around."

She crossed her arms, scowling. "Uncle does not play like that," she grumbled.

"I would imagine he does, just not against you. Was it he who taught you to play?"

"My papa taught my uncle *and* me. He was a champion at Cambridge," she informed him archly.

"It is to your credit that you have learned as much as you have, for one so young," he gave a little mock bow of his head, inspiring her twinkling smile to make a return. "I believe that I myself had barely begun to play by your age. Your father is perhaps wise to begin teaching you early."

He did not add his thoughts that it was unusual for a girl to play at all, for he meant to begin teaching Georgiana as soon as she could concentrate well enough. It made for a pleasant way to pass time with a female, and in his mind, more girls ought to learn chess than dancing.

"Papa lets me use his library, too." She offered him a conspiratorial grin. "Nobody else at home is allowed."

"He permits you, or you simply ignore his disapprobation?" He fixed her with a suspicious expression. Yes, he thought he knew how it was with this little minx. It had been similar with himself at that age, when his father did not trust him in the library, but he had enlisted the help of one of the maids... until he had been caught. George Darcy's wishes were not to be flaunted, but perhaps this little hoyden's father was less firm.

She was not cowed by his challenge, which was truly all the answer he needed. She smiled, shrugged lightly, and replied, "I never use it when he is there, of course. He only makes a show of disciplining me so that Mary and Kitty will not follow."

"Indeed." Fitzwilliam chuckled, shaking his head in greatest amusement. What a puzzle this little girl was! He had enjoyed their chess match more than he could have expected, though it was hopelessly one-sided now. Even were they to switch sides of the board, the light side was irredeemable, and there was no point in forcing her king into check.

"Here." He lifted his own king and handed it to her with a playful flourish, one such as he might have reserved for Georgiana. "For the lady. May all kings fall so willingly into your hand."

She took it with a small giggle, causing a dimple to pop on her cheek and her dark eyes to sparkle. She really was a rather engaging child, if he were forced to confess it. He sighed and straightened his torso in a refreshing stretch, then looked to little Georgie. She still slept in an impossible curled ball at the window seat, but just through the glass, he could see the weather beginning to settle once more under good regulation. He was almost sorry for that.

"Will you take her home now?" The girl's suddenly sober voice wondered.

"I cannot put her back on a horse again today," he mused thoughtfully. "She has been frightened and is far too weary. My father would not approve. I imagine that Father or his steward will find us soon enough."

"Oh," she chirped brightly, "so you *do* live here in Lambton?"

"I?" he queried, turning to face her with some measure of his typical hauteur. "Why, no, child. My father owns a great estate near here, but I do not suppose you will have heard of it."

"My father owns an estate as well." She preened a little.

"Of course, he does," he commented neutrally, not seeing any point in detailing the differences between Pemberley and whichever gentle hovel had birthed this rather interesting creature. He frowned again, his eyes still on Georgiana. "I've no doubt that Father has sent out riders, and possibly a carriage, in search of us. I would expect them almost momentarily."

"In the hail?" his companion objected incredulously.

He turned back to her, his eyes narrowed curiously. "Naturally. It is only their duty, if my father sends them, to go."

The little imp crossed her arms. "That is not nice," she asserted, with all the practical eloquence of a very young child.

He scoffed, looking again to Georgiana at the window. "*'Not nice!'* she says! It is rather consequential, do you not think, if the master's own family are caught out in a storm such as that? It would be shameful if the staff did not do all that could be done!"

She stuck out a petulant lip. "Did you ever ask them if *they* liked riding in the rain and hail?"

He swept his gaze to her again, thunderstruck. "What does it matter if they like it? They are paid, and rather handsomely, too!"

"You are more important than they are?" she questioned, with a sharpness he might not have expected from one of her age.

"Well, of course I...." He stumbled to silence, recognizing how neatly she had trapped him into confessing his pride. Who *was* this meddlesome little sprite? Whoever she was, her seeming power over him ended *now*. To think that the future Master of Pemberley should feel obliged to explain himself to a child barely out of leading strings! He straightened and brushed a little dust from his sleeve, rising at last from the chess table. "It is a matter beyond your understanding," he dismissed her flatly.

He left her behind at the chessboard, trying not to imagine her look of either triumph or disappointment in him. Why should he care? She was but a child, yet once more she had baited him into losing his temper! His one consolation was that within a short while, he would have left that inn and would never have to bear the humiliation of seeing her again.

Feeling all the more compelled to show himself a more considerate person than he had just given her reason to believe, he bent over his sleeping sister with soft words. "Georgie? Sweetling, it is time to wake." A low, reluctant groan met his efforts. "Come, little love, I expect we shall be on our way home soon. You ought to eat a little more before we go."

She stirred groggily; her youthful face creased with the lines of the blanket she had snuggled into. "Don't go, Will," she mumbled, then flopped over into his arm.

"Georgie, come, we shall be going together this time," he soothed. It was with no great degree of surprise that he perceived his new little "friend" come to peer round his elbow. She was certainly an inquisitive creature. "Georgie, you must wake now," he admonished, trying to ignore the pest at his side.

"She told me earlier that you were leaving her soon," the little maid informed him, as if she thought he desired her input.

He turned sharply on her, though not unkindly. "She said what? When?"

"When you were seeing to your horse. She said you go away often. I think she misses you."

He studied the girl's earnest face in some dismay. "Well... yes, that is true. I am away to school again in a few weeks. It cannot be helped, but I am surprised she said as much."

She shrugged wordlessly, then the curly brown head turned away. A moment later, she returned with a bite of jellied scone left over from before. She knelt beside Georgiana on the window seat and crooned gentle words to the surly child in the blanket. Slowly, the blonde head raised, eyes were rubbed, and the scone consumed.

He straightened the blanket over his sister's shoulders, grateful that her mood seemed rapidly improved. "Thank you," he told the girl sincerely, once again humbled by the youngster's success in easing his sister where he had failed.

She spared them both a wistful little smile. "I wish I had a brother," she sighed.

He paused to stare at her. It was a rather revealing sentiment for her to have expressed. A modest gentleman's daughter with no brother would be under considerable pressure to marry well. Even he, at age fourteen, understood that—though he doubted that she did. It seemed more likely in this moment that she admired his own brotherly abilities enough to speak the desire for a protector of her own in his hearing. Perhaps she truly did not think him such an ogre as she might have, and some small part of him found contentment in that.

He began to open his mouth to make reply when the door to the inn slammed open. It was only a man come in from the storm; a tradesman by the look of him, and Fitzwilliam turned away to dismiss him as of no importance to the moment. His young friend, however, underwent an immediate transformation.

"Uncle Gar'ner!" she cried, leaping from her seat, her face alight. She rushed to fling her arms around the man's rain-soaked neck as he bent down.

"Lizzy!" the man swept her up and embraced her so warmly that Fitzwilliam almost felt as though he should not be watching this private family moment.

The girl kissed her uncle freely on the cheek, then leaned back in his embrace. "Uncle, Miss Fairbanks was so worried! I am glad to see you are all right. It will make her feel better."

The man's face brightened. "She was, indeed? Well, I shall go assure her that I am quite well. You were not frightened by the storm, Lizzy?"

"No! I made some friends, Uncle."

"Good girl. Go on back now, I must look in on Jane. I will be back down in a few moments for you." He set her back on her feet and turned, still dripping and anxious, to address himself to the flight of stairs.

She wandered back to him then, smiling beatifically. He arched a brow. "That is the uncle who plays chess with you?" he wondered aloud.

She beamed proudly. "Yes!" she asserted. "Is he not wonderful?"

He frowned. Not only did she have unconventional manners, but an uncle in trade! Charming as she was, this girl would have a difficult time of it one day, but in an effort to not annoy the girl who had so comforted Georgiana, he decided to say no more about it. He never would have had a chance anyway, for at that moment, the door to the inn opened once more.

"Master Fitzwilliam!" Mr Wickham enthused. "Thank heaven you and the young miss are safe!"

"We are, thank you Mr Wickham," he answered, unable to help catching that little girl's eye once more. "Did my father send the carriage?"

"Indeed. George!" he called to his son. "Help Master Fitzwilliam settle Miss Darcy into the carriage while I see to matters with the innkeeper."

Fitzwilliam stiffened. "I am quite able to carry her, thank you. My horse is at the livery, perhaps..." But Mr Wickham had already hurried off to do his business. George, who had tailed his father, stood smirking before him.

"Caused a to-do, you did!" his counterpart chortled. "I expect your father will have some words for you on your return."

"It is none of your concern, now, is it?" Fitzwilliam shouldered his still-drowsy sister, turning her so that she could huddle her sleep-flushed cheeks into his chest. The dark-haired miss by her side started forward to help with the tangle of blanket, but he shook his head slightly, waving her back.

George did not fail to notice, unfortunately. "Oh, what have we here? A foundling, eh, Fitz?"

"Let her alone," he growled. "She is a gentleman's daughter, George."

"I see, then," the other replied with a knowing smile. "So, I'm not fit to tweak those little curls?"

Fitzwilliam twisted the blanket, which was wrapped around Georgie, and tugged it free. "Your father instructed you to help Georgiana. Take this to the carriage and lay it out."

George's shoulders slumped. He snatched the blanket with a disgruntled scowl. "Ever the gallant, aren't you Fitz?" he sneered under his breath.

He turned to go, but before he did so, he tugged his grey cap from his head and bowed theatrically before the little brunette. "I beg you would forgive my good friend, Miss. It is certain that he left his manners back at the mansion, but we Derbyshire folk are not all such curmudgeons. I wish you a very pleasant stay in the neighborhood." With a smug little jerk, he replaced his hat, grinned serenely at Fitzwilliam, and sauntered out the door.

Little Lizzy was staring after George in vague distaste. He groaned, adjusting Georgiana's weight on his shoulder. "I am sorry about that," he began.

She lifted clear brown eyes to his. "He is not nice at all, is he?"

"Sometimes he is not," Fitzwilliam agreed. "However, my father wishes me to call him a friend, and so I shall."

She pressed her lips into a thin little smile. "We are to go away in a few days. I expect I shall not see you again."

He blinked, suddenly realizing that fact was to his regret. It was a pity, really. Georgiana could use such another little girl for a companion—and he found her unpredictable company rather less than tedious himself. Gripping his sister's inert form more tightly, he made her a little bow of his own—less formal, perhaps, but far more genuine than the one George had offered her.

"I wish you safe travels, Miss. Perhaps one day our paths may cross again."

She grinned, those dark eyes sparkling. "Only if you should come to Hertfordshire."

He laughed. "I just may. I will look forward to another chess match."

She dipped him a cheerful curtsey, and he left her behind in that homey little inn.

Chapter 17

MADELINE HAD TWITTERED HER fingers nervously for the last hour. Occasionally she would attempt to read, or fuss over Jane's blankets and tea things, but the girl was soundly asleep and her book had become suddenly dull. If only the rain would cease!

She moved to the window once more—not that she had strayed very far from it—but a glance down the street revealed only the beginnings of the exodus from dry quarters throughout the town. Those who were not far from their intended destinations now hurried back to them, but those who had a distance to travel were likely still waiting out the rest of the rainstorm. If Edward Gardiner had returned to the livery stable before the worst of the storm had struck, he surely would have come back to the inn by now! Her hopeful eyes searched and did not find that dark blue coat among the walkers below.

She sank morosely into her seat, then chided herself. He was a grown man, after all! Surely he was well. As another half an hour came and went, however, her stomach turned sickeningly. What if he truly had been hurt? What if he were thrown from a frightened horse, alone in a strange terrain with no shelter? Her mind began to conjure all manner of dreadful scenarios. She clenched her slim fingers into a fist. No one in this area might think to send anyone out to search for him, save for herself!

Resolving to do precisely that, she leapt to her feet and was almost upon the door when it swung open. Still dripping and breathless, the man she had looked for thumped into the room, grinning broadly. "Miss Fairbanks!" he cried in some surprise as she nearly careened into him.

"Oh!" Madeline put up her hands to halt her headlong rush to the door, almost stumbling instead into his arms. "Mr Gardiner! Oh, you are safe!"

"Quite safe," he smiled more gently, catching her hands in his own. "You were concerned?"

"I... well, naturally! A hailstorm is a very dangerous thing, Mr Gardiner."

"It is, indeed." He seemed rather too cheerful as he agreed with her fears. "Frightfully dangerous. Why, a man could meet his maker at a moment's notice! Is it that which troubled you, Miss Fairbanks?"

"Of course!" She was still standing rather close to him, her hands trapped in his, as her cheeks burned red. "Should I not have been concerned?"

He flashed her an easy grin. "Well, as it turns out, I met with some rather amiable fellows who shared their cave with me, but..." He glanced down to her hands and kneaded them comfortingly, "... It is good to know that I might be missed."

Madeline found herself quite incapable of speech. What could he mean by caressing her hands, smiling down at her like that? Why, in another moment, he might... he might.... She made a small noise in her throat and nervously tugged her hands free. She had not thought Edward Gardiner a rake, but there was no sense in allowing... whatever she had been about to allow. She turned back to Jane's bed, her cheeks stained brightly.

"Miss Fairbanks," he spoke at her elbow, his voice now subdued. "I hope I have not distressed you."

Her neck prickled at his closeness, standing just behind her as he was, and she shivered in a way she had never done before. She tried to shrug it off. "It is well you are returned, sir. I had feared the worst," she forced herself to confess softly. It would not be truthful to claim her fears were on behalf of Jane and Elizabeth alone, but surely a woman, in her feminine compassion, was permitted to show concern for a man's welfare and still maintain some semblance of modesty.

"Yes..." Gardiner murmured, but by the tone of his voice, she felt he was speaking less of the storm and more of other matters. "I am sorry to have caused you to worry, Miss Fairbanks. I should not like to be the source of any such unhappiness to you."

She turned shyly to meet his gaze. "It was quite unintentional, I am certain, sir."

"Indeed, it was, but I think I shall not be taking any more long horseback rides during my stay. Fishing seems a much safer endeavour."

Madeline started into a giggle, bashfully covering her mouth with her fingertips. He was smiling down at her—smiling with kind, sincere eyes and a warm, artless expression which spoke volumes. Madeline felt a little tug at her heart and suddenly began to hope that little Jane might take several more days to recover.

"Well," Gardiner gently took her hand again and bowed over it, "I must go tend to my wildly unkempt appearance, Miss Fairbanks. Might I persuade you to take a little tea with me later?"

She dipped her head, unable to quell the brilliant smile which grew on her own face. "I would be delighted, Mr Gardiner."

THE BELEAGUERED LITTLE TOWN of Lambton was a disaster for the rest of the day. The summer sun finally made a reappearance at half-past three, and the remaining hail which had not been washed away by the rain, finally vanished. The storm's other effects were felt for much longer.

It was soon reported that three local homes had their roofs destroyed, with several others claiming more minor damages. A goodly number of livestock had succumbed to the hail, and it was discovered that the remaining flocks and herds might find their forage scarce that winter, as the hay fields had suffered terribly.

What Edward had anticipated as a restful evening after his ordeal became quite the opposite. As a willing and able-bodied man, his services were called upon to help move the dead animals as they were found and to cart them away to be burned. It was a mercy that the larger cattle had all fared decently well, but the sheep had an unsettling tendency to drop from stress and cold, even several hours after the storm had gone. It was filthy, stomach-turning work, but Edward stripped to his shirtsleeves and laboured with a good will beside the town's residents until dark.

When he did return to the Lion's Head, bone-weary and covered in mud, he found Mr Fairbanks just coming away. He was not wearing his fine peaked beaver—nor, indeed, any hat at all, as he had returned the rugged one he had borrowed for the day's work—so he merely swept a polite bow. "Good evening, sir!" he greeted the older man.

"Gardiner, there you are, my good fellow!" Mr Fairbanks returned his salutations. "I fear you have not had the most hospitable welcome to our town."

"Think nothing of it, sir." He waved a hand. "I was glad to be of service, though I am hoping the worst is over."

"I doubt you shall be needed on the morrow," Fairbanks assured him. "Mr Darcy of Pemberley—a fine estate, if you ever have a chance to tour it—he sent word that his men will arrive in the morning to help with whatever remains to be done. He has even pledged his assistance with the damaged homes."

"That is generous, indeed! This Mr Darcy must be a charitable fellow."

"The Darcys have always been so," Fairbanks agreed. "It seems that Pemberley's own damage was limited, for that estate sits in a curious little corner of Derbyshire, somewhat protected from the worst of our weather. I feel badly for all the others, though," he sighed.

"Indeed, I imagine it will make a deal of work for you, sir. Have you been called out to tally the losses?"

"I shall be tomorrow." The man brushed a hand over his eyes, suddenly looking ten years older.

"Sir...." Edward hesitated, not wishing to slight the young lady of his recent acquaintance, but he was well aware of the hardship her new occupation would cause her father. He felt duty bound to offer what help he could. "Is there any capacity in which I might be of assistance? If the men from Pemberley are to arrive tomorrow, I shall have no other employment for the day."

Fairbanks brightened instantly. "You would not feel it an imposition to dodder about with an old clerk?"

"Not at all, sir! Why, I am of little use here with my nieces—I feel I am more in the way than anything else," he lied. In truth, he felt it very much of an imposition, but there was little else to be done. "I expect it may be a day or two before I have word from my brother regarding his plans for our return to London, and I may as well make myself of some use."

"I will accept your help, and gladly, then!" Fairbanks nearly glowed in relief.

Edward was less enthusiastic but would not allow his disappointment to show. Another full day of matters other than courting his favoured lady... his heart sank a little. Perhaps he could not injure his standing with her by working alongside her father, but he would greatly have preferred to remain near Madeline herself. He bade Mr Fairbanks a good evening on the steps of the inn and turned gloomily to the door.

Most of the guests had retired to their rooms, and the local denizens who typically occupied the common room remained out on the same business which had kept him away for the afternoon. Mrs Porter was no longer bustling about with her accustomed air of industry, and a low fire crackled warmly at the far corner of the room. Only two other patrons, both looking as exhausted as he felt, cradled drinks at the tables, but moving among them was a light figure with a mug of cider and a welcoming smile.

Madeline.

He sighed in pure contentment. It was almost like he imagined it would be to come home to a wife, and that notion brought him more cheer than anything else could have. She drew softly near and handed him the mug.

"Is Jane resting?" he asked lowly.

"Yes, she and Lizzy both are—at last! Was it very bad?" she wondered, tipping her head toward the street from which he had come.

"It might have been worse, but I do not see how," he confessed. "There will be a deal of hardship for the local herdsmen this year."

"I feared as much," she cringed, a pained look coming to her eyes. "But come, you must need to rest!"

He glanced down at his bedraggled person and gave a rueful little chuckle. "Perhaps I ought to change again. Might I join you in a few moments?"

That sweet, ingenuous smile lit her face. "I will wait for you here."

Chapter 18

T HEY SPENT THE DWINDLING hours of the evening ensconced by the fire. Neither desired the warmth it offered, but the light was welcomed. By its soft glow, Edward shamelessly admired smooth golden curls, earnest eyes, and the faintest dusting of freckles on a sun-kissed nose. Madeline Fairbanks, he settled with himself, was an angel.

Some might have argued that she smiled almost too much, but to Edward, her sparkling wit and vivacity were tempered most agreeably by her gently sociable manner. Oh, yes, she was clever—deliciously so! He discovered a new favourite pastime in lightly baiting her into revealing her opinions on books, music, and even dancing. It seemed the young lady had few opportunities to enjoy that amusement—a thing which, Edward decided—he would actively attempt to remedy.

"What of you, Mr Gardiner?" she inquired at length. "Do you often attend country dances? I am told that private balls are more pleasant than public ones—perhaps you know something of the matter."

"Oh," he looked down modestly, "I spent much of the last Season in Meryton, attending my father's affairs when he died. I am afraid that I have not been to any such events at all in some months. I..." he winced, cast an uncomfortable glance to her, and forged ahead. "I did spend a deal of time earlier in the Season at private gatherings in London... with one or two notable families."

The significance and hesitation in his tone caught her attention. Her smile froze, and one caramel brow twitched. "I take it you were in... particular company, sir?"

He sighed, rubbed his hands together, and forced himself to confess the truth. She would hear of it one day, if she cherished the same hopes as he, and it was only fair that he should be completely honest with her. "I had believed it to be so at the time, Miss Fairbanks. It happens that I was mistaken."

Her features relaxed and he could see the tension drain from her. "I am certain that was an uncomfortable circumstance, sir," she offered kindly.

His gaze faltered, then jerked back to her sweet countenance. Was she truly extending consolation for his disappointment at the hands of another woman? A careful examination of her manner, and the intensity of her eyes, yielded the answer. She had indeed caught his full meaning, and his heartbreak pained her! What woman would respond so? *Only this one.* He smiled, his determination to win her quickening. It would be worth as many trips to Derbyshire as his pocketbook could afford, just to court her!

She had dropped her gaze uncomfortably away to take a sip from her teacup, and he realised that he had been staring like a lovesick puppy. He shook his head. This was no way to begin! "Miss Fairbanks," he started over, stumbling for thoughts which did not revolve around her graceful figure or delicious complexion, "I believe you said you had a brother in London. May I ask where he resides?"

"To be quite truthful—" she cast her eyes down, her face pinched—"I believe he lets a room in a rather less than fashionable part of town. He did not wish for his living expenses to place any greater burden on my father...."

Edward held up a hand. "Forgive me for asking, Miss Fairbanks. Far be it from me to look down on a man for living economically while trying to establish himself. For goodness knows, I did the same."

She released a tight breath and smiled her gratitude. "What of your family, Mr Gardiner? Are they all still near Meryton?"

"Yes, I was the youngest, and I had two sisters. One, as I have said, married my father's successor, and the other is Mrs Bennet. Bennet has a small estate named Longbourn near the town." He chuckled lightly, fingering his teacup. "Fanny was quite delighted to marry a gentleman! A real distinction for the daughter of an attorney, you must understand."

She smiled indulgently. "Little Jane and Lizzy are so delightful, I am certain she must be a noble, wise lady—without her equal, I am sure. Oh, Mr Gardiner, are you quite all right?" she started in concern, for he seemed to have inhaled a portion of his tea.

He waved dismissively, shaking his head and attempting to breathe properly. "I am quite well, Miss Fairbanks!" He cleared his throat gently and regarded her with some bemusement.

She was still gazing back in wide-eyed anxiety. "Oh, dear, was it something I said?"

"I only thought," he laughed, "how—er—*flattered* Bennet would be to hear your praise of his wife. Perhaps one day I shall have an opportunity to introduce you to my sister, Miss Fairbanks."

Her eyes widened. This was tantamount to a declaration on his part! He seemed to catch himself as well, as his face first blanched, then darkened with embarrassment. Madeline swallowed nervously, but it seemed that he suffered more greatly than she. She cast her eyes to the side and found the inspiration she required to salvage the moment.

"Mr Gardiner," she returned swiftly, "you have mentioned an interest in fishing on a few occasions. Did my father tell you that there is a very fine stream not two miles from here?"

He brightened, once again at ease. "He did not, Miss Fairbanks. I expect we shall be occupied enough about his business tomorrow, but perhaps I might persuade him to point me in that direction for another day."

"Oh, it is not difficult to find if you know where to look, although very few venture to it. It lies to the northwest. I believe it has its source from that far peak you can see in the distance, and I am told it trickles through a part of Pemberley before flowing in this direction."

"Capital! I wonder where I could obtain the proper tackle and bait? I suppose I might enquire of your father or Mr Porter."

"I imagine so. Mr Porter likes to escape the inn for the brook whenever his wife allows it," she smiled.

Edward laughed. "It seems that few in this neighborhood dare to defy Mrs Porter! She rules with a laced glove, does she not?"

"She does, indeed!" Madeline chuckled. "Lambton will not be the same when she leaves."

He tilted his head. "Mrs Porter is going away?"

Madeline's smile faded. She had not intended to reveal so much, but now must explain herself. "Her son has established himself rather well in Leeds. He has an inn of his own there, I am to understand, which is far larger and more prosperous than the sweet old Lion's Head. He sent word to his mother and father recently that he would have them come to him—to help out, you understand, but only in a modest way. It would really be a retirement of sorts for them, but they must first sell this place. I believe a prospective buyer named Mr Williams is to stop by in only a few days."

His brow furrowed a moment in thought. "Mrs Porter is one of your particular friends, I understand?"

She stopped breathing for a second, wondering at the peculiar light which had come to his eyes. "Yes. A few others are also... away at present."

He held her gaze for a long while, both studying her and offering some silent commiseration. "Perhaps you also will one day venture to new places, Miss Fairbanks," he answered softly.

Madeline felt her cheeks scorching crimson. Edward Gardiner was the most courteous, refined man of her acquaintance, but he was certainly making no secret of his intentions! She ought to feel flustered or imposed upon—after all, they had known one another only a couple of days! He was so gentle and candid with her, however, that she felt almost as naturally at ease in his company as in Mrs Porter's. She could not help rewarding his bold comment with a shy smile.

The evening continued to fade, and one by one, the few souls who had passed through the dining room while they had spoken together retired to their own rooms. The amount of time they had shared in intimate conversation would have never done in London, but here, in this quiet, respectable little inn, the only expectation was that he would behave honourably—a thing which he had every intention of doing.

At last, Edward was forced to concede that their interlude must draw to a close. Mrs Porter had returned after her own evening meal and had busied herself with odd jobs about the room. Some tasks were vital enough, but others—such as dusting the already pristine mantle over the fireplace—seemed rather unnecessary. When she began unfolding and refolding the napkins, Edward at last understood her rather pointed hint.

"Miss Fairbanks." He rose at last and offered his hand. "I must thank you for a delightful evening."

Blushing in Mrs Porter's direction, Madeline rose to meet him. "I believe the pleasure was mine, Mr Gardiner."

He bowed gallantly over her hand, and would have liked to escort the lady up the tiresome case of stairs—for surely, she must be fatigued by now, and it was only the gentlemanly thing to do! Alas, it would not do for them to be alone on the stair together. "I will bid you a good night then, Miss Fairbanks," he murmured huskily.

Her sparkling eyes raised to his, and Edward had never desired to kiss a woman more in his life. "Good night, Mr Gardiner."

Chapter 19

M R Fairbanks' work was not terribly back-breaking labour, but it was rather monotonous. Edward spent the day with him, going about from place to place and meeting with various local farmers who must now estimate their losses. It was during these travails that Edward discovered Mr Fairbanks' infirmity. The man could scarcely see the paper before his own face, let alone pick out the portion of hail-damaged fields or count the livestock still standing. Edward found his own keen eyes in great demand and began seriously to wonder how Mr Fairbanks could possibly go on with his work many more years.

It was not a subject of which he could speak openly. Mr Fairbanks tended to ask Edward to do the looking and counting while he tallied in his books. "It goes so much faster, do you see," he would explain a little self-consciously. Edward simply complied without objecting.

By afternoon, however, Mr Fairbanks brought himself to concede the truth. They had just completed the second to the last stop they intended to make for that day, and as Edward clucked along to the horse pulling their little cart, he tipped his head to the left. "Sir, Miss Fairbanks told me of a particularly good trout stream nearby. Is it there, just over that bank and below that far stand of beech trees?"

Fairbanks strained to see, but to no avail. "It must be, Mr Gardiner, for it ought to be in that direction, but I am afraid I cannot verify that for you. My eyes are not what they once were." He faced straight ahead once more, his mouth set in discouragement.

Edward only twitched the reins, sorry that he had so inconsiderately brought it up.

"Mr Gardiner..." The old fellow hesitated, then peered up to his companion with a myopic squint. "Do you think you will remain long in Lambton?"

"As long as need be, sir. I expect my brother only just arrived at his destination yesterday, and goodness knows what he will need to settle there before he comes away."

"I take it, sir, that you yourself are not in any particular hurry to return to London without him, in case he is detained longer than expected?"

Edward turned to study the older man. "I have a few capable clerks who can see to the affairs of my business for the time. I had made arrangements to stay away for as long as a few weeks, if necessary, but I have already been away for some while. I should think that we will remain possibly as long as another se'nnight, though."

Fairbanks smiled a little. "That is well, sir. I believe Madeline is growing quite fond of your nieces."

Edward swallowed. He had not expected to discuss his intentions with the father so soon, but... he cleared his throat, bracing himself. "I believe they are equally enamoured with her. Miss Fairbanks is an enchanting young lady, sir."

Mr Fairbanks looked pleased. "She has been a kind daughter to an old man," he beamed proudly. "I ought not say so, but it must be apparent to you—I have little enough to offer her in the way of a future. I hope that someday, she may be made happy."

Edward was warmed. The man was extending more than an olive branch—he was practically begging him to make an offer to his daughter! His face softened. "I hope that for her as well," he answered sincerely.

Fairbanks' mouth quivered, and he drew an emotional breath, then nodded in some satisfaction. "Well, Gardiner," he put on a brave smile once more, "suppose we drive over in the direction of that stream you saw. We have got quite a lot done, and it is still earlier in the day than I had anticipated. I just happen to have a pair of rods in the back of the cart."

Edward grinned and gave a little tug on the rein to turn their path from the road. "A capital plan, sir!" he agreed.

"JANE! OH, YOU ARE awake!" Elizabeth pounced on the bed near her sister, upending the carefully arranged tea tray and nearly setting Madeline's teeth on edge.

"Lizzy! You must not-" Madeline gave up with a sigh and a roll of her eyes. The counterpane was drenched and little bits of bread crumbled everywhere, but Jane was smiling contentedly as her sister accosted her.

"Are you feeling better, Jane? Uncle is away, but he promised he would walk with me when he returns. Did you truly sleep through the storm yesterday? I met the most interesting people! Oh, did you like your tea yesterday? Miss Fairbanks promised it would set you right, and so it has! Is she not clever? Miss Fairbanks, may Jane come below with me?"

A little stunned by the barrage of questions, Madeline held up a pleading hand. "Lizzy, look what you have done to Jane's bed!"

The little scamp finally ceased talking to take in the mess she had created. Her slim shoulders rounded in genuine regret. "I'm sorry, Miss Fairbanks."

She shook her head and sighed. "I suppose the linens needed changing anyway, as Jane's fever has passed. Do not tire her needlessly, Lizzy! I will go speak to Mrs Porter."

"Oh, there is no need, Miss Fairbanks!" the helpful little maid supplied. "She told me a moment ago that she was sending fresh things up. She said also that an express had come for Uncle, and I was to be certain to tell him of it, but she would not let me bring it up here. I do not understand why, for it must have come from Father, but she said I had best not take it myself."

"Fancy that," Madeline intoned drily. "I expect your uncle may be a few hours yet, Lizzy. I do hope the express was not one which required an immediate answer!"

She spoke this last to herself, and under her breath, for the girls were already otherwise occupied. Elizabeth, boisterous though she often seemed, was truly a good girl, after all. She was industriously putting to rights the upset tray and doing her best to make her sister comfortable.

Jane, though still weak from her fever, was already much improved. She thanked her younger sister, and the two settled companionably under the blankets. Madeline looked on with a touch of yearning. She had never had a sister, but perhaps one day she might be blessed with little girls of her own... if she were very fortunate! Her lips tugged into

a quiet smile and her stomach fluttered when an image of Edward
Gardiner's parting smile came to mind.

"WILLIAM, COME HERE, PLEASE."

The young man clenched his eyes and his jaw, then his
expression cleared and he turned to face his parent. "Yes, Father."

The elder Darcy, composed and dignified as ever, lifted his chin
and strode to his study. His son, with a doleful cast to his shoulders,
followed. There was no ambiguity as to the subject of this conversation—the wonder was only that it had been a full day in coming.

"Sit, William," the father commanded.

Fitzwilliam obeyed.

George Darcy observed his son in penetrating silence until the lad
began to perspire. He was too well-schooled to squirm in his seat, but
his adolescent nerves insisted on betraying him in this, at least. He
willed his limbs to lock and his breathing to steady as he gazed stoically
back at his father. Was he about to lose his riding privileges? Sent back
to school early? Sentenced to work in the ruined hay fields?

That last, he thought, might not be such a bad fate, but he shivered
faintly in horror at what discipline his father might have devised. He
certainly had taken enough time about it, and the suffering of waiting
and imagining had been nearly as bad as the punishment itself could
possibly be!

"William, you did admirably in keeping Georgiana safe."

The flinty jaw slackened. "Excuse me, Father?"

George Darcy narrowed his eyes and slowly smiled. "I have spoken with her at length. If she did not worship you enough before, she does even more so now."

Surprised and humbled, Fitzwilliam's gaze dropped to the floor. "It was I who put her in harm's way! I took her too far, and I was not aware of my surroundings until it was nearly too late. I deserve no such praise, Father."

"Which is why I am all the more willing to bestow it. You acknowledge your errors, but you behaved manfully, William. Through storm and uncertainty, you thought quickly and did what you must, to keep my daughter safe. I am well pleased."

The boy's lanky frame eased somewhat with a long, relieved breath. "I only wish I had not taken her out yesterday. It was foolish of me to ride with her so far."

Darcy pressed his lips and tapped a finger on his desk, weighing his words. "William... what you did, and what you have been doing—trying to cheer Georgie... do not give it up. She needs you, I suspect, more even than she needs me just now."

The younger Darcy blinked and his eyes fell to his father's hands as he spoke. "I would do anything to protect her, Father," he promised.

The fingers drummed again. "William, the real reason I called you in here this afternoon was to tell you that I have changed the terms of my will. I only wait on my solicitor to finalise the details."

At this, the dark eyes flashed up again to the father's face. He attended with bated breath.

"You are nearly a man, William. I hope it will be many years yet before it shall be of concern, but I have removed your aunt Catherine as one of Georgiana's guardians. I do not feel that her guidance will be either necessary or helpful. Should anything happen to me while you are both young, the Earl and the Countess will have charge of her until your majority. I would not wish," he admonished, "to leave the full burden for her upbringing—as well as the entire estate—solely on your shoulders, so after that time you will share guardianship with your cousin, the Viscount."

"With all due respect, Father," Fitzwilliam rasped, his voice raw with unbidden emotion, "If I am to take on such guardianship, I would prefer to share it with Richard. He has ever been tender with Georgiana, while Langton is...."

A sly smile appeared on the father's face, growing quickly into a chuckle. "I had hoped you might be quick enough to respond so! Richard, it shall be, for you are quite right about Langton."

Fitzwilliam tried not to shudder in relief. "Thank you, Father. I certainly hope, however, that you shall never leave us so."

"As do I, William, but I have not yet done. It is time we had a serious conversation about your own future. We agreed that you would take the summer after..." he sighed bravely, "...after losing your mother. You must resume your studies again soon. Now," he studied the boy with a tight expression, "every Darcy for the last two hundred years has attended Eton, but under the circumstances, I would not be opposed to you taking a year at Rugby. You would be a few days nearer—it might be possible for you to come home on holidays."

Fitzwilliam sucked in a bracing breath and faced his father. "Sir, I had hoped rather to study here this year with a tutor."

The elder Darcy's brows arched. "I thought you enjoyed school. Champion boxer, winner of the chess tournament as a freshman, and I hear your fencing is improving dramatically."

"Yes, sir, but as you said, perhaps I ought not to leave Georgiana now. She said something to... to someone else, yesterday after the storm, and it has troubled me ever since. I think she will suffer more than I had realized when I leave again."

The father stared hard at his son. "You will lose an entire year, falling behind your classmates."

Fitzwilliam shifted uncomfortably. "I would not mourn that, Father. I have few enough friends among them as it is. I can join another class as easily next year."

George Darcy's fingers resumed their pensive drumming on the burnished desk. "What will you do with your time here, should you remain, William?"

He already had an answer for this. "I hoped to learn more of the duties you would have me perform one day, Father. It has become plain to me that I do not know enough of our tenants and our staff. I would not become the sort of master who gives no thought for the people on his estate."

Darcy's eyebrows jumped in astonishment. "Whence came this notion? Indeed, you have never been ignorant or abusive with the staff, but I have noted a tendency toward a little excess pride in your station."

The boy hesitated. "It was brought to my attention that my carelessness forced men out into the elements to search for me. It is a mistake I do not wish to repeat."

Darcy studied his son in silence for a long moment. "William," he answered at length, "your response is a much more mature one even than I had looked for. I will give consideration to your wish of remaining here for the year. I do not pretend that I have no further misgivings regarding the consequences to your own education, but I am touched by your concern for you sister, and for the estate." He smiled wistfully. "I would not be sorry to see you remain another year myself," he added with an uncharacteristic softness. He blinked a few times, cleared his throat, and then nodded matter-of-factly to his son.

Fitzwilliam, sensing the conversation over, rose and jerked a pleased little bow to his father. "Thank you, sir!" He rose to go as his father dismissed him but was immediately called back.

"Oh, William, there is one thing more."

He turned. "Yes, Father?"

"I've a man coming to see me about buying the wool from our flocks this year. I expect him tomorrow or the next day. He owns an exceedingly prosperous woolen mill about forty miles from here. He has been seeking out landowners with large flocks. If he buys directly from us rather than purchasing many smaller lots, he can pay a little higher price than we have received in the past. It is an excellent proposition for both parties.

"I am concerned, however, about our losses yesterday. Most of the flock were already shorn and the market wool stands in the shed, but next season may be rather bad for us. I have not yet had time to look over everything with old Daniels, but I need his counts. I would like you to take that on and report back to me by tomorrow."

Fitzwilliam straightened yet taller, nearly a match for his father in height when he did so. "Yes, sir!"

Chapter 20

"Gardiner, I declare, you shall make a splendid angler with only a little more practice."

Edward's face split into a flattered grin as he held the door of the inn for Mr Fairbanks. "It is the work of my excellent teacher, I assure you, sir."

"No, no." The man shook his head. "You have a natural way with the line, and a knack for seeing just the right places in the stream. I've no doubt you shall easily surpass my own humble skills."

"I thank you, sir." He bowed to the older man, then turned to commence an undisguised search of the crowded dining room for a particular young lady. A cursory glance did not reveal her, but Mrs Porter happened to be passing by and caught his eye.

"Mr Gardiner, there is an express for you." She drew the missive from a pocket of her apron and tipped a knowing smile toward the stair. "I believe Miss Fairbanks will be happy to hear you have returned. She will want to tell you that your young niece was faring better this afternoon."

"Excellent news!" He thanked the woman and turned to the letter in his hand. Fairbanks glanced away in deference for his privacy, but a groan from Edward quickly drew his attention back. "Oh, this is dreadful indeed!" he cried. "Mr Bennet's brother has died of his illness—just after he arrived, it seems. Apparently, it was more serious than Thomas had wished to believe."

Fairbanks adjusted his spectacles. "My condolences, sir. It must be most distressing to lose a relative so suddenly."

"Indeed, though I knew very little of Thaddeus Bennet myself. I was still a lad when he left for the north, and I'd no notion then that we should one day be related. I am sorry for what this will mean for my sister and her children, for now I do not know who Bennet's heir is to be. There was a cousin, if I remember correctly... but perhaps it is not yet too late to hope for a son."

"Perhaps," Fairbanks agreed. "Does..." His voice became hesitant. "Does this mean your family will be departing from the area immediately?"

Edward lowered his letter, his stomach sinking with the same realisation. "He does not say—only that he expects his brother's affairs will be resolved quickly, as Thaddeus had little to call his own." *Dash it all!* He grumbled inwardly, raising unhappy eyes to the hopeful father.

Fairbanks' weathered cheeks drooped somewhat in disappointment, but he quickly braved his typical, genial smile once more. "Well, I suppose nothing more can be done just now. Come, Gardiner, let us seek out Madeline. I think I should prefer to sup here tonight, rather than alone at home."

"I would like that as well." Edward brightened. He began to start toward the stair, but a fair-haired traveler, a little older than himself, had been walking just to his left when Edward inadvertently bumped his shoulder.

"Oh, my good man, I do beg your pardon!" he apologised. The man he encountered was still wearing his traveling suit, and looked, by his clothing, to be a well-to-do businessman like himself.

"No!" the other answered quickly. "Think nothing of it, I beg you. I say, are you a guest here, sir?"

"I am," he answered. "This is my third day. You are lately arrived, I take it?"

"Yes, I've some business in the area, and my son and I were looking for lodgings tonight. I was expected to stay at the Rose and Crown, but I am told that the establishment sustained some damage yesterday—windows broken by that hailstorm, an unlucky affair! I wonder, sir, have you found this to be a comfortable place?"

"Quite hospitable," Edward assured him. "It is rather snug if you are accustomed to finer lodgings, but if it is only yourself and your son, I think you shall not be discontented."

"I thank you for your recommendation, sir." The other traveler dipped his head amiably. "I shall no longer trouble myself about the change in lodgings. Charles," he called to a boy of perhaps twelve standing behind him, "I think we shall be well suited here."

Edward left him with a friendly nod and made his way to the stairs without allowing another second of delay. If his time in charming little Lambton with the bewitching Madeline Fairbanks was to be limited, he meant to make the most of every moment.

JANE HAD SO WELL recovered her strength by the next morning that Madeline felt it would do her no harm to attempt breakfast in the dining room. Accordingly, she descended with both girls, though keeping a watchful eye on the eldest as she negotiated the stairs. "Are you quite all right, Jane?" she inquired at the landing, when the child had paused out of either faintness or simple disorientation.

"Yes, Miss Fairbanks," Jane smiled pleasantly. "I was looking for Uncle."

"To your left," Madeline directed. Jane looked, and Madeline allowed the children to lead. Elizabeth, calmed by her sister's serene influence, seemed an entirely different girl on this day! Patient and gracious, she had looped her arm through Jane's and acted to lend support, though it was not needed. She was scarcely even speaking, and had it not been for the characteristic roving of her mirthful dark eyes, Madeline might have suspected her swapped out for a changeling. Madeline only shook her head in relieved wonder. Perhaps there was a future lady to be found in her, after all!

"Jane!" Edward had stooped to greet his niece—the first time he had seen her out of bed these last days. "Dear one, are you feeling better?"

"All better, Uncle Gar'ner!" Jane answered brightly. She tipped up on her toes then, and whispered, "I am hungry, though!"

Edward laughed, teasing a blond curl at her forehead. "We shall see what can be done for that. Come, I have a bench set aside. Do not be troubled, Jane, it is rather crowded, but there is plenty of room for us. Miss Fairbanks?" he extended his elbow hopefully.

Madeline accepted it readily. He was so warm, and... well, comfortable! His affability set her so at ease, short though their acquaintance was. With greatest consideration, he assisted her to a seat at the table nearest the hearth, then turned to Jane, who had taken his other hand. Madeline watched him with almost hungry eyes, eager to catch every nuance of his interactions with his nieces. Was it possible that he truly was as generous and thoughtful as he seemed? He looked to adore children and had ever been perfectly solicitous of her own comfort. How was such a man still unmarried?

She looked modestly to her lap when he turned back to her. "Will this suit?" he asked, gesturing to the arrangements he had secured for them.

"Quite well, sir," she replied, and was rewarded by one of his open, honest smiles.

The foursome set in on the meal, which was promptly brought—Jane more ravenously than any. Madeline looked on in satisfaction. After quite frightening her two days earlier, now the girl was mending outstandingly well—thanks, perhaps, to the fortitudes of youth rather than her own unremarkable nursing skills.

"Miss Fairbanks," Edward ventured as they finished their meal, "how do you think Jane is getting on? I was wondering if you thought she might tolerate a short walk today. It is such a fine country. I should be sorry to see her left in her room rather than out in the fresh air."

"Oh, Mr Gardiner, I do not feel myself the proper authority on that point." She bit her upper lip. "She seems strong enough at present, but I should not wish to tire her. I do not know her well enough to say, I think."

He frowned. "Of course, you are quite right. Forgive me, I ought not to have asked. Perhaps..." he cast a pensive glance at his other niece, "it might not be too much for her to remain here by the fire for an hour? Lizzy could keep her company. It would spare you the discomfort of another full day in that little room."

She stilled, gazing through lowered lashes. "How else would you have me occupy myself, sir?"

"I was hoping perhaps I might persuade you to show me about Lambton a little," he smiled modestly.

She gave a light chuckle. "Sir, there is little enough to be seen! The entire tour would take less than half an hour."

"That allows us another half an hour for a picnic, does it not?"

"Why, I... I suppose," she conceded, though a little uncertainly. "That is rather a short picnic, sir."

"Yes," his face fell. "Yes, of course. Perhaps we might forego the tour?"

"Or perhaps," she laughed, "you might ask Jane herself how she is feeling. She seems a steady, sensible girl, and I believe she will answer you honestly. If she feels herself strong enough, perhaps the girls might join us for a leisurely outing?"

"Excellent! There was a charming little trap at the livery—perhaps if I hired that for the afternoon rather than walking, she might fare better? I wonder if I might even convince your father to join us."

Madeline could not help smiling agreeably at his enthusiasm, but he had yet to enquire of Jane. She tipped her head significantly in the girl's direction.

He nodded. "Quite right. Jane, dear?" he turned his head to speak to his niece. She did not seem to hear. "Jane?" he called a little more loudly.

Still, she did not turn her head. "*Jane Bennet,*" he spoke more firmly. Lizzy, seated next to her, gave her a sharp nudge, and her head finally snapped round.

"Uncle? I am so sorry. I did not hear you!"

He peered at her in renewed concern. "Why, Jane, your cheeks are flushed. Has your fever returned?"

"N-no, Uncle!" the girl stammered. Her eyes shifted guiltily to the side, but straightened back to his face before he could determine the source of her sudden awkwardness.

This was strange behaviour for placid, sweet Jane. He stared in some confusion until Elizabeth, her impish grin threatening to return, pointed surreptitiously behind herself, over her shoulder. Jane nearly melted into the long oaken table in embarrassment.

"What...? I do not understand," he faltered, until his searching gaze caught the bright pink ears of the boy at the opposite table, who seemed to have only just turned away himself. It was the young lad he had seen last evening, arriving with his father. He glanced back to his nieces.

"Jane dropped her napkin," Elizabeth furnished helpfully. "The boy picked it up for her, and now they keep smiling at each other." Jane groaned in misery and covered her rosy face.

He stared hard at his eldest niece. She was only eight years of age! How was it possible a boy had already caught her eye, and she his? *Gracious.* He shook his head. *Another Fanny!* Bennet would do well to lock up his daughters until they were out!

"Well," he sighed, "I suppose I need not ask how you are feeling, Jane. Indeed, I think the sooner I take you out of this building, the better!"

Chapter 21

"FATHER? YOU WISHED TO see me?" Fitzwilliam waited patiently at the entrance to his father's study, the door cracked only enough to permit his voice.

"Yes, come, William. You have those figures for me, I trust?"

"I do, Father." He had come prepared and presented his father with a pad of paper whereupon he had made his remarks.

George Darcy's brow furrowed deeply as he took the paper and studied it while he paced back to his desk. "Mmm," he mused, "it could have been much worse, but yet it might have been a great deal better."

"We have still the Herdwick flock on the northern slopes, which have yet to be accounted for," his son reminded him. "These numbers encompass only the Southdown flock, which grazes on the flatter pastures."

"Not as hardy," his father nodded, his eyes focused only on the paper as he began to lose himself to one of his great passions. Fine estate though Pemberley was, it was, at its heart, a farm, and its master by necessity, a proficient husbandman. "A gentler animal for the shearers," he continued, almost to himself, "but they are not thriving. Your uncle's herdsmen have had some success in crossing the Norfolk... but that is perhaps a question for another time. What are we to do for next year, with nearly twenty percent of our ewes and forty percent of our young stock either ailing or perished?"

"Are you asking," his perceptive son answered, "what are we to do about replenishing our flocks, or what measures may be taken with regards to this woolen miller you are expecting?"

George Darcy lifted his face with a pleased curve to his mouth. "The latter. I expect only time and care will remedy the former, but if I am to do business with this man, I must know my own means. I would not promise him what I cannot deliver."

"I had considered that some, Father. You said that this man is willing to pay a higher price for his wool? Can that really be true?"

"He is from an old clothier family; quite well established in Gloucester they were, until perhaps ten years ago. He has since moved his operation to Yorkshire, and I understand he has installed some new sort of engine at his mill so that he is not wholly dependent upon the strength of the river. As a result, he is in great need of more wool, but expects to turn a higher profit."

"Sir, there must be any number of indigent herdsmen in the area whose flocks were also diminished by the storm. Do you suppose they also might be aided by a better price?"

A dark eyebrow twitched. "Perhaps. What, specifically, did you have in mind, William?"

"If it is indeed mutually beneficial for Pemberley to sell wool to this miller instead of another, and if our yield should fall short, might we not offer to buy from other herdsmen at the same price? They also might reap the benefits of your agreement. It would be no loss to us—rather, it might strengthen your partnership if we keep this man in good supply with lesser need to search abroad."

George Darcy had been standing behind his desk, leaning intently forward on his knuckles in a most unseemly posture for the Master of Pemberley. Now he straightened, a satisfied expression on his still handsome face. He said nothing, but his approval needed not be voiced.

A knock brought the butler's graying head to the door. "Sir, a Mr Bingley and a Mr Bingley are here to see you."

Darcy's features warmed still more. "Excellent timing, Hughes. Show them in, please. William, I would like you to remain," he spoke to his son, who had begun to withdraw. "Mr, Bingley, sir, you are most welcome."

A sandy-haired man of middle years and a genial aspect entered the study, followed by his own exact duplicate as a youth. "Mr Darcy." He came forward cheerfully, and offered a polite bow as his son followed suit. "Thank you for receiving us. This is my son Charles."

Fitzwilliam gazed at the pair somewhat askance. It was not typical for any of the men of business who regularly called upon his father to bring a child.

It seemed, however, that George Darcy was thoroughly unsurprised by the lad's presence. "I am very pleased to meet you both." He bowed in return. "May I present my son, Fitzwilliam." This remark was accompanied by a sternly arched brow. Fitzwilliam bowed stiffly in obedience.

"Fitzwilliam," Darcy spoke gravely, "Mr Bingley intends for Charles to study at Eton. We have written some of it during our other correspondence."

"Yes, indeed," the businessman affirmed. "He is to take up residence next month!"

William apparently had yet to learn to conceal his horror and astonishment, for his face bled of all composure. *A tradesman's son!* What travesty had compelled the school officials to accept the man's application?

His father made a discreet noise, calling back his attention. "I understand you are twelve years of age, Master Bingley, and an able student?" the elder Darcy inquired.

The boy, who had been staring somewhat indecorously at Fitzwilliam, stiffened respectfully when addressed. "Yes, sir."

"I've no doubt you shall get on well," Darcy answered kindly. Then, to his own son, "Fitzwilliam, I asked Mr Bingley to bring Master Charles to Pemberley so that the two of you might be known to one another. You may, perhaps, have some valuable guidance to offer a prospective Freshman while we conduct our business here." The subtle lift of his chin emphasised the father's wishes.

Fitzwilliam's teeth set, but there was nothing else to do. "Yes, Father." He gazed down reluctantly at the somewhat younger lad. "Perhaps we might walk the grounds?"

Charles Bingley assented with enthusiasm. Fitzwilliam Darcy tried not to sigh as he led the boy away. Another tuft-hunter to brush aside as readily as may be—would he be forever thus plagued? What could his father have been *thinking?*

"AND THE WESTERN wing, which was remodeled in the time of William III...." Fitzwilliam Darcy looked to his young companion as he gestured toward the house and found that Charles Bingley's eyes had glazed over. He valiantly strove to point his head in the proper direction, but his gaze was searching the treetops in the distance.

Fitzwilliam dropped his hand. Whatever else might be said against his guest, the young Bingley had not the least interest in ingratiating himself to his host by excessive attentiveness. "Perhaps you would prefer to see the gardens," he suggested.

The youth looked somewhat abashed. "Forgive me," he apologised—though his manner was modest and simple, rather than groveling as many did. Fitzwilliam could not quite dislike him for it. "I am afraid I've little head for architecture," Charles confided. "It seems so lifeless and dull—I confess, my mind wanders completely."

Fitzwilliam spread his hand in another direction, inviting the other to follow. "It is something of a walk, but there is a very fine trout stream. Perhaps you would care to see it?"

Charles brightened. "Indeed, I should! You have a remarkable prospect here of the fields," he noted, pausing briefly to gaze from their rolling vantage out over Pemberley's pasturelands, hazy in the distance. Here and there, the green was dotted with his father's blood-stock mares and their scampering youngsters.

Fitzwilliam tilted a puzzled look at his guest. Most of the visitors to Pemberley preferred to enthuse over the antique gardens or the stately house, but Charles Bingley's honest appreciation of his own favourite vistas intrigued him.

Unable to restrain his curiosity any longer, he finally decided to question the boy. "Why is it that your father desires for you to attend Eton?"

Clear blue eyes, brightened by exertion and merriment, tipped up to him. "Is it not a fine school? I suppose he expects that I shall make a gentleman someday," Charles grinned—an easy, authentic expression if ever Fitzwilliam had seen one. "He thinks to purchase an estate of his own, and it will be for me to manage it one day, I presume."

"Purchase an estate?" Fitzwilliam was astounded. "Why, I..." he stopped himself short of the indelicacy he had been about to propound. He straightened. "Your father has been successful in business, I trust?"

"Oh, yes," Charles agreed nonchalantly. "Enough so that he feels my education ought to be that of a gentleman rather than a businessman." His gaze continued to drink in the landscape, but there was an earnest admiration in his manner, rather than the vulgar fawning one might have expected. "I understand you attend Eton yourself?"

Fitzwilliam had clasped his hands behind his back as he walked, and he turned his shoulders slightly toward his companion. "I attended last year, until my mother's death," he answered quietly. It was a thing of which he never spoke, but something in this forthright youth unbound his typical reserve.

His sudden confidence, it seemed, was not ill-placed. Charles' clear, sincere gaze swept up to him in surprise. His cheerful smile faded, and he regarded Fitzwilliam with genuine empathy. "My mother is gone as well. I am sorry," he replied.

That was all that was said. No meaningless platitudes, no prying into his sentiments, and no promises of how he would forget his grief in time. A simple exchange of feeling, an offer of understanding, and their friendship was sealed. Fitzwilliam felt his throat tightening, and he swallowed hard before resuming their walk.

"I had not thought to return to school this year," he continued heavily. "It is my father's decision of course, but I had hoped to remain one more season with my younger sister."

"Oh! I am quite happy to be escaping my own sisters!" Charles laughed. "You must be very fond of her."

"I am." He spoke no more on the subject, but it was not necessary.

With the intuition of a much older lad, Charles Bingley let the matter rest. He had been regarding the path thoughtfully, then stopped as if pricked. "Why, if you do take a year, we shall be in the same class when you return!"

Fitzwilliam paused. A strange warmth tugged at his mouth; a sensation which, until the day before, had been completely foreign to him for months. Connections and status be hanged, there was a liveliness about this Bingley chap which wholly offset his own melancholy. First that bright little minx from the inn, and now this tradesman's son—it was as though they had been messengers sent from above by his mother, granting him permission to live once more.

"That would be most agreeable, Bingley," he smiled. At this address—the name by which he would be known at school—Charles almost grew a full inch before his eyes. He grinned—a most unpretentious and heartfelt expression—and gave a firm nod.

Fitzwilliam happened to be turned toward the house as he was speaking, and it was with no little surprise that he perceived George Wickham sauntering back from his chores in the stables. He was making himself conspicuous, as always, by swinging a short hank of stable rope in his hand and whistling jauntily—both undignified behaviours for which any of his betters would promptly have trounced him, had they seen. Fitzwilliam chose to turn a blind eye, but a whisper of inspiration struck. If George had finished his punitive chores in the stables for the day, that would be the very place to take himself for some peace.

"Bingley," he turned to his new friend, "have you much experience with horses?"

The sandy head jerked toward him, the bright blue eyes rounded with zeal. "I thought you would never ask!" he cried.

Chapter 22

"W HY, MISS FAIRBANKS! A lovely afternoon, is it not?" Mr Lawrence lifted his hat to reveal his wavy, thinning locks plastered down with pomade. His gaze drifted immediately to Jane and Elizabeth, who stood nearby. "And who have we here? The little travelers I have heard so much about? These must be the reason you have been little seen of late," he smiled, tipping his hat again to the girls.

For a wonder, there was no slur to his speech on this day, and Madeline almost congratulated him in her heart for cutting a more dignified figure than he had on other occasions. Perhaps the rumours she had heard yesterday about Mr Kent's cellar being plundered while he was away with his stock had nothing at all to do with Mr Lawrence, as had been originally suspected.

"Indeed, I have been most occupied, sir," she answered. "Is it not a beautiful day? We are just about to take the air with their uncle, Mr Gardiner—he and my father are coming with the carriage just now," Madeline gestured with the tip of her bonnet.

Lawrence glanced disinterestedly over his shoulder, but his gaze quickly returned to Madeline. "I am sure your father enjoys the condescension. These London folk are always so very fine, are they not?

It is a pity they always move on so quickly, for Lambton enjoys their patronage, I daresay."

Fine lines appeared near the corners of Madeline's eyes. "Indeed, Mr Lawrence, though I am told the tavern keeps busy enough even without them. If you will excuse us, I am afraid we must be going." Giving a firm tug to Jane and Lizzy's hands, she brushed the man aside to wait for Edward Gardiner to assist them to the carriage. He loitered, a lazy smile twisting his face as he watched them for another moment before proceeding up the street.

Madeline almost shivered in revulsion. She had never been comfortable in Lawrence's company, but something about the way he looked at the girls sent quivers down her spine. She did not think him necessarily evil, but certainly an opportunist—particularly when corrupted by drink. She was still gazing over her shoulder at the man's retreating back when Edward's voice spoke her name. Gratefully, she accepted his hand as he helped her settle into their hired carriage.

The drive proved to be just as lovely as any could have desired. Edward had hopefully offered Madeline the seat next to himself, and Mr Fairbanks was more than satisfied to recline in the rear with a little girl on either side of him. Their sharp eyes and his kindly way of telling stories ensured utter contentment on the parts of the passengers in the rear, leaving the driver and his lady to their gentle conversation.

Edward guided the horse to the same little spot where he and Mr Fairbanks had done their plundering of the stream, although it was not fishing which held his interest on this day. He had earlier noted a slightly elevated little knoll beneath a spreading beech, and nearby a wild flowering hedge cast its fragrant spell over the spot. Acres of untamed field rolled behind them, forming a private meadow of sorts. The only thing which could have improved on the spot was if he and

Madeline were quite alone, reclining beneath that tree with soft words and tender looks only for one another.

It happened, however, that their "chaperones" were less than interested in the prospective couple's activities. Mr Fairbanks had already settled with himself that it would be a very fine thing for his daughter to capture this man—who, despite his obvious interest, seemed honourable enough for him to wander beyond conversational distance with Elizabeth for ten minutes.

Elizabeth was eager to exploit Fairbanks' knowledge of the area, and it was fortunate that he was still a spry gentleman, for she took the old man by the hand and insisted on a full accounting of all the springing wildlife she could see. They made a rather amusing pair, really, with Elizabeth leading and describing in vivid detail, and Fairbanks squinting, scratching his chin, and drawling out his responses. Jane divided her own attention between watching them and lying peaceably by the rippling brook, gazing up at the blue, cloudless sky.

Edward and Madeline strolled briefly about the area, he proudly offering his arm, and she blushingly accepting. "I wish," he mused after some while, "that such venues were to be found in London. I do miss the peace of the country!"

"London must have its diversions, surely," she returned, keeping her gaze carefully averted so that too much hope did not shine in her eyes.

"Indeed. I think you would like the parks. They are much finer, you understand—everything manicured and pristine, but there is not the perfect serenity one finds here. It is difficult to seek such seclusion in London."

"That does not sound objectionable. I have often felt the lack of new faces here. I expect that does not trouble you at home."

He checked his steps to smile down at her. "No, it does not," he murmured. "New faces London has in abundance, but friendly ones can be another matter." They walked on for another stride, their eyes still holding, until their momentum failed and all of their energies diverted instead to the warmth glowing between them.

"Miss Fairbanks," he spoke huskily, his chest tight, "do you think you might ever be content in a place like London?"

Her lips parted in surprise. Did he intend to declare himself now—so soon? Her breath staggered and she swallowed nervously. Every impulse of hers yearned for this to be *it*—that moment which every girl was taught to anticipate with all of her devotion—the one question which would define her future and all that she was to be. With sudden clarity, she at last recognised that former expectation to be but a pale shadow of all that she might aspire to.

With Edward Gardiner, she would never be relegated to frilly drawing rooms with her lace cap and needlework, losing all of her own identity to the cares of maternity and wifely obedience. Her identity would change, to be sure—if she married this man, she would become an honoured partner, a respected confidante, and a woman in a fair way of falling madly in love with her husband. She had never longed to speak the word "yes" more in her life, but he had not yet asked *that* question. There were other matters of import which must be sorted first.

"I believe I could be quite content in such a place, sir," she spoke haltingly, "but I do not know how my father should manage alone here."

The moment of hesitation before her answer had caused a cloud to pass over his face. At her response it broke, and such a ray of light beamed forth that nothing might dampen it. He brought his free hand to rest on hers, gazing down in speechless awe for half a moment.

When he did find his voice, it was soft and a little hoarse. "I would never presume to disrupt the close bond you share with your father, Miss Fairbanks. Indeed, I find your regard for him most admirable."

The breath she had held eased from her, leaving behind a look of such tenderness that it was all he could do not to bring his hand to her cheek... *and then he could lean close...* but it was too soon!

She glanced down to their hands and allowed her fingers to lace through his. He had given her every assurance she had hoped for, and logically all that remained was to allow their feelings to blossom to the full fragrance of their maturity. She raised shining eyes to his once more, her lips pressed tightly into a quivering smile.

He caught up her sense of pleasure for his own, and for the first time, he dared to press the back of her gloved fingertips to his lips, delighting in the gentle reciprocation of her hand tightening round his. He stared for a heartbeat as he returned her hand to his elbow... *now what?*

If he allowed his fancy to run freely, he would have her wrapped in his arms in another moment! It was too much, surely—he already frightened himself with the force of his feelings and dared not terrify her. He must allow her some little time for her sentiments to catch up to his! He cleared his throat uncomfortably. "Shall we open the picnic basket, Miss Fairbanks?"

Her petite frame swelled with a long breath. "Yes, Mr Gardiner, I think that wise."

He escorted her to the tree and returned a moment later with the basket and a blanket which Mrs Porter had sent. He found Madeline gazing intently at the bark of the old beech, her fingers lightly touching on some marks she had found. At his approach, her smile broadened and she flicked her eyes to indicate the thing which had held her interest. "It seems we are not the first to enjoy this place."

"Oh?" He came near to inspect. "Why, they are initials—a very young couple, no doubt. 'GD' and 'AF'. They look to have been carved a number of years ago, do you not think?"

She nodded, a whimsical little crease playing about her mouth as she lovingly traced the deep grooves in the thin bark. "I wonder if they found happiness," she sighed. "Oh, I do hope so!"

He drew near and rested his own index finger over hers. She froze, looking doubtfully up to him. This touch, this sympathy in faith, seemed far more intimate than the kiss to her hand but a few moments ago. He was stepping willingly into her feminine heart, sharing in her poetic fancies and claiming her romantic hopes. "I am certain they did," he whispered.

It was well that he kept his eyes on the scarred tree as he spoke, for had he looked on the face uplifted to him, there is no doubt that he would have made a rather poor example for the impressionable young girl lying not fifty feet away on the grass. He drew in a sharp breath. "Right, then." He turned quickly away to address himself to the basket, leaving Madeline to smile at his back as he did so.

He spread the blanket and assisted her to it, and they settled themselves just beneath the shade of that old tree. Edward at last opened the basket and his eyes lit in delight. Clever Mrs Porter had, at his request, packed them a delectable array of refreshments. The blessed woman had not neglected to include a bottle of decent wine, nor had she forgotten that favourite food of lovers—a juicy, sweet cluster of grapes.

Chapter 23

"WHERE DID YOU LEARN to ride, Bingley?" The younger Darcy pulled up his horse for some air, turning to regard his companion with a deepening appreciation. Few boys of his age, and certainly only a handful of Bingley's age, could keep up with him over the hedges and stiles of his home estate. This tradesman's son had truly taken to the sport as a natural and had clearly been taught well somewhere.

"There is a riding master not far from my home. I convinced my father that I ought to be learning the sport with the sons of gentlemen, but the truth is, I was only trying to avoid more school lessons!" laughed the young fellow.

"I thought you got on well enough in school. Is that not what you told my father?"

"Well," Bingley twisted a little in the saddle, "I do, I suppose. I find it dreadfully hard to sit and read for hours on end. I much prefer to be out of doors."

"It is the duty of a gentleman to discipline himself, and to improve his mind through extensive reading," Fitzwilliam admonished, only belatedly realising that he had just quoted his father's words to himself.

"I suppose it is," Bingley sighed, his gaze unfocused as he scanned the horizon. Brightening, he turned to his new friend. "I am very glad to have made your acquaintance, Darcy. I feel your society might do me much good."

Fitzwilliam lifted a sceptical brow.

"Oh!" the perceptive Bingley reddened. "I did not mean... why, surely, you must be weary of being sought for... I suppose what I meant was that I admire your discipline. I hope to profit by your example."

The corner of Fitzwilliam's mouth twitched and he appeared to turn his attention back to the trees in the distance. He would never confess it aloud, and he could not in the course of a century imagine himself baring his sentiments to *anyone* as freely as Bingley routinely did, but he thought it possible—only somewhat possible—that he might gain by their friendship as well. It would do him no harm, at least.

"Come," he beckoned at last, once their horses had sufficiently blown. "I think we have time to venture a little farther, and then we may circle back by another way."

The two boys touched their mounts with their heels, and Fitzwilliam Darcy led Charles Bingley down a sweeping stretch of grassland. They passed his father's cattle, his father's broodmares with their foals sired by Pemberley's stallions, and they could see his father's flocks not far in the distance. Everything the eye touched on belonged to Pemberley and the Darcy name, and perhaps that is why Fitzwilliam was so eager to show his friend the nearest corner of land which he would *not* one day stand to inherit.

At last, their destination approached, but as they dropped down to the final valley, Fitzwilliam drew his horse abruptly to a halt. Someone had already discovered his meadow! It was the first time he had ever encountered another there, and as it was a smallish little hollow in the land, he was nearer than he liked to the strangers by the time he became aware of their presence.

"By Jove!" Charles exclaimed beside him. "It's that same family from the inn!"

Fitzwilliam's gaze snatched to him, but Charles was turning red again. He refused to explain himself further. It was not necessary, for by no means could Fitzwilliam Darcy fail to recognise the dark-haired little maid scampering between the tree and the brook. A nest of Georgiana's yellow blossoms festooned her bare head, and she assailed whatever amusements could be found in the little meadow with a vehemence which could belong to no other girl.

He watched in stunned fascination as she sneaked up behind another young girl, her dripping hands full of some treasure from the muddy stream bank. From the corner of his eye, Charles Bingley stiffened and almost yelped out a warning, but Fitzwilliam's little friend must not have been as stealthy as she might have hoped. The blonde girl sat up only just in time to avoid having some squirming creature dropped into her lap.

The boys could not understand her words, but her chiding tone was clear. The younger girl's shoulders drooped and she opened her hands to release a great, fat frog, which leaped immediately for the freedom of the stream.

Fitzwilliam could not decide whether he was more scandalised or diverted by the scene. He choked on a silent laugh; his shoulders shaking, but his mouth welded resolutely closed against any sound. Charles Bingley, it might be noted, only exuded apparent relief that the innocent party in the whole business had been spared a most unpleasant surprise.

At that moment, Fitzwilliam found sparkling dark eyes seeking his own. Even from this distance—too far for words—he could read that impish expression and needed not wonder if she recognised him. She tilted her chin, lifted her hand, and offered him a playful salute.

He responded in the only way a gentleman could—a gallant tip of his hat, and a little bow from the saddle. When he replaced his hat, he found Bingley gazing at him in undisguised wonder, but it is likely that he was never aware of the broad, unaccustomed warmth pulling at his mouth which occasioned his friend's surprise.

"Well," he coolly lifted his reins, reclaiming his typical reserve, "I expect we will be wanted soon enough. Shall we?"

Bingley cast a curious glance once more to the girls, then drew himself up. "By all means."

IT WAS WITH NO little surprise that Fitzwilliam returned to his home and found an ostentatious carriage gracing the drive. He pulled up, his stomach balling into a fist. That monstrosity belonged to none other than his infamous Aunt Catherine. He was too well-disciplined to scowl, but he could have imagined a good many more pleasant ways to have passed the next few weeks—for Aunt Catherine never came to stay for less than a month together, and seldom waited for an invitation to do so.

It was well that the carriage's inhabitants had already disembarked and the horses were just then being led away. Once within the sanctuary of the house, his aunt would have taken herself to her customary rooms and it was likely he would not see her until dinner that evening.

At least he would be permitted a decent interval to bid his new companion a proper farewell!

"Charles, there you are." The senior Bingley came at that moment from the house, alerted to their arrival by a sharp footman. "I wondered where you had gotten to! I ought to have expected you to be on a horse," he grinned cheerfully.

George Darcy followed his guest, and as the boys handed their horses off to the groomsmen, the men exchanged their final felicitations at the steps of the carriage. "Master Bingley—" the elder Darcy turned—"Fitzwilliam brings you back just at the last moment, I see. Do you require any refreshment before your departure?"

Charles tensed, his face aglow. It was apparent that he was not at all accustomed to speaking personally with such great men as George Darcy, but he rose admirably to the occasion. "No, sir, I thank you."

"Very good. I will bid you good day, young man." Darcy's eyes softened, a subtle shift in expression which his son knew to convey hearty approval.

"And to you, sir," Charles bobbed quickly. He looked next to Fitzwilliam. "I shall look forward to seeing you at Eton," he offered hopefully.

"I as well," he replied, "this year or the next. It has been most agreeable to make your acquaintance."

The final farewells were exchanged, with one or two obligatory references to a fruitful business relationship, and at last the Bingley carriage rattled away. George Darcy turned twinkling eyes on his son. "Well, William, what think you?"

"They are most respectable, Father," he answered dutifully. "Am I to understand that you and Mr Bingley came to a suitable agreement?"

"Indeed, we did, but it was Charles Bingley of whom I should like your opinion."

He could not bring himself to the quick, automatic answer which he had been trained to deliver. He slowly mounted the steps to the house beside his father, his gaze fastened on his feet as he walked. As they gained the top, he spoke at last. "I like him very much, Father. He is an earnest, friendly fellow—much like Richard, in fact—but he is not uncultured, as I might have expected."

"He could use a friend at Eton," his father commented neutrally. "As a tradesman's son, it will go hard for him, but a word from you will carry much weight."

Young Fitzwilliam tensed. "Have you decided that I am to return this year, then?"

"I have not decided." Darcy turned to enter the house, drawing his son into step beside him. "However, I expect your aunt may have one or two opinions on the subject, and we shall have ample opportunity to canvass them in the next days."

This time, the boy was unable to repress an audible groan.

Chapter 24

THE FIVE SUMMER REVELERS returned to the Lion's Head late that afternoon—the girls boasting rosy cheeks and wind-sweetened hair, and the hopeful couple fresh in the consecration of new love. Only Mr Fairbanks seemed unaltered by the outing, but one who knew him well and gave himself the trouble to notice would have detected an easiness about his countenance which had long been absent. He had every reason to believe his daughter's affections to be secured by the man from London, and her future no longer in doubt. It was with calm serenity that he parted from them at the door of the inn to set about some tasks he had neglected earlier in the day.

Edward handed his nieces and Madeline down at the front steps of the inn, thinking in contentment on the perfect day they had passed and the plans they had made for the morrow. Mr Fairbanks had offered to take him fishing again in the morning, and the afternoon was to be spent walking with Madeline and the girls about the town. Could Edward Gardiner have submitted his opinions on how the Almighty ought to craft paradise, it would have looked very much like these two days.

His flights of fancy tumbled to the ground the instant he walked the lady through the door of the inn. Thomas Bennet reclined at the darkest and most private of the corner tables, nursing his pipe with the road dust still clinging to his boots. A wry curve defined his mouth, and those cunning eyes of his twinkled brightly when he observed the party just entering.

"Papa!" the girls cried in unison. Both flung themselves into his embrace, which was a good deal warmer than usual. It seemed that even the sardonic Thomas Bennet was not immune to genuine sentiment. It might be supposed that the sudden loss of his only brother and lingering concern for his eldest daughter had left him visibly shaken, and at a startling loss for his typical witticisms.

He sighed loudly, clasping his two favourite daughters, before pushing Jane back by her shoulders. "Dear one, how are you feeling?" he asked gently.

"Quite well, Papa!" she answered brightly.

Her father rewarded her with a pat on the cheek, then turned his attention to his other child. "And Lizzy, you have not been unwell?"

"No, Papa, and I have ever so many things to tell you!" she gushed.

"I am sure you have," he smiled, his eyes shining curiously. "You can tell me all about your stay on our way home tomorrow. Run along to your room, girls, and dress for dinner!"

They obeyed promptly, and some of Bennet's unaccustomed tenderness left with them. He cocked a brow at the couple who still lingered, arm in arm and gaping at him. "Well, Miss Fairbanks," he tapped his pipe and at last rose to do her proper courtesy, "you have survived your ordeal, I see."

Madeline shifted her gaze to Edward, who self-consciously began to disentangle their arms. "I am delighted to see you returned safely, sir," she murmured. The grim set of Edward's mouth troubled her, and she did not yet know him well enough to understand it.

"Yes, the horses performed their work admirably, I daresay. Tell me, Miss Fairbanks, how many times did you have to set off in search of my Lizzy while I was away?"

"I..." She tilted her head slightly, "... Why, none at all, sir. She is a charming girl, and certainly a credit to you and Mrs Bennet."

At this, the older gentleman openly chortled. Why, even Edward seemed to be biting back some involuntary response! What was it about Mrs Bennet that engendered such sly mirth whenever her name was mentioned? Madeline fisted a hand at her hip, a thing she had not done for many years. "Forgive me, but I do not understand what I have said that can be so amusing."

"Oh, do not trouble yourself, Miss Fairbanks," Bennet chuckled, waving dismissively. "I've no doubt that you will meet my wife soon enough."

Edward stiffened and cleared his throat. Madeline took the rather pointed hint, assuming she would be safer to withdraw until Bennet had exhausted his acerbic wit at Edward's expense in privacy. She straightened. "I should be honoured to meet her if I ever have the opportunity. If you will excuse me, Mr Bennet, I shall retire with the girls." She dipped him a curtsey, then offered another to Edward. "Thank you for a lovely outing, Mr Gardiner."

"The pleasure was mine, Miss Fairbanks," he assured her. He watched her go, his longing eyes trailing after her Grecian form until it disappeared up the staircase. Reluctantly, he turned back to the satirical gaze of his brother. *Drat Bennet for returning so soon!*

"Thomas, I had not expected you for another day or two, at least. How is it that you return so quickly? Certainly, there were some affairs to settle, were there not?"

Bennet's eyebrows twitched in that queer way of his, and he held up a finger. His mouth twisted downward as his other hand sought within the pocket of his waistcoat, and he withdrew a plain, battered pocket watch. "Behold: my brother's estate. What little else he possessed has been left to the landlord—and I think my brother got the better end of the bargain."

"How is that possible? Your father left him some sort of stake, as I recall. He should not have been impoverished."

Bennet shrugged, replacing the watch and resuming his seat. "Indeed, he did—and depleted the estate's coffers before his death to do it. Thaddeus was always a spendthrift. What other employments and diversions he found, I shall not dare to speculate, but it is well that my wife and the wagging tongues of Meryton will know nothing of it."

Edward heaved a weary sigh and dragged the mate to Bennet's chair under himself. "I am sorry, Thomas. Had we—any of us—known that his circumstances were so dire, we should certainly have offered what aid we could."

"Had he accepted such aid, he would have been bound by our strictures, and well did he know it," mused the older man. "No, Thaddeus did not wish to be rescued. I think he rather liked his squalor—or, at least, he liked his utter liberty and lack of responsibility."

Edward shook his head in vague misunderstanding. "I cannot fathom a man of such a disposition."

"Come now, Edward, I might have done the same myself, had I not the estate shackled round my neck," was the laconic reply. "Had I a decent library and table, I would want for nothing else. It is very greatly to my credit that I decided to own up to my responsibilities."

Edward snorted. "It is well that you have only daughters, then. The trouble of properly rearing up a son might have proven too much for your preferences."

Bennet took a long draw at his pipe and lifted a brow. "You have met my daughters," he retorted drily. "Have you not wondered where my hair is starting to go? They shall prove my undoing!"

"Oh, come, Thomas, your daughters are all... mostly all... perfectly enchanting. And after all, it is not likely that a daughter will run off and ruin the family name as Thaddeus tried to do! It does trouble me, however, that you no longer have an heir in your family. On whom will the entail fall?"

Bennet's lip curled. "My cousin, Gerald Collins—or his son. I think his name is William. It galls the pride, Edward, I will confess it. Would that I had some means of breaking the entail!"

"Shall I be expecting a new nephew to arrive in the spring?"

Bennet tapped his pipe out at last, inspected it, then tossed it haphazardly upon the table before making a response. "I should think you will have a son before I will. When am I to wish you joy?"

"Why, I had not... that is, I have only known Miss Fairbanks a few days!"

"Would your cause be better served if I should return to Sheffield for a fortnight?"

"Indubitably." Edward groaned, resting his forehead on his fist. "I cannot offer for her so soon, surely. And yet, if I return to London without securing her promise, I've no idea how I shall beg leave to court her at such a distance."

"You can still read and write, can you not? Or has your clerk taken over that duty?"

"I have never thought a letter a good means of coming to a right understanding on sensitive matters, and even less do I think it so when writing to a woman. It would be acceptable, I suppose, if that is all I have, but how shall I write what I wish to tell her? I do not have it in me. Speaking to her face, at least I may know how she receives my words. I fear I may frighten her with everything I would say in a letter!"

"Sounds a hopeless business," Bennet chuckled, crossing his knees and reclining somewhat more in his chair. "You are right. Best leave well enough alone, then."

"Thomas, I want this woman in my life! I would come back to court her, but..." Here he heaved the sigh of the lovesick. "I do not think I even wish to return to London without her."

"That might prove awkward. Where will you put her, in your trunk?"

"Thomas! You are the most contrary man I have ever known!"

"A man must have his amusements," Bennet winked. "See here, if you and the lady are both set on this notion, I see no reason for delay. You would not be the first man to marry on a short acquaintance," he pointed out. "My father met my mother only once before their marriage."

"There is a deal of difference between a suitable match arranged by prudent parents and a near elopement!" Edward objected.

"Her father disapproves of you, then?" the sage lips curved into a cunning expression.

Edward's brow furrowed. "Not at all. No, why, I believe he would be most pleased."

"It sounds a 'suitable match', then, does it not? I see no obstacles. You've no need to wait to draw up marriage articles, unless you have become more prosperous than I had realised. If that be the case—" he raised a finger—"I will be keeping those books I borrowed."

Edward stared at his brother-in-law. "Thomas, I would not have expected your advice regarding Miss Fairbanks to be so obliging—reckless, even! Why, if I listen to you, I should offer for her this very moment, and then immediately hie me to the parson's home to arrange for the banns to be read this very Sunday!"

Bennet offered a thoughtful frown. "You might take the trouble to procure a ring. Yes, now that I remember correctly, that seemed to be a rather important element in the process."

"You are serious!"

"Quite. As I am serious about starting for Longbourn in the morning. I am run out of books, do you see." He stretched, glanced about the quiet of the common room with an appreciative little smirk, and rose. "Just now, however, I am in want of a clean set of clothing. Will you be so good as to ask the mistress of the house to send up some fresh linens?" With that, he strode nonchalantly to the stairs, leaving his baffled brother to sort out a fresh torrent of plans and feelings on his own.

Chapter 25

FITZWILLIAM DARCY WAS IN hiding. It would not be long, of course, before he would be summoned to give audience to his aunt and to pay respects to his cousin, but before he could be sent for, he must first be found.

None observing his actions this day could have accused him of such, for it was well known that his aunt never stirred from her rooms before ten. A young gentleman was expected to employ himself somewhat better. He had arisen early that morning to take a long ride on Saul, and now he occupied himself in his father's orchard with its caretaker.

He had been pleased to find that there was much to be done even so early in the season and had applied himself devotedly to the pursuit. He had already learned a great deal, and felt he was making profitable use of his time this day. That no one would think to look for him in the orchard for some while was merely a bonus.

He was nearly ready for his midday meal when his occupation was discovered. "Master Fitzwilliam?" One of the younger footmen approached respectfully. "The master and Lady Catherine de Bourgh desire for you to attend them in the blue drawing room."

His face never altered. He did not sigh in vexation, nor did he make any sort of excuse. He was a Darcy, after all. "Very good," he replied. With a polite glance of acknowledgement to the orchard's keeper, he strode to the house, his adolescent bearing as stately as he could make it.

Lady Catherine de Bourgh awaited in all her opulence, with Anne sitting demurely by. He presented himself with a bow, and she beamed in satisfaction. "Fitzwilliam," she blinked slowly—the only approximation of a courtesy he would receive.

"Good morning, Lady Catherine," he greeted. "I trust you are well this morning?"

"I am always well," she intoned graciously, "and so is Anne. The very picture of health, is she not?"

He bowed briefly, as indicated. "Cousin Anne, it is a pleasure to see you in such spirits today." He spared her a quick evaluation—she had looked dreadfully weary at dinner the previous evening. The night's rest and leisurely morning had worked only modest wonders at restoring her colour, but he must say *something* complimentary toward Anne, for his aunt would continue to salt the conversation with references to her until he did so.

"Darcy," Lady Catherine now addressed the senior personage by that name, "Fitzwilliam is looking very robust. I am quite satisfied in his appearance. How does he get on with his studies? No gentleman of superior birth must be permitted to while away his holidays. If I had a son, I should have kept him at all times with his masters, for no excellence of manner or education can be attained without constant diligence."

"He is doing admirably, Catherine." George Darcy—one of only a handful of people in the kingdom who dared omit her title—smiled at his son with a spark of his old conviviality. "As a matter of fact, we had been discussing some alterations to his education of late, have we not, Fitzwilliam?"

"Indeed, Father," he agreed.

"Discussing it? I never heard such an idea! The boy has no say in this. Tradition, position, and the duty to his family name dictates what must be done, Darcy! I wonder that you have permitted him to remain so long at Pemberley. He ought to be taken back to London, to refine his dancing and all other gentlemanly pursuits!

"That is why I am come, naturally, for he shall be quite ready to return to school at month's end, and he may, of course, ride with us. Anne and I can certainly make way in the carriage, and Mrs Jenkinson may ride on top of the box, as the weather will still be suitable. It is time enough that he ceased mourning for my sister, George, for he has a responsibility to the family to enter Society and to prepare himself for his future obligations."

"Fitzwilliam has his duties here as well, Catherine," Darcy commented mildly. "He must learn to manage the estate, of course."

This seemed to check her. Nothing was more dear to Lady Catherine than the honours and marks of station, and short of a title, no finer feather existed for the cap than the name of Master of a sprawling, luxurious ancestral estate. "Well... yes, indeed." She paused a moment in silence.

Fitzwilliam marveled at his father. Never could he imagine himself so easily capable of governing his aunt as his father seemed to be! George Darcy had the knack for dropping a few syllables, delivered carelessly to the ear of the casual listener, and somehow even Lady Catherine was often brought to heel. He resolved to make a careful study of his father's manner and spare use of words. Perhaps one day, he too might master the trick of speaking in such a way as to amaze the whole room.

"Perhaps, Catherine—" Darcy came round the large sofa which he had appropriated for its commanding position in the room—"Fitzwilliam's education would be better served by bringing to Pemberley the best masters to be found. He might benefit from private instruction for a year, while honing his abilities at stewardship. I think it possible that he will finish school well ahead of his classmates in knowledge and experience."

Her eyebrows lifted speculatively, but the worn lips still frowned in his direction. Fitzwilliam kept his eyes properly fixed on a portrait above her head—a particularly ghastly visage of his mother's uncle, the late and not terribly regretted Viscount of Matlock, whose bilious and scowling mien had always terrorized him as a child. It saved him from exhibiting a triumphant gleam in his eye at his father's seeming support against his aunt's wishes.

"I do not deny, Darcy, that the boy must learn the management of the estate," she conceded at length. "To shirk his responsibilities to Society, however, is unpardonable. Why, I never heard of such a thing! What you propose might do very well for any other young man, but he is a *Darcy*. The demands of him are greater than of others!"

"Indeed, they are, Catherine," Darcy agreed. "To that end, I had intended for Fitzwilliam to begin assuming the annual tour of Rosings in my stead. I shall accompany him for a year or two, of course, but I believe that soon enough, he will be found more than capable of advising you without my assistance. I am certain that your guidance and support will prove invaluable during this time."

Lady Catherine verily preened. She swept a calculating gaze between her nephew and her daughter—no doubt reflecting that this scheme of her brother-in-law's would supply ample opportunity for the young couple to form their attachment. Fitzwilliam rolled his eyes very subtly in his father's direction, but George Darcy only lifted a brow in reply.

"We will speak more of this, Darcy," she declared, as though the decision had been properly hers to make. "Fitzwilliam, Anne desires an outing in the barouche after her luncheon. See to it that she does not take a chill!"

He bowed, concealing the gritting of his teeth. "Yes, Lady Catherine."

"Mr Fairbanks, sir? I was hoping to have a private word with you." Edward hesitantly entered the older man's study, sorry to be disturbing him at such an early hour.

"Mr Gardiner! What can I do for you?" Fairbanks seemed tense—pleased, perhaps; hopeful, certainly. There was a tightening in his weathered features which suggested that he was not at all certain of the younger man's intentions, but he had a fair notion. He offered a chair, which Edward politely declined.

Edward's entire core was taut and wound. He clenched and unclenched his fingers as his palms were beginning to perspire. He had no reason to expect his wishes to be denied, but the last time he had thought himself on the cusp of happiness, his hopes had been most painfully dashed. Though it had stung his pride bitterly, the cost of losing Miss Rutherford would be nothing compared to the wrenching agony of losing Madeline!

Mr Fairbanks had tilted his head forward in some expectation, a doubtful quiver starting about his lips the longer the younger man delayed. Edward cleared his throat, hoping his voice would not waver when he spoke. "Mr Fairbanks, I wish you to know that I am very fond of your daughter," he croaked.

Fairbanks eased a little in his chair—but he was not wholly comfortable yet. "She is a fine girl, Mr Gardiner—much like her mother! I have been a very blessed man."

"Yes, sir, indeed." Edward shifted his hat under his arm. "I would like to ask permission to court her. I understand, sir, that you know little of me, but I can assure you that my intentions are noble, and that I can provide for her most satisfactorily. Should you require a character reference, my brother-"

"Mr Gardiner!" Fairbanks waved a hand, chuckling a little, "I have watched you most carefully with those dear little nieces of yours, you may be assured. I am already quite confident in your character and have no doubt of your means. Pray, do not trouble yourself on that account." He sat back a little, lacing his fingers as a faint frown troubled his forehead. "I must ask what you intend by a courtship. You are returning to London this very morning, are you not?"

"Yes, sir," Edward answered miserably. "My brother is making the final arrangements even now, and Miss Fairbanks was helping my nieces to make their own travel preparations. I was hoping I might write to Miss Fairbanks from London, and perhaps come again for a visit in a month or two."

"Your business, sir... can you so easily come away again?"

"I have an able clerk, but you are quite correct, sir. I can manage planned departures well enough, for a fortnight or so at a time—infrequently, of course. If it were possible, I would wish to remain behind in Lambton when my family returns to Hertfordshire. I could naturally travel home by post-chaise, but I would be obliged to leave myself rather soon—it seems hardly sensible. I have contracts which require my personal attention, and I had not anticipated any need to extend my plans before I left...."

Fairbanks smiled gently. "Love has a way of altering a man's plans, does it not?"

Edward at last relaxed, an easy pleasure gracing his features. "That it does, sir!"

Fairbanks sobered, perhaps sensing that it was his duty to at least catechise the prospective groom a little. "Tell me, Gardiner, what are your expectations? I do not desire for my daughter to be left with only a vague notion of your intentions."

Edward swallowed. "I would wish to marry her by year's end, if she found it agreeable," he almost whispered.

Fairbanks' eyebrows shot up at this. "So soon!" He brought his forefinger to his mouth, rubbing his lips thoughtfully. "That is not long for a courtship. It seems scarcely worth the trouble of calling it such."

"No, sir. It is not." Edward tightened his right arm about his hat. "I think, however, that both you and the young lady might be distressed by an immediate engagement. My feelings and wishes are fixed, but I would not expect hers to be so immutable on such a short acquaintance."

Fairbanks gazed silently at the floor, then pressed his lips and raised his head. "If Madeline finds it all acceptable, you have my blessing, sir."

Edward felt his heart soar. He had not expected a refusal, but the affirmation of all of his hopes was heady... intoxicating, even. That such a woman might be his! It was too glorious, too astonishing, that he might have found such a creature and be welcomed into intimacy with her. "Th-thank you, sir!" he stammered, his regular features flushed with pleasure. "Her happiness shall be my highest priority. You have my word!"

Fairbanks' mouth tugged wistfully. "I've no doubt of it, Mr Gardiner, but I shall miss her! You will let an old man come to see you by and by, will you not?"

Edward grinned, playing his trump card. "I had hoped, sir, that I might persuade you to remove to London permanently, once you have retired. I intend to purchase a house of my own upon marriage. I am certain that it shall come equipped with far too many empty rooms, and if Miss Fairbanks should agree to become my wife, nothing would give me more pleasure than to welcome you to our home."

The lines of care washed from the elder man's face. His weakened eyes grew wide and misty, and he seemed to choke with joy. Blinking rapidly, he rose and took a tremulous step near. "Bless you, sir!" his strangled voice came at last, and he grasped Edward's hand between both of his own. "It is a good man who would take his father-in-law into his home!"

Edward shifted his weight uncomfortably. He did not like to be given credit for such a notion. It was only the decent thing to do—no man violently in love with a woman could do less for her! He knew not what to say in response to Fairbanks' effusions, but another moment of embarrassed silence settled the issue for him.

Fairbanks withdrew a small handkerchief to dab his eyes. "You must go, Mr Gardiner. If you are to leave today, you have better things to do than to talk to an old man!"

"Of course! I thank you, Mr Fairbanks." He bowed humbly, then rushed from the room.

Fairbanks, left alone in his dim little study, chuckled softly to himself in pure relief and fell back into his desk chair. "A good man, that," he murmured to himself. "Ah, my girl, you have done well!"

Chapter 26

"**A**RE YOU COMFORTABLE, COUSIN?" Fitzwilliam solicitously checked the thick lap robe draped over Anne's skirts to see that it was clear of the wheel. He then personally saw to the shade of the carriage, inspecting all minutiae of the vehicle for safety and comfort. He did not hurry.

"Step the horse forward ten paces, Wickham," he called out.

George Wickham, still suffering his punitive month of stable work, frowned at the horse's head. "The wheels are quite sound, Fitz," he objected with a faint scowl to his tones.

Fitzwilliam clamped his tongue between his teeth. He *hated* that nickname, and George knew it. The surest way to disappoint him would be to reveal no reaction whatsoever, but thus far at least, the strategy had not yielded the desired effect. "I want to be sure the horse is, as well," he answered reasonably. "Please walk him forward."

Wickham released an audible growl but turned and did as he was bidden. Fitzwilliam was watching Wickham far more than the horse. Wickham would *never* dare to affect such an attitude before his father—or even the senior staff at Pemberley! No, George Wickham reserved all of his sullenness for Fitzwilliam Darcy.

He narrowed his eyes thoughtfully. That bitter attitude would surely grow and lash out most devastatingly if not checked, and it would all be focused at himself. As his father's wishes made it impossible to command George's respect, his only recourse against the almost certainty of such an event was to make a friend of him where possible.

"Thank you, Wickham," he waved to the other boy as the horse halted. "The horse is well turned-out," he complimented. George only turned his back.

Fitzwilliam frowned with the cold weight of another realisation. Each admittedly stiff attempt of his own at amiability or encouragement would only be seen by George as insulting condescension. In order to pay a compliment, one was asserting authority, and there was simply no way to prevail against another determined to assume the worst. He thinned his lips in resignation and turned his attention to other matters.

"Are we to set out soon?" Anne's plaintive voice sounded from within the carriage. "I should like to have returned before the worst of the afternoon heat."

"Naturally, Cousin," he agreed. He moved to re-examine the horse's harness, though it was, of course, in perfect condition and precisely fitted to the horse. George cast a baleful eye his way, no doubt wondering what he was about. Douglas, the head coachman, would tolerate nothing less than excellence in the stables, and everyone knew it. Wickham likely took his lingering inspection as a lack of trust, perhaps even an unspoken accusation of sabotage on the harness. There was no way to win!

At last, the interruption he had been waiting for arrived. "I am sorry for the delay, Master Fitzwilliam!"

He peered over the horse's back. "Ah, there you are, Miss Tuttle. Is my sister quite ready for her outing?"

"Yes, sir. Pardon me, sir, for taking so long about her dress!"

Fitzwilliam came around the horse and leveled a stern look at the small child, who squinted confidently up to him from beneath her starched bonnet. "Georgie, did you argue with Nurse over your attire again?"

"Not much, Will," she cocked her head, tracing one toe in a semi-circle before the other. "I wanted to wear my pink flowers," she sulked.

He sighed, shaking his head briefly. "Thank you, Miss Tuttle. I apologise if my sister caused you some vexation over the matter."

Fitzwilliam cocked an eyebrow at his little sister. "We will speak of this later," he whispered firmly.

She clasped her little hands sheepishly behind her back and shrugged. "I'm sorry, Will."

"I should hope so. Come, you shall sit facing our cousin Anne." He lifted her into the barouche, then snuggled another lap robe about her. Georgiana primped a little, thrilled to be treated as a young lady sitting opposite her much older cousin.

Anne stiffened. "What is this, Fitzwilliam? You cannot intend to bring Georgiana on our ride! She had much better stay here with her nurse."

"Georgiana is very fond of outings in the carriage. I believe you will find her excellent company," was his unfluttered response, accompanied by a smooth bow. He took the ribbons at last from George and mounted the driver's box.

"Fitzwilliam, you cannot be serious!" Anne objected. "I thought the coachman was to drive us so that we could speak to one another!"

He turned sedately about. "I could not entrust your safety to another, Cousin Anne. I would be distressed indeed, should one of our coachmen inadvertently jostle you. My aunt has given me specific instructions on how gently the carriage is to be managed."

Anne's pinched face withered to a scowl. She possessed all of her mother's petulance, but none of her grandeur. He had made a dedicated effort over the past few years to teach her to expect nothing of him, and it appeared to be working, for at each interaction, Anne protested the less and relented the more quickly. One day, he hoped, they might succeed at occupying the same room while ignoring one another completely.

He turned to the horse once more in satisfaction, but a movement from George halted him before he could set out. A peculiar spark glimmered in his eye—perhaps it was amusement at the way he had managed his cousin, or perhaps it was some mischief of his own. Whatever the cause, he moved close to the passengers, drawing something from his pocket. Fitzwilliam paused curiously.

"Miss de Bourgh, and dear little Miss Darcy," he bowed gallantly, "perhaps you might enjoy this on your outing." He presented them with a cloth wrapped about a fistful of sugared almonds and a few stubs of licorice. It looked to be fresh from the kitchen, still untouched, and brought specifically for their pleasure.

Anne glanced at it with suspicion, but Georgiana's entire countenance brightened. She spun in the seat toward her brother. "May I, Will?" she gasped.

That hope vanished quickly, however, when George looked back to him. The open, courteous look reserved for the young ladies dissolved into smug triumph. What George thought himself to have gained, Fitzwilliam could not imagine, but unease entered his heart once more. He moved the horses off, refusing to glance over his shoulder at the smirk which he knew was still directed his way.

The outing was by no means as tedious as it might have been, for he was able to turn his gaze in any direction he fancied. Anne was sulking, ignoring Georgiana's company. There was no need to point out to her any of Pemberley's vistas or items of interest, for she knew them all well, and so it was a silent carriage which made its stately tour about the shorter loop round the pond.

Within an hour, they were drawing up once more to the front of the house, and beside Lady Catherine's enormous carriage. Horses were already harnessed to it, and his aunt's liveried footmen attended them. Fitzwilliam narrowed his eyes curiously, turning in the driver's seat to query of Anne, but his aunt spared him the trouble.

Amid a flurry of verbiage, Lady Catherine whirled and stormed and swept down the steps of the house in a tirade. "I have never been so spoken to in all of my life!" she spat over her shoulder. "You would deny the claims of duty and tradition, and aye, your own daughter's interest! George Darcy, I shall speak to the earl of this! Your name shall no longer be mentioned by the rest of the family—you will face censure wherever you go! To think of the great folly-"

Here she ceased her vitriol as she gained the lowest steps. She glared up at Fitzwilliam, still poised mutely atop the barouche, and her lips pulled into a terrifying sneer. "A mere boy! Such arrogance I never could have thought my sister's son capable of. Fitzwilliam Darcy, I take no leave of you! You are no credit to your mother, and not worthy of my regard! I am most seriously displeased. Anne! Come away this moment!"

Fitzwilliam dismounted the carriage to assist his cousin, then his sister to the ground. Anne spared him a haughty glance before one of her mother's footmen came to escort her to her own carriage. Within mere moments, the equipage of Lady Catherine de Bourgh rolled grandly away from Pemberley.

Fitzwilliam had stared, somewhat baffled, at his aunt's furious departure, but now joined his father as Darcy sedately watched after the retreating carriage. He seemed thoroughly untroubled as he lifted a hand in an unheeded final salute.

"Father, I do not understand. What has happened?" he demanded in a low voice.

George Darcy surveyed him with a sidelong glance. "I explained to your aunt the altered terms of my will regarding Georgiana's guardianship. She is most seriously displeased."

Fitzwilliam gaped openly. His father's face was a mask, but a glimmer of mischief appeared in the elder Darcy's eye—one which had long been absent.

"She left over that? It is the middle of the afternoon already! Where can she go by nightfall? She is displeased with my uncle at present as well, is she not? Surely, she will not go to Matlock!"

A sly tug appeared at his father's cheek. "She is welcome to return here, naturally."

"She will not. Aunt is very determined, Father. It will be months before she is speaking to us again."

"Indeed. I pity the poor Lion's Head inn. Lambton is the only village she might find worthy of her regard within three hours, and the Lion's Head the only place open just now, I understand. Perhaps I will have Mrs Reynolds arrange for a fine smoked ham to be sent to the mistress of the inn."

After a moment of companionable quiet, Fitzwilliam ventured, "My aunt will be unable to escort me to school in a few weeks, I presume."

The father's mouth turned very slightly. "It seems unlikely. I find myself quite occupied at present as well, William. Perhaps you ought to remain here."

Fitzwilliam felt the whole of his tall frame fill with air and life, but he made answer with perfect dignity. "Thank you, Father. Georgiana will be pleased."

"Indeed. I do ask that you not tell her just now, however. I believe her nurse wishes for her to take a rest, and poor Miss Tuttle has had enough trouble today."

He laughed—very softly, it must be noted. "Yes, Father."

"Did she enjoy her outing in the carriage with Anne?" George wondered aloud. "It was very thoughtful of you to provide your cousin with a companion for the ride."

Fitzwilliam stiffened and found it suddenly necessary to clear his throat. "I... I believe so." He hesitated, then by some wild impulse, decided to blunder ahead. "Father... I do not wish to marry Anne."

George Darcy turned fully to face his son. "Your aunt has determined that the marriage is to take place once you have completed your Grand Tour."

"I shall regret that I must disappoint her." He clasped his hands behind his back and made answer stiffly, gazing out over the long drive to the receding dot of his aunt's carriage.

"Your mother also spoke favourably of the marriage." Darcy straightened his shoulders and assumed the accustomed posture which his son now emulated. He allowed his statement to hang as a challenge, waiting on his son's response.

"Mother..." His voice trailed off. For a hideous moment, he panicked. He could not dare disappoint his dear mother's memory, but surely Lady Anne Darcy would not have expected him to wed his cousin against his will! His stomach turned nauseatingly.

George Darcy had been watching his son's expression carefully, and now rested a comforting hand on his shoulder. His voice, when he spoke, was low and pained. "William, I would not see you suffer as I have. The women of the Fitzwilliam line are not strong—your aunt is the exception, and I hope Georgiana shall be as well. My Anne was all that was good and gentle, but she ought never to have borne children, nor taken on so much as Mistress. I knew that from the beginning, but I hoped..." He heaved a ragged breath, pressing his lips to a thin line. His gaze returned to the horizon, and his old air of authority heartened his inflections once more when next he spoke. "Do not assume that your cousin will be any less frail in ten years than she is now."

Fitzwilliam's astonished eyes drifted from his father's countenance to his feet. "Yes, Father," he husked, blinking rapidly.

"That was the least of your concerns, was it not?" queried the perceptive father.

"Yes, sir," he confessed. "If I thought I could ever care for Anne, I should do as you, Father. I believe I could overlook a great many obstacles if I found a lady I could admire—so long as her family and background were suitable, of course," he hastened to add. "Anne resembles my aunt too closely for my taste."

George Darcy choked back a most unsophisticated noise. "Well, you will have to sort that yourself," he coughed. "I have done battle enough with Catherine Fitzwilliam for one lifetime. Come, I was thinking of a ride over the northern slopes to see to the flocks there. I would appreciate your company."

Fitzwilliam's face nearly blossomed in delight. His father had not openly requested the simple pleasure of his company for longer than either could remember. His heart aglow, he stretched to his full height and gave his father a firm, dignified nod of agreement. "Yes, Father."

Chapter 27

Elizabeth Bennet stuck her lip out slightly as Miss Fairbanks knotted her bonnet under her chin. "I wish we could stay another day," she sighed.

"As do I," Madeline replied, affectionately touching her sweet little cheeks. "You will take good care of Jane as she continues to recover her strength?"

"I am quite well already, Miss Fairbanks!" Jane protested.

"I suppose you are." Madeline bit her lip, as she had been doing all morning. She had known as much herself, but could not think what else she might say, for all of the usual parting assurances seemed presumptuous. She could not be certain of ever seeing the girls again—not until Edward had spoken openly of his intentions—and there seemed an embargo on every possible profession of regret at their parting.

"Have you all of your books, Lizzy?" she thought to ask. "You would not wish to misplace any, I am sure."

"Oh—" Elizabeth shrugged—"they are mostly Uncle's books anyway. You may just give it back to him if I should forget one."

If I bite my lip any more, it is going to start bleeding! Madeline thought to herself. She cleared her throat and made answer lightly. "Suppose I do not see your uncle again for a long while—if ever?"

"Why, of course you will," Elizabeth maintained. "I heard him talking to Papa this morning before he went out walking. Do you know where he went?" Elizabeth laced her fingers behind her back and swirled her skirts, in the manner of a pert youngster who knows too much.

"Lizzy!" whispered Jane fiercely. "You mustn't speak of such matters!"

"He did not say, and it was not for me to ask," Madeline retorted, fixing the younger girl with a grave, albeit not displeased expression. "I had assumed that he was seeing to his coach and horses at the livery."

"Oh, no," Elizabeth insisted. "Papa was seeing to the horses. Uncle went *mmrfmrh*—"

"*Lizzy!*" Jane—gentle, sweet Jane—had clamped a tight hand down over her sister's noisy mouth. "Shhhh!"

Madeline was slowly shaking her head, her sore lips curved into a knowing expression. "You girls ought never to go into the business of secrets and intrigue," she chuckled.

A knock sounded at the door, and Mr Bennet's greying head poked in. "Are the girls quite ready, Miss Fairbanks?"

Madeline rose to face him. "They are, Mr Bennet."

"Very good. I must thank you again, Miss Fairbanks." He shifted his feet and his tones took on a deeper seriousness than she had previously thought him capable of. "Were it not for you, I would have been troubled most greatly to leave my girls behind."

"I did but little, sir. Your brother saw to all of their wants with prodigious care, you may be assured."

"Yes, well..." He appeared unconvinced, flashing her that cunning smile of his. "It might interest you to know that I have settled my accounts with Mrs Porter... and I left a healthy... er... gratuity."

"Mr Bennet," she laughed, "I appreciate your efforts at delicacy for my dignity and reputation, but I am far from a gentlewoman, sir."

"Mmm," was his only reply, but his eyes twinkled far more articulately. Madeline felt herself flushing anew with nervous anticipation. Did Mr Bennet expect, as she hoped, that one day soon she might claim him as a brother rather than a one-time employer?

"Come along, then, girls, for the carriage awaits," he beckoned his daughters. "Miss Fairbanks, it has been a very great pleasure." He bowed lackadaisically, took his nearest daughter by the hand, and sauntered away.

Madeline followed at a respectful distance—after all, there was no further point in lingering in the girls' vacated room. How strange, though, that Edward should be nowhere about! Only when the Bennet family were mounting their carriage did she at last glimpse him, striding quickly toward them from three blocks away.

Bennet reached to close the door, and his head emerged from the window of the carriage. "Put the steps up, please, Jones." The driver did as he was bidden, then mounted the box.

Madeline was glancing in confusion between Edward, who now had quickened his pace, and the quirky gentleman in the coach.

"Well, Miss Fairbanks, do you recommend Matlock, Dovedale, or Chatsworth for our outing today?"

"I... sir?" she turned back to Bennet. "I thought you were for London!"

"Oh, no, no, do not be silly," he waved. "Dovedale sounds a fascinating place, I do not think I shall be content until I have seen it. Drive on, Jones." He then procured a book from somewhere within the carriage and had it open before his eyes before Jones had quite sorted the ribbons.

The carriage rattled away, in entirely the wrong direction. Madeline's last glimpse of its occupants was a mischievous little grin from Elizabeth as she sent back a gleeful farewell. Edward had run the last block, waving his arm and shouting to no avail. He now appeared beside Madeline, somewhat out of breath and flustered.

"I... I believe your brother's carriage has left you!" she managed lamely.

He was still staring after the retreating vehicle, sputtering a little in anger. "That is *my* carriage, and I paid for the horses! What can he be thinking?"

"He mentioned Dovedale," she offered hesitantly. "I do not understand, I thought you were leaving straightaway!"

The annoyance had faded from his countenance, replaced slowly by an appreciative chuckle. "Bennet!" he laughed. "I ought to have known." He shook his head, then turned to her at last with a gallant bow. "It would seem, Miss Fairbanks, that I am at my leisure today. Might I request the pleasure of your company?"

She blinked, glancing again at the departing carriage, then back to Edward. Her body began to quiver with laughter, welling up from within until she was obliged to put her fingers to her lips to squelch a most unseemly outburst. When she could finally speak, she curtseyed in reply, "I would be most honoured, Mr Gardiner!"

"**P**APA, ARE WE REALLY going to see Dovedale?" Elizabeth was poring over her geography book, flipping the pages as she sought the aforementioned locale.

"Of course not, my pet—much too far for my taste. I should prefer a comfortable drive and a peaceful location to enjoy my book. No, I asked Jones to select whichever is the nearest popular attraction. I am certain he will procure us some noteworthy sights."

She dropped her book, disappointed, but strained to gaze out of the window. Only her eyes and the bridge of her nose might have been visible to an onlooker, hence only the skyline and distant horizon were within her field of view. "I met a boy who said he was from a fine estate near here," she mused, craning her neck to look farther down the road.

"Every boy has a fine estate," her father commented neutrally, scarcely even looking up from his book. "Nothing affords the gentry more pride, nor lends the dissembler such credit, as claiming a connection to ancestral lands."

Elizabeth squinted. She could not quite decipher the meaning of some of her father's words, but she understood his tone well enough. "He was not pretending, Papa. Mrs Porter said—"

"Oh, aye, my girl," he chuckled, shaking his head, "I give you leave to think well of the young fellow. Next to a genuine acquaintance with the same, I should say that a girl likes to have been brushed off by a lord. It gives her a certain distinction among her peers, does it not? You may have an entertaining tale with which to amuse your mother and sisters for years to come."

Elizabeth withdrew, not quite liking her father's cavalier treatment of her brief friendship. In Jane alone she found sympathy. "I am certain he was quite a *nice* person," Jane insisted with a pat to Elizabeth's shoulder.

She thought for a moment. "I think he *could* be very nice, if he wanted to be. I think he only pretends to be cross so nobody bothers him."

Jane nodded generously, fully believing everyone to be pure and noble of heart if they had once shown a morsel of kindness to her dear sister. "What was the boy's name, Lizzy?"

She paused, twisting her little forehead into a frown and puckering her lips. "I don't remember. I never said his name. He was just the tall boy with the curly hair and the little sister."

Whatever response Jane or the chortling Mr Bennet might have made were lost in a sudden jarring of the coach, followed by the sound of splintering wood. Jane cried out, and Elizabeth bit her tongue most painfully. All three occupants of the carriage were tossed about, and no doubt the driver atop the box nearly lost his seat.

When all had come to rest, the carriage was sitting at a comical angle, with Jane and Elizabeth thrown into their father's lap and the girls' strewn bonnets and little personal items littered haphazardly over the floor. Mr Bennet groaned—not in pain, but with the effort of lifting both girls off his person. Jane was sobbing and clutching at her ankle.

"Mr Bennet, sir!" Jones' voice carried inside the cab. "Are you well, sir?"

He groaned again. "Never better, Jones. Fine day for a broken wheel, is it not?"

From without, they could hear the driver assuring them that he would have them free straightaway. The carriage lurched as the horses were unhooked, for Jones apparently feared that in their startled state they might upset the crippled vehicle even further. A few seconds later, the door opened. "I do not know why the wheel broke, sir!" he was apologising. "I saw no rocks or ruts in the road!"

Once Mr Bennet stepped down, the two men bent to investigate the skewed undercarriage of the coach. "There it is." Mr Bennet pointed. "Two of the spokes were cracked before—do you see the age of this splinter? What could have occasioned that, I wonder?"

Jones was shaking his head. "Part of the way from Sheffield, sir—you remember the state of that road. Mayhap a crack started from the ruts."

"I shall have to repair my brother's carriage if that be the case, but I suppose it matters little for now. Do you know where we are?"

The driver looked about. "I was told that Pemberley lies another two or three miles up this road, sir. You wished for pleasant sights, sir, and I am assured that is a fine place to visit. Would you like that I go on to the estate to see if the head coachman will send help?"

"Oh, no, surely it cannot be necessary to trouble some great gentleman and his stables. We are approximately the same distance from Lambton, are we not?"

"Very nearly, sir."

"And neatly situated here—why, a quieter spot for reading I could not have fancied. I am afraid Jane cannot walk just now, but the girls and I may wait comfortably by that little stand of trees while you send for assistance."

"Yes, sir," Jones touched his cap. He went next to the team, sorting their harness to suit his purpose, then mounted the lead horse exactly like a post-boy. "I shall return or send someone straightaway, sir!" he promised.

Chapter 28

"How old, precisely, did you say this church was?"

Edward was desperately searching for anything sedate, natural, and commonplace to say. It was a difficult task, as his brain seemed suddenly disconnected from his tongue. *She* was standing beside him, her hand resting on his arm, the fractured light from the many-faceted windows shimmering off her hair... and he had her father's blessing! It was taking all of his concentration not to spiral toward that sublime event, that happy day when he might give her his name—quite probably in this very church!

"I believe it dates only some three or four hundred years. There is a much finer church in Derby, and another in Matlock." Her gentle, serene features softened luminously as she contemplated the tall, slim window before them. "Most people forego humble Lambton's church if it is a historical tour they desire, but I have always thought it beautiful."

"It is, indeed." There was something husky in his tone as he spoke. He watched her blink a little self-consciously, though the tinted glow of the stained glass concealed her certain blush. Did he dare speak now? "Miss Fairbanks?" he whispered.

She turned to him; her lips slightly parted. "Yes, Mr Gardiner?"

"Miss Fairbanks, I—"

"Did you wish to see the frescoes, sir?" a thin, high voice interrupted. "We have some very fine examples on this wall." The rector of the little church gestured importantly to his mid-day guests. The reedy, balding gentleman was a most informative and attentive tour guide—*too attentive*.

A small growl of disappointment rumbled in Edward's chest. He had no intentions of compromising Madeline, and consequently made no objections to the rector's chaperonage, but the man's timing left something to be desired. He pressed his lips tightly together, affecting a smile with his cheeks, but his eyes spoke only frustration. "We would be delighted, sir," he answered as soon as he could do so civilly.

Was she laughing at him again? Madeline had tipped her face away from him, but the roundness of her cheek betrayed her. Amusement was a more hopeful prospect than annoyance, but it was far from the sentimental longing he had been hoping to inspire in her. He clenched the fingers of his far hand, for they were cramping nervously. How did a man create the proper moment to speak of forever with a woman he had barely met?

"Oh, yes, very fine," he assured his eager host when they had crossed the room. "Indeed, yes," he nodded again as the man pointed out a particularly exquisite rendering of the holy family. He might have appreciated it more on another day, but it little held his attention at the moment. Madeline's fingers still curled round his elbow, her shoulder incidentally brushing his as he guided her about the little church. If he continued turning to his right, he discovered, it brought her into inevitably close proximity with each step....

"Mmm, now that is an interesting portrait," he mused thoughtlessly.

"Mr Gardiner?" she whispered.

"Yes, Miss Fairbanks?"

"We have viewed that same fresco thrice already. In fact, we have circled the church nearly half a dozen times."

"Have we?" he stopped abruptly. "No more than that?"

Her eyes, those gentle, warm eyes, narrowed laughingly. "Sir, are you searching for something particular?"

He caught a sharp breath, counted to three, and slowly spoke. "I was. I never thought to find it here, but I believe I have done so." Hesitantly, he reached for her free hand with his, then stood speechless for another moment as he tried to assemble his thoughts. It had never been so difficult with Mae Rutherford!

Perhaps it was not natural that it should have been, for that first blush of infatuation had been no more than that—a passing fancy, easily forgotten once compared to the real passion. Love had not then commanded his heart, seizing his very pulse and causing his breath to falter with each attempt at speech. There had been then no difficulty in forming the logical proposal he had designed for himself. Until the shock of Miss Rutherford's refusal, he had been the same man as always; confident, sensible, well-spoken. Faced now with the certain knowledge that what he asked of Madeline would answer for every hope he had ever held, the few, simple words he could form seemed inadequate to the momentousness of the occasion.

Her eyes were fixed breathlessly on his face. Her shoulders rose and fell more quickly now, and he could see the delicate curve of her white throat trembling in uncertainty. "It is well, sir," she choked at last, "that you have found what you sought. Many never do."

Some guilty conscience prickled the back of his neck, and he darted a quick glance over his shoulder at the ever-present rector. "Miss Fairbanks," he spoke softly, "may we take some air?"

She assented readily, and he led her out to the open street. Here, they could be assured of any number of eyes to ascertain their level of propriety, but no ears were so close at hand. "Miss Fairbanks," he began, still uncertain of his course, "I once had a vision for what I wished for in life. The respect of my peers, happy relations with my family, a promising business, the ability to purchase a comfortable home... all of these I have achieved."

Her gaze trailed the ground before them as they slowly paced the cobblestones. Coming to a sort of nook in the exterior wall of the church, he drew her out of the main path, encouraging her to look into his face. "One thing remains. I have long hoped for a partner—a companion. I wish for love and children, and the dearest possible friend of my heart with whom to pass the rest of my years."

Those light blue eyes had gone nearly black now as she stared back at him. She spoke not a syllable, but her entire being seemed centred on his words, hanging perilously by his inexpert declarations.

"I had begun to think," he continued gently, "that sort of ami-ability—the sense of fellowship and friendly belonging—could not co-exist with the deep feelings a man ought to have for the woman he would marry. The two notions had begun to appear to me so diametrically opposed, so impossible to join to one another in a single being, that I had been ready to give up altogether." He reached to clasp her hand once more, his gaze intense. "Madeline Fairbanks, you have changed my thinking on this matter."

Her lower lip trembled slightly. "You speak rather plainly, sir," she murmured, casting her eyes up the street at the other passers-by.

"I regret that I have not time to do otherwise. I know I ask much, and far too soon... but I hoped, Miss Fairbanks, that before I leave for London, I might persuade you to consider a courtship."

Her small fingers flexed within his. She parted her lips as her form went rigid with agitation and her eyes flashed briefly over his face. He waited in silent hope as she set her teeth, swallowed, then nodded jerkily. "Yes, Mr Gardiner," she managed in a hoarse whisper.

He nearly laughed for joy, for having once spoken so boldly, the lady's beautiful face repented of all its former trepidation. An easy smile blossomed, her cheeks pinked prettily, and her eyes sparkled her pleasure.

He gasped a little, delirious with relief that his beautiful Madeline was as brave and held such faith as he had dared to hope! Were he not a grown man, he might have shed a tear or two, such was the very depth of his heart's contentment—and if he blinked a little more than was his wont for a few moments, he could certainly be excused.

"May we go now and speak to your father again... Madeline?" he pleaded.

Her shining eyes danced gaily. "Yes, Edward!"

As the couple set out for the little dwelling a few blocks distant, a certain window lace across the way fell back into its place. The hand which had released it now touched sentimentally to smiling lips, then dabbed at moist eyes. "Benjamin!" cried Mrs Porter. "Will you fetch down my fine red shawl from the garret? It seems I shall have a wedding gift to prepare!"

"**P**APA, IS THE DRIVER ever coming back?"

Elizabeth tumbled over to her father, placing a hand in the centre of his book page. "We are hungry!"

Mr Bennet casually reached within his pocket to retrieve his watch, his eyes never leaving the page until the watch was open and ready to be viewed. "Well past two of the clock already! Indeed, I should think you are. There ought to be a basket in the boot with our luggage. You girls may help yourselves."

"Papa, we are not tall enough," Elizabeth reminded him.

"Eh? Oh, I suppose not." With a martyred sigh, he heaved himself from his comfortable position under the tree to procure the requested victuals. "Jane?" he thought to inquire as he passed. "Is your ankle much better?"

"Yes, Papa," Jane replied softly.

"She is lying, Papa. She tried to walk and cannot manage more than ten steps. I thought the driver was to return!"

"Indeed, it seems strange. He may well have encountered other difficulties. I've no doubt we shall see a rescue soon enough."

Even as he spoke, the girls' sharp ears detected the merry jingle of harness and the rattle of a heavy carriage. The sound came from the opposite direction, and the attention of the stranded travelers fixated on the approaching team. Mr Bennet released the basket into Elizabeth's care, then turned to present himself to the driver. It was clearly a smart, luxurious vehicle—likely quite safe as strangers on the road went.

"Pardon me, my good fellow!" he hailed the driver.

The coachman drew up the horses. No explanation of their plight was necessary, but Mr Bennet spoke regardless. "We seem to have been too much for our poor carriage, sir. Our driver has not yet returned, and my daughter's ankle was injured in the accident. Might I impose upon you and your good master to—"

"How dare you importune my carriage!" A shrewish voice lashed out from within the compartment.

Accordingly, Mr Bennet looked to the principal passenger, whose face now appeared at the window. "I believe, Madam, that it was your driver whom I importuned." Coolly, he turned his attention back to the man. "As I say, sir, my daughter is unable to walk the distance. Would you find it within your means—"

"Absolutely not!" vowed the mistress of the carriage. "You *dare* to speak impertinently to a member of the nobility! You address Lady Catherine de Bourgh, sir!"

Had that distinguished personage been more familiar with the queer sort of smile overspreading Mr Bennet's face, she might have experienced a flash of trepidation. Lady Catherine, however, had never in her life known such a sensation.

"Forgive my mistake," he returned mildly. "Be it as your ladyship is, as I am corrected, a member of the nobility, then quite certainly your ladyship is well acquainted with the privileges and obligations of rank."

She sniffed a little. "Quite so. Drive on, Matheson!" she commanded.

Bennet held up a hand. "One moment, if your ladyship pleases. Our driver is competent enough, but like most, I fancy, is a chatty fellow. Should his efforts to deliver another conveyance have been frustrated, he will quite naturally expect that any other honest travelers could not fail to render aid to an injured girl. So much will certainly be assumed at the livery and hotels in Lambton—I presume your ladyship is to pass through there?"

"My affairs are no business of yours!" she proclaimed.

"Indeed not, my lady. And surely, I would not wish for your ladyship's name to be misrepresented. One never knows what talk may propagate."

The lady visibly bristled at this. "Miscreant! Sir, I shall have you before the magistrates for defamation!"

"Completely unnecessary, I assure your ladyship. A truly great lady's character could never be in doubt," he bowed theatrically. "It is perpetually evident in her gracious manner and ready condescension toward the unfortunate."

"I am *always* generous toward the unprosperous," she retorted icily. "Vagabonds on the roadway are quite another matter. Matheson! Drive on immediately!"

The carriage started to roll away—the driver scarcely daring to look the stranded folk in the eye. While the lady was still within earshot, Thomas Bennet sang out, "I applaud your ladyship's caution. One never knows when vagabonds will take on the guise of eight-year-old girls!"

No further response issued from within the carriage, nor was one expected. Mr Bennet turned back toward his daughters, chuckling happily to himself. "It has been too long since I had the pleasure of speaking with the nobility. Is that a wedge of cheese, Jane? Excellent. Most comfortable, I should say." With that, he settled himself once more on the grass, and enjoyed a capital picnic.

Chapter 29

With thanks, Edward accepted the cup of tea from Madeline's hand, then turned his radiant countenance back to Mr Fairbanks—the man he might one day call his father!

"Have you any expectations of when you might return to the area, Mr Gardiner?" Fairbanks asked.

"As soon as I possibly can, sir." Edward's smiling eyes found Madeline. "You may be assured that my thoughts will not be far from Lambton while I am away!"

"That I understand well, sir." Fairbanks' eyes crinkled over his cup as he took a sip.

"It will certainly be some weeks," he elaborated, glancing regretfully to his love once more. "As I have already been away from my business quite some time... I wish it could be otherwise, Madeline," he apologised.

"Edward, you are a man of responsibilities," she spoke cheerfully. "I could not admire a man who did not look to his affairs with diligence, even at the expense of his own pleasure."

At this pronouncement he stilled, gazing on raptly, with an even greater appreciation for her generous nature. Blessed indeed was the man who could claim the treasure of such a woman's heart, steeped in both grace and wisdom! Such an easy spirit, untroubled by jealous or vain inclinations, only intensified his desire to please her. "A month—five weeks at most, even allowing for travel time!" he promised fervently.

"Do you think, sir," the father awkwardly interrupted the tender looks with a clatter of his cup on the saucer, "that you and your family will leave directly on the morrow?"

He released a sorrowful breath. "I do. Bennet is a curious fellow, a little difficult to predict at times, but I believe he wishes to return home immediately. He has never cared much for travel. Today... I shall count it as an unexpected gift," he smiled.

"But I dare not thank him for it, for he is a proud fellow, in his way. He dislikes displays of either generosity or capitulation, and so conceals whatever goodness or humility he possesses beneath that wit of his. It makes for a rather unique character."

"I think him endearing, now that I understand him a little better," Madeline defended the gentleman stoutly. "I do hope that he and the girls are having a pleasant outing today, for it *was* good of him to delay."

The gazes of the blushing lovers caught and held once more—this time undisturbed by the father. Fairbanks merely looked away and drained the contents of his teacup. Perhaps it was fortuitous, in that moment, that the knocker sounded firmly on his front door, so that he might be pardoned for excusing himself momentarily.

He was back almost directly. "Mr Gardiner, there is a fellow come who says there was some trouble with your carriage. It seems that your brother and his daughters are even now still awaiting his return, somewhere along the northern road from town."

"Good heavens!" Edward bolted to his feet. "Are they hurt?"

Fairbanks beckoned for him to follow to the door, where he met with the soiled and tattered person of his driver. "Jones!" cried he. "What has happened!"

"The wheel, sir, it's completely broken. It would be easy enough to repair, had I another and some tools, sir, but I did not." Jones passed a hand over his eyes to catch the sweat running from his forehead.

"What of Mr Bennet and the girls? Where are they?"

"That's the worst of it, sir. One of the girls was knocked about. I don't think it is serious, but she cannot walk back in her state. Mr Bennet said they might be safe enough to wait until I could send help, but that was some while ago, sir. I had a little difficulty of my own in making it back." He hung his head, clearly somewhat ashamed.

"I can see that! Come, Jones, out with it!"

"Well, sir, I was on my way back with the horses when I saw a fellow lying in a nearby field. I thought to myself that he might need some help too, so I called to him. There was no answer, so I called again with no success. I feared him badly injured, or perhaps dead! I dismounted and went up to him, sir, and that was when he kicked my feet from under me."

Edward coughed in surprise. "He did what?"

Jones grimaced. "Yes, sir. Rolled me on the ground, mumbling some oaths. I think he was greatly the worse for drink, sir, for he smelt badly and his speech was slurred even when I was not striking him back."

"What happened then?" Edward demanded.

"Well, sir, he pushed me down a little bank—not too hard, sir, as I said, he was suffering for drink—but by the time I climbed back up, he was gone and so were the horses."

"The horses!"

"Oh! Do not fear, sir. They did not go far. I started back for Lambton on foot and saw them over a rise not a quarter mile farther on. The fellow had passed out and fallen off the beasts. He was by the road, but the horses had a merry time of it. Took me hours to catch them both again! A dreadful wreck they made of the harness, sir."

"Jones," he clenched his eyes again in thought, "how long ago was all of this?"

"I left Mr Bennet around eleven of the clock, sir. I thought they might have met with some other travelers by now and had help back to Lambton—that's why I looked in at the inn before the woman told me to come here."

"They may have encountered someone traveling another direction, and taken whatever immediate help they could get," Edward reasoned. "Where else does that road go?"

"We were bound for Pemberley, sir, and it was about half-way when the carriage broke down. I'm told that is the nearest estate, but about four miles beyond the turn-off for Pemberley there is another town called Chesterton. Anyone might have been going there."

He pressed his fingers into his eyes, groaning. What a disaster! His carriage broken down, his driver imposed upon, at least one of his nieces injured, and his relations still unaccounted for! "Stay a moment, Jones, I will join you."

He hurried back to the little parlour to explain to Madeline his predicament. "Oh, dear!" she exclaimed. "I will ask of my neighbors if anyone has passed that way today and might have seen them! Certainly, we can find two or three who are able to help recover them."

Edward thanked her with a quick kiss to the back of her hand, then rushed out after Jones. "Which of the girls was hurt, and how badly?" he snapped out as they marched.

"The elder, sir. I think she only turned her ankle, but I did not stay to find out."

Edward stopped in the middle of the road, struck with a sudden realisation. "I know not where to begin!" he confessed. "Perhaps I will inquire of the Porters—they have ever been my friends in town. Surely, they will know whom I should seek out." So reasoning, he bent his steps in that direction, with Jones trotting briskly behind.

Even from far down the street, the two were surprised to observe a massive carriage blocking the entrance to the little inn. It did not deter them from their course but did cause Edward to slow hesitantly as he approached. Some august visitor had arrived... and was displeased, from the sound of the tones carrying out to the street. His heart sank a little, realising that Mrs Porter likely would be unable to spare him even a moment just now. He waved Jones back and slipped quietly inside.

"What can you possibly mean, you have *no* accommodations!" an imperious voice echoed. "Why, I saw five windows facing the street on each level, and you must have more besides. I shall require the whole of the top floor at the very least!"

"I regret, your ladyship, that those rooms were all taken days ago," Mrs Porter answered reasonably. "The guests previously residing at the Rose and Crown have all lodged here, and I had my own guests besides. I am afraid I simply have no more available space."

"You must *make* space!" the woman retorted obtusely. "You know quite well who I am!"

Edward was standing at such an angle that he might observe her expression, and a more determined, inflexible look he could little imagine. The woman was attempting to stare down Mrs Porter, clearly aghast that anyone could dare be unavailable for her complete disposal.

Mrs Porter never flinched. "I cannot, your ladyship, much as your patronage would honour me and increase my consequence." Here, Edward detected a faint twinkle in Mrs Porter's eye. "I cannot in all conscience evict paying occupants of seven rooms at your ladyship's pleasure."

"You've a stable, have you not?" the lady thundered—if, indeed, it is polite to say that a lady's voice might thunder. "Let them have clean straw for the night! Heaven and earth, what is it come to that indigent tradesmen should take precedence over a member of the nobility? I am by the twin virtues of birth and marriage of superior station, and I absolutely insist that you make way!"

"Your ladyship might enquire at the Rose and Crown," Mrs Porter answered with every politeness. "They've hung oilcloths over the windows and the bedding is all laundered by now. They are not opened again for regular business, but they might consider—"

"With oilcloths over the windows! What do you take me for, woman?" she roared. "And where is your husband, the keeper? Why may I not see him?"

Mrs Porter crossed one hand over the other, in a nonverbal assertion that she would not yield. "My husband is about his duties, my lady. Many of them are out-of-doors in this season."

"Oh! So, he is a farmer into the bargain! Shameful that your establishment should be so poorly run that it does not maintain you! You lack economy in your ways. Upon my word, I see at least half a dozen candles more than is needed for a room this size. And that window! Why, it faces full west. It is little wonder your room here is so stifling!"

Mrs Porter smiled sweetly. "I regret that our inn is not up to your ladyship's discerning standards. I shall consider your advice and make what humble remedies I am able. I dearly hope that you will find matters so much improved on your next visit that you will decide to honour us with your patronage."

Edward snickered... silently. If Mr Bennet's mother were still alive, he imagined she might have been something like Mrs Porter!

The great lady dominating the room seemed utterly at a loss. Her brow furrowed and jerked, her lips puckered in contempt, and her incredulous eyes studied the woman who would first defy her authority, then insult her intelligence. She seemed to be carefully evaluating her options and considering how humbly she wished to lodge for the night—the inn did, after all, have one empty bed that Edward knew of, but not seven.

At last, her decision set in iron. "This establishment is beneath my regard," she sneered coldly. "I shall be certain that no business of mine ever diverts through this odious little village, and my brother's estate shall conduct no further business here either!" She swirled her skirts about and stalked to her carriage, with a strident, "Matheson! We are for Matlock by nightfall!"

Chapter 30

Temporarily forgetting his own troubles, Edward started toward Mrs Porter. "Dear lady!" he cried. "I would not have wished you to incur the wrath of the local manor. Will this incident not ultimately bring economic harm to you and your neighbors? I would certainly have been willing to give up my room."

She chuckled. "Fear not, Mr Gardiner. I have not had personal dealings with Lady Catherine de Bourgh before, but she is well known in Lambton. This happens about every seven or eight years. She is related to the Darcy family, you know, and would only come here if she had a falling-out with Mr Darcy. We will suffer no hardships for the withdrawal of Pemberley's business, nor that of Mr Darcy's tenants."

"I am relieved to hear it. Oh! Mrs Porter, I had nearly forgotten what I came to you about! My carriage—"

He started to tell her the entire tale, but sudden shouting from out of doors halted him. Trading quizzical looks with his hostess, he darted out the front of the inn. The de Bourgh carriage had only just taken on its passenger once more, with the door facing the inn still open. On the far side, however, was an open window to the carriage, so that all of the occupants might be seen easily from either side.

This detail might have passed unnoticed, but for the voice Edward now heard. "*That* lady is not nice! She refused to help us!"

Relief and dread spiraled together, as Edward clearly recognised Elizabeth's tones. Fearful of what he might find, he crept round the carriage and spotted a humble farm cart, drawn by a single old plug of a steed. The cart itself was heaped with woolen bundles and people, with Elizabeth standing securely in the middle of it all as it creaked to a stop. She was pointing at the elaborate carriage. "*That* lady right there!" she repeated.

"Elizabeth," Mr Bennet was correcting casually, "what have I taught you about raising your voice?"

Elizabeth cast one more dark look to the carriage. It could not be known whether Lady Catherine de Bourgh took any notice of Elizabeth's outcry, but she must have heard it, at least. Certainly, everyone else on the street did, and perhaps that might account for the vehemence of the hand which now drew the shade.

Edward watched Elizabeth frown, purse her lips while looking toward her father, and lift her voice in quite a different way. By the time he had reached the side of the little cart, she was humming most charmingly and helping her wounded sister into their father's waiting arms.

"Why, 'tis yo', sir!" a voice surprised him at his shoulder.

Edward turned and recognised the younger shepherd from the mountains. "Indeed! I had not thought to see you again, my good man."

The fellow thumbed his hat a little higher on his forehead, a pleased look on his face. "Well met, sir. Do yo' know this folk? Found 'em in a bad way, sir!"

"I should say I do! They are my relations, and I only just learned of their predicament. I am much obliged to you for your kindly aid."

The young man beamed. "A favour turned is a favour returned, sir. 'Tis no longer in yo'r debt I am."

"I had never considered you so," Edward smiled. "Thomas!" He turned slightly to grant his brother a share in the conversation. "I am very glad to see you safe!"

"Much thanks to our friend here. Ah, Miss Fairbanks," Bennet tipped his hat smilingly to the lady, who approached Edward and took his arm. Elizabeth promptly claimed the lady's other hand.

"Mr Bennet, sir, we were very troubled to hear of your misfortune! I am relieved that you and the girls are safe."

"Well, apart from Jane's injured ankle and the damage to the carriage wheel, I would not count the day's events a misfortune." He drew a book from the wagon, tapping it with satisfaction before handing it to Edward. "You really must order more of this volume. Most diverting!" From his coat pocket, he withdrew several coins, handing them to the shepherd. "I thank you, my good man, for turning back."

Edward's brows rose. "You were not even coming to Lambton?"

"Nay, sir, to Pemberley. Th' master's promised a fine price on my fleece for next year, if 'e likes the quality, and I've some small bits left for 'im to see."

"It sounds a profitable scheme," Bennet put in, "but before Mr Darcy mistakes him for some rather poor-quality wool, what are you to do with our other passenger?"

Edward looked again to the cart in surprise. Lying flat on his back amid thirty or so bundles of wool, was a groaning, tallish fellow, caked in dust and bruises. Beside him, Madeline touched her hand to her mouth. "Why, it is Mr Lawrence!"

"I dinna' 'is name, Miss, but there's a deal o' the devil in 'im."

"Where is the nearest magistrate?" Edward asked. Inwardly, he cringed. Surely this was the man who had randomly attacked Jones, which would mean an investigation and delay if they pressed charges.

"'Tis the same, Mr Darcy at Pemberley," the man answered. "'E looks poorly on a man 'o lives in the bottle. Bad morals, 'e says. Mr Darcy will like as not set 'im to better work—keeps a man clean, 'e says. And since I've business there anyway, 'tis no trouble to take 'im."

Quite rapidly, however, the shepherd had cause to rethink that assurance. Lawrence sat up, clutching his head with one hand and wrapping the other lovingly over a bale of wool. He ceased stroking it abruptly when his eyes opened and he took in his surroundings. "What's all this, then!" he demanded, sounding as though he were trying to speak round two or three large stones in his mouth.

"You are intoxicated, sir, and this good fellow has found you in a shocking state along the road," Edward replied.

Lawrence rubbed his eyes and began, slowly, to disembark from his equipage. "Intoxicated! One drink, that's all I had," he grumbled.

"One might ask how long it took to swallow that drink. Sir, you must remain to be taken before the magistrate."

"That's a fine way to talk before a lady!" slurred the man. He reached for his hat but found none. "Miss Fairbanks, how do you do today?"

Madeline shrank somewhat closer to Edward. "Mr Lawrence, you are unwell," she murmured. "Please, you must do as Mr Gardiner has said!"

Mr Lawrence, tottering only slightly on his feet, stared back and forth between the couple. "So, it's the London dandy for you now? What sort of woman leads a man on, then takes up with the first fancy man she finds?"

"Sir!" Edward cut in, his voice steel and his eyes hard. "I will not tolerate such words to Miss Fairbanks, nor to any other lady! If you do not mount the cart again of your own will, you will be taken by force.

In that case, I shall accompany you to the magistrate and report that my driver was accosted along the road! What say you, sir?"

The man's face darkened. "What right've you? Why, I...." Mr Lawrence took a great swinging step forward, well within striking distance, but suddenly swayed heavily and stumbled, falling flat to his face in the dirt of the road.

Edward had braced a protective arm around Madeline, snatching her away from danger as Mr Lawrence fell. The man lay moaning in the street, utterly harmless, but she still trembled faintly in astonishment.

"It is all right, my dear," he soothed, stroking her shoulders.

"Edward," she spoke, turning her face up to him with a tip of her rosy lips. She needed say no more. He glanced about.

They were standing in the centre of the street, she wrapped securely in his arms, with a dozen of her neighbors staring at them. He caught Bennet's eye, which was not difficult, for his brother-in-law was sniggering and winking most suggestively.

"Miss Fairbanks," he turned back to her with a blissful expression, "would you do me the honour of accepting my hand in marriage?"

She was laughing and nodding. "Yes, Mr Gardiner!"

T HE NEXT SEVERAL MOMENTS passed by in a fog of pure delight. Edward was nearly heedless of the young shepherd, who, with the assistance of Mr Bennet, once more got the intoxicated Lawrence back into the wool cart.

He was the last to notice when a Mr Kirk arrived on the scene, apparently quite put out with the same man and vowing to accompany him before the magistrate to bring the charges of theft and general nuisance.

He scarcely acknowledged Jones, who passed by with a quick congratulation and a promise that he and a man from the livery would have the carriage repaired and returned to town by nightfall.

That his swirling delirium and focus of his attention all centred upon the being of the happy young woman who now received the congratulation of her neighbors need not be in doubt. Nothing else existed for a few moments but her radiant smile. Assorted hands clapped him on the shoulder, several ladies' voices wished him joy, but it was Mrs Porter who was at last successful in beckoning the young couple off the street.

"Well, now." She directed the party to a table. "It seems we've a wedding to plan!"

Edward clasped Madeline's hand after she took her seat and stared intently into her eyes. "My dear, will you marry as soon as may be? Have you any wish for a longer engagement so that we might come to know one another better?"

"None at all, Edward," she squeezed his fingers back. "I will miss you these few weeks, and it is a feeling with which I do not wish to become too familiar."

"Then it is settled!" he declared with growing excitement. "But can it be managed in just over a month?"

"Lord bless you, Mr Gardiner, you needn't fret about that. When you return, all shall be in readiness," Mrs Porter beamed comfortably. "Just step on over to the church across the way and see to the reading of the banns, and while you do so, Madeline can help me prepare this lovely ham which is just arrived."

His feet light and his heart thrumming, Edward leaped to Mrs Porter's suggestion. This final errand made their engagement official! Whatever else might happen, he would be returning to quaint little Lambton in but a few short weeks, and when he did so, Madeline Gardiner would be coming home with him.

Chapter 31

Five Weeks Later

FITZWILLIAM DARCY PAUSED HIS writing when he heard the hurried tapping of small shoes outside the library door. He slanted a small—and not at all undignified—smile in the direction of the door, watching patiently for that amusing moment which always came when Georgiana defeated the door latch and thrust it open.

He had not long to wait. Lavender was apparently the colour choice of the day, and her prim little dress boasted more ribbons and bows in that shade than he could count. She squealed in delight when she spied him at the writing desk and hurried confidently to his side.

"Will! Papa said I might stay with you this morning!"

"Did he? Where has Miss Tuttle gone, to visit her mother?"

"Her friend is getting married," she informed him blithely. "Papa said she might go. She promised to bring me back a flower." She hopped up to his knee and tipped her little chin with serene pride. It did thrill her so to have the advantage of information!

"I see. Well, then, you can help me decipher this letter from my friend Charles Bingley." He held up the correspondence with a helpless frown.

Georgiana squinted, looking from the page in his hand to the one on his writing desk. The contrast in penmanship was remarkable, even to a girl of not quite four. "He broke his pen!" she declared bluntly. "So many splotches!"

"Bingley's letters always look that way," he sighed. "He will fare rather poorly in Master Langley's writing class—I imagine the poor chap will scarcely scrape by. I expect we will have much to study together next term."

"You're going back?" Georgiana seemed at once subdued and hesitant.

"Yes, little love, I am afraid I must, but not until next year."

She snuggled her head into his chest, her little rosebud lips pursed in distress. She sniffled once, but countless hours of observing her brother had not been fruitless. He could verily watch the brave façade fall once more as she blinked and straightened. "Your friend will be happy," she decided graciously.

"I think so," he agreed gently. "Perhaps you can help me finish my letter, and then we may do something else together?"

Accordingly, he turned his attention to his letter, with Georgiana still perched upon his left knee and leaning over the writing desk. It was awkward to balance her and reach his hand around her little body, but it was worth every bit of the trouble her presence cost. As he finished the last line, he cast his eyes affectionately over her. She propped her chin on her hands and her elbows on his desk, and her bright blue eyes rounded in awe at his flowing script.

He tapped out the very last punctuation and set the pen down with an air of finality. Georgiana turned to him in surprise. "You're done? You write so fast!"

"Not at all. I write rather slowly. You should see Father. What shall we do next?"

She pressed her little mouth in thought. "May we go riding?"

"No!" he cried, jumping a little. "Er… what I mean is, it looks like we could have some rain later this afternoon. I think the certain dry days of summer are almost behind us, and any further long outings will have to wait until next year."

Her little face fell in disappointment. "Will, there is *nothing* to do!" she whimpered.

"Perhaps it is not too early to teach you a little about chess," he mused. He glanced furtively between his sister and the marble chess board across the room. "Indeed, I think not. Come, I will teach you the names of the pieces."

They settled together on one side of the board, he nestling her close and resetting the board. "Now, look here—this is the queen. She always goes here… and here is the king. Over here are the bishops, and these are the knights, and here are the rooks."

"What are those?"

"I am just coming to those. They are the pawns. Do not let the name fool you—each is valuable. Occasionally during the game, you must sacrifice one of the pawns, but it always comes at a cost. Never take them for granted, sweetling."

She glanced from left to right, taking in the whole board with furrowed brow. "How do you win?"

He squeezed her a little in encouragement. What a surprise to see that she was interested, and what a treat it might be over the next years to enjoy this particular pursuit with her! That little lass from Hertfordshire was not the only child who would be able to challenge him, he promised himself.

"It is rather complex. Each piece has its own role—fear not, dearest, I will teach you all of them in turn. Eventually, however, a player must move his pieces to the other side of the board, to force the other king into check."

She nodded, her eyes wide with interest. "The king is the most important?"

He laughed silently. "He likes to think so, but the real power belongs to the queen. It is she who directs the king's movements, and she who protects him when he advances."

She stared hard at the carven piece, contemplating it deeply, before at last turning to him. "You need a good queen, then!"

"Indeed," he chuckled.

M ADELINE SWEPT TREMBLING HANDS down the front of her gown. It was such exquisite material! How was it that she, a humble clerk's daughter from a simple farming village, was so attired?

"Madeline, dear, you look lovely!" Mrs Porter fussed a little more over her hair, then turned her about by the shoulders. "Ah, perfect!" she declared. "The blue ribbon was a splendid choice. Sets off your eyes, it does, but I daresay any of the samples would have suited. Your Mr Gardiner has excellent taste!"

Madeline swallowed and tried to still her quivering limbs. "He should not have sent so much! Oh, Mrs Porter, how shall I manage? He must have such a large warehouse, and so many fine things. I do not know the first thing about trade and London fashions!"

"Calm yourself, my dear," Mrs Porter commanded sternly. "There, now, that's better. You are a clever young lady, you know, and your Mr Gardiner seems most generous and thoughtful. Surely you will learn your way soon enough. Now, let me look at your bonnet." She plucked up the fashionable new millinery, with its saucy little feather and ribbon to match her gown and settled it over Madeline's curls. "There. Oh, how proud your papa will be!" she decreed. "It is a shame that your dear mama could not be here."

"It is," she agreed sadly. "Nevertheless, I know she would be pleased that it is you helping me this morning. I am among friends today." Madeline impulsively leaned close to drop a kiss on the older woman's cheek, then embraced her with all of the force of her sorrow at their imminent parting.

Mrs Porter returned the embrace, then fought back a rush of sentiment and pulled away. "There, there, my dear. We were to part soon enough as it is. Mr Williams comes next week, and then Mr Porter and I are off to Leeds. You and your Mr Gardiner must come see us one day."

Madeline nodded vigourously, swiping a stray drop from the corner of her eye. "And we will write often! I know that Edward is so very fond of you both, and we are so grateful... Oh, Mrs Porter, how grateful I am that you helped to bring us together!"

"There, there, Madeline. The gentleman has eyes, after all. He could not have failed to take note of you about town when he was here before, though he might have met with even a dozen others first! Come, now, I think I hear voices below. I believe they must be ready for you."

Madeline hurried to the window and looked down. They were back in that same little room where she had attended Jane, with her father waiting in the dining room for her to finish dressing. Edward and all of his connections had arrived only late the evening before, in two separate carriages, causing something of a to-do among the knowing matrons of Lambton. Edward had taken his old room in the Lion's Head, but the Bennets and Philipses had settled in immediately at the more spacious Rose and Crown with its newly refurbished rooms.

With Edward had ridden her dear brother Robert from London, who had reported confidently that she had caught herself "a fine fellow, if I ever did see one." Robert had spent the last evening regaling Madeline and her father with details of Mr Gardiner's establishment; the fine flat where he resided, the handsome houses in Cheapside which he intended to propose to his new bride, the large warehouse, which was his, but his most particular praise was reserved for Mr Gardiner's offer to retain his legal services once he had completed his license. That Robert approved of Edward Gardiner would be an understatement.

Edward had walked Robert to the house the very moment he had arrived last evening, lingering for a few stolen moments together before their wedding day, but she had not yet met her future sisters. She longed to rush down to greet them—so genteel they appeared! Madeline pressed up against the glass, her curiosity washing over her.

How should she get on with such refined ladies? Their apparel, their manner of walking, even the dainty shoes poking beneath their gowns were all simply exquisite. They must attire themselves every day—why, several times per day!—in the lavish manner of clothing which she herself now wore. She fingered her skirts again. It was a dramatic alteration from the simple, serviceable clothing to which she had always been accustomed.

What might they think of her? She bit her lip. She dearly hoped they would not find her a disappointment and would greatly have desired to at least meet them before the ceremony. Alas, propriety dictated that she wait for her father, and then proceed directly to the church across the street, where Edward and his family were now entering. She would be related to the two ladies below before ever exchanging words with them.

"Oh!" Mrs Porter clucked in disappointment, peering over Madeline's shoulder. "Mr Bennet did not bring those charming daughters of his!"

"No," Madeline sighed wistfully. "Edward wrote that he had some affairs with his business at the last moment, hence they were traveling in haste so that they might arrive in three days rather than four or five. It would not do to bring the children. I am certain I shall see Jane and Lizzy again soon, though, as well as their younger sisters."

"Be certain to keep an eye on those two for me! I've quite a fancy for them, particularly that youngest. Mark my words, Madeline, those two will make fine young ladies one day."

"I will!" she promised with a laugh. "I think we must go now, for Papa ought to be ready downstairs."

Chapter 32

WITHIN MERE MOMENTS, IT seemed, the father had offered up his most treasured possession into the keeping of another. With solemn pledges and a precious, binding display of affection, the ceremony passed quickly into memory. Madeline would forever bear the vision of Edward's cherished face alight with love for her as she made that fateful journey to the altar, and Edward himself treasured the sight of his angel, descending to him in the divine sweetness of bridal surrender. They stood now, hands clasped and heads bowed together, just before the first well-wishers streamed into the great room of the Lion's Head.

"Madeline." He brought her little gloved fingers to his lips. "I know it sounds trite, but you have made me the happiest man alive! Not so very long ago I thought I would never be so fortunate, but you have blessed me beyond measure, my dear."

"I might say the same," she blushed. There was so much on her heart, and so much more she might have said. Fate, however, decreed that any further nuptial reminiscence would have to wait, for at that moment their guests entered.

"Oh, my dear brother! Oh, sister, let me greet you!" Madeline's attention was now demanded rather forcefully by a curious personage. She was no longer a particularly young woman, and she crowded first through the door before the others. Behind her fluttered a great billowing shawl, her bold auburn curls were primped inside a floral bonnet which, upon closer inspection, could only be called gaudy, and her hazel eyes rounded wide in transports of delight.

Edward cleared his throat. "Hrm... Madeline, may I present my sister, Francine Bennet."

"Mrs Bennet," she dipped a polite little curtsey. "How pleased I am to make your acquaintance. I had the very great pleasure of coming to know your daughters this summer, and I have been looking forward to meeting you!"

"Oh! Edward, such a charming girl! I knew how it would be, brother! Mother always said you could not be so agreeable for nothing. Is he not the most wonderful fellow, and such a generous man!"

Madeline glanced uncomfortably toward Edward. "Uhm..." she stammered—a mannerism most unlike herself. "He is indeed, Mrs Bennet. I count myself most fortunate."

"Naturally, sister! Now, you must call me Fanny. Come, here is our sister Philips, but of course, you may call her Geraldine." The woman draped her arm comfortably about Madeline's waist, drawing her far away from her new husband.

Madeline cast a panicked glance behind herself, seeking Edward's sympathetic, cringing face. He lifted his shoulders helplessly, for he could not shield his wife forever from his sister. Perhaps, the unspoken understanding passed between them, it was best to allow the effusions to flow now, rather than needlessly protract Fanny Bennet's joy at the expense of a delayed departure. Madeline drew a deep breath and turned once more to face the woman who was not at all what she had expected.

"Has our brother not secured us the most lovely new sister?" Mrs Bennet was gushing to Mrs Philips. "Why, she is ten times the beauty that *Miss Rutherford* was, is she not?"

Madeline blanched in horror. She was aware of the lady's existence, for Edward had, in a fit of naked honesty, written her all of the relatively innocent details of his prior almost-attachment. However, for Mrs Bennet to blurt out the other lady's name on her wedding day was... well, nothing could have prepared her for the woman's vulgarity!

Mrs Philips clasped her hands lightly together and tilted her head into a composed greeting. She cast an evaluating glance from bonnet to shoes over Madeline and appeared satisfied. Her cool reserve seemed to be in every way the opposite of her sister... until she spoke. "I quite agree, Fanny. Miss Rutherford," she disclosed intimately to Madeline, "had *no* taste whatsoever! Silks at all times of day and in every season! I used to tell my brother what abominable lack of breeding it showed, and I am glad to see that he at last took my advice. A terrible disappointment he gave her, to be sure, but he shall be much better suited with you. You are most welcome to the family, Madeline Gardiner."

She tried to gasp out a reply but managed only a strangled little noise in her throat.

"Now then, Madeline," Fanny Bennet bent near to whisper her loud confidences. "You mustn't worry about a thing once you come to London, for we have your rooms all settled for you. Edward, of course, could not be expected to know how everything must be arranged, so we naturally took it upon ourselves to decorate and appoint your chambers for you. We did recommend a ladies' maid for you, but my brother is so stubborn! He had someone else in mind, but do not hesitate to write me for recommendations when you find my brother's choice unsuitable. Oh, but your chambers are so elegant and charming! I cannot wait until you shall see it all, for my brother would spare no expense for you! Only imagine how we shall appoint your rooms in your new house once we have all chosen it! If only Mr Bennet would allow me such pin-money, I should do my own rooms at Longbourn over!"

She darted quick eyes to Edward and found him tugging at his collar with a grimace. There was no possibility that he had not overheard the conversation, and she guessed by his look that he had had little choice in the decoration of her rooms.

"I am sure," she fumbled diplomatically, turning back to her new sisters, "that there will be a great deal of material and other items... left over. I believe Edward usually obtains great quantities when he receives the shipments for his warehouses—more than my humble rooms can need, you understand. Certainly, he could give you a very fine price for anything you might desire."

"That is precisely what I was hoping! Oh, I *knew* you would be clever," Fanny Bennet tapped her expressively on the shoulder with a little fan from her reticule. "I shall be sure to bring Mr Bennet to London again when you have returned from your wedding tour, so that we may look over everything. Oh! Have you settled all you will need for your trip?"

"I believe so," she smiled. "I have never been to Brighton, but I have heard that it is lovely."

"Oh! If only Mr Bennet would take me to Brighton! I am quite sure that a little sea bathing will set me up forever. Do you not agree, sister?" she nudged Mrs Philips.

"I always thought sea bathing most scandalous," sniffed the other. "Why, you remember how Lady Lucas saw that young woman's dress slip from her shoulder when she was taking the bathing machine in Lyme! It could happen to anyone, Fanny dear."

Madeline was slowly overcoming her mortification. The two women before her were not vicious—simply ridiculous. Across the room, she could see Mr Bennet speaking with her father, but he was, in truth, watching his wife with that cynical twinkle in his eye. At last, she understood his cryptic phrasing when he spoke of his wife, and if she bit back a small ripple of sympathetic laughter, it is not likely that Mr Bennet took any offence.

"I think," she chuckled, "I may assure you quite decidedly that we have lost the season for sea bathing, but I believe we will find ample amusements there. There must be any number of activities which do not require a dip in the cold water."

At this, Mrs Bennet and Mrs Philips each contrived an expression which bore a striking similarity to the other. Their eyes widened, their mouths puckered to scandalised little smirks, and they turned quickly to one another with their fans fluttering near their faces. "Ooooh!" Mrs Bennet sucked in her breath, looking to Mrs Philips for assurance and receiving it in the form of a prod from her elbow. "Dear sister, you cannot have had any... *warnings*, can you?"

Madeline's brow crumpled. "I am afraid I do not.... Can Brighton be so very dreadful?" She glanced from one to the other, sure by the rosy stain of their cheeks that she was somehow the brunt of a scandalous joke.

Mrs Philips leaned confidentially close, tapping a fan on her arm. "Someone may as well tell you—you need not bend to your husband's *every* whim. Be certain that he..." here, she glanced uneasily to her sister, "... *ahem*... takes you out to the shops, my dear."

"Aye!" seconded Mrs Bennet with energy. "And you must insist that he buy you whatever you wish, and you must not be afraid to lock your door, sister! Surely, it is not too late for you to bring a companion—why, I spoke to the most charming young girl just before the ceremony, I forget her name, but I believe she said her mother was a widow—"

"*Thank you*, Fanny," Edward's deep voice at last interrupted. Madeline had been again struck dumb, gaping in open-mouthed astonishment. She came to herself when Edward's hand cupped firmly round her elbow. "If you will excuse me, my sisters, there is someone else I wish to introduce to my wife."

She leaned on him rather heavily as he drew her away, her eyes still wide and staring in shock. "Are you well, my dear?" he whispered from the side of his mouth.

"I... why, I hardly know! I thought Mr Bennet unpredictable, but I have no words for his wife!"

He chuckled under his breath. "And that is why he married her, if I had to guess. Marriage to my sister cannot be monotonous. Did she frighten you too terribly, my dear?"

"I do not know that 'frighten' is the proper word. I simply wonder how you can possibly be related. Oh, my, Edward, you must introduce me to this friend of yours before I prattle on further! Where is he?"

Edward stopped her, a proud grin overpowering his features. "Jones? Why, he is with the horses, and waiting to drive us to Leicester."

"Ah, the very man I have been longing to meet!" she teased. "Are we to see him now, or shall I wait?"

"In a few moments. Let us see to our guests here for a little longer."

Accordingly, they did so. Madeline could have preferred a much simpler wedding breakfast, but Mrs Porter had overruled her. "Your new station warrants a generous display, my dear," she had chided. "I may consider it my own farewell from the neighborhood as well, you know."

Even so, Mrs Porter's machinations and Mrs Bennet's giddy chatter proved not as powerful as Edward's desire to carry off his bride, and it was not long at all before he was tugging at her arm. "Let us begin our retreat," he murmured low in her ear.

She complied, smiling all the while at the sly glimmer in his eye. Standing before the door of the inn was yet a different carriage from the ones which had arrived the previous night. It was either new, or newly made over, with well-built springs and plush upholstery. She turned to him in some confusion. "Where is your carriage?" she asked softly, not to be overheard by the small throng of well-wishers following them out of the door.

"This is it," he beamed. "I decided that my old carriage, which was suitable enough for a bachelor who traveled little, would not do for my bride. This is yours. I am leaving the other for your father's use until he is ready to join us in London, and then I doubt we shall need it further."

"Edward!" she touched fingertips to her lips. "This is simply too much! Why, it is so large!"

He leaned very close and whispered, "We will simply have to set about filling it then, my dear."

She giggled but sobered quickly as a press of humanity surrounded her. *This is it*, she realised with a shiver. This was the last moment of her girlhood, the last time she would embrace these dear folk as a neighbor. The moment her foot touched the step of the shining new carriage, she would belong to Edward in fact, as well as in ceremony. His world was now hers.

Not all of her dear friends were in attendance, for some had gone on to their own futures already. Sarah Tuttle had managed to procure a holiday from her employment at Pemberley, and Jenny Burke, née Mayweather, stood by with her new husband. These were the only representatives present of Madeline's most particular friends, but they were to visit briefly with the former Miss Perry and her new husband in Leicester on the morrow, before continuing on their travels. The remaining faces were dear and familiar, but less intimate. All of these passed by in a dreamy haze for the new bride, until Mrs Porter and her father were the only souls remaining.

Mrs Porter had exhausted all of her motherly sentiments earlier in the day. Ever the proper house mistress, she gave Madeline one last demonstrative embrace, then fled back within the inn. She would not shed her tears before others, but her sincere depth of feeling was not lost to the young bride.

Her parting from her father was less sentimental, at least on his side, than it might have been. "Well, well, my dear," he smiled proudly. "I shall miss you, my girl, but I shall see you in London in a month's time, or perhaps two if matters here take longer to settle."

She dabbed another misty tear from her cheek, nodding vigourously. "Yes, Papa, I shall be looking for you!"

"I will be the one in that strapping carriage your husband is leaving me!"

"Of course," she grinned. "Do come to us soon!" She kissed her papa on the cheek before he stepped back to allow Edward to help her to the carriage.

"Oh, my dear," he paused and held up a finger as an afterthought. "If your husband should disappear some morning on your journeys, do not judge the man too harshly. I have given him my rod and tackle as a wedding gift."

Laughter bubbled from her. "Oh, dear papa! Thank you, I am sure!"

"And most grateful I am, but I shall restrain that particular passion for the duration of our wedding trip," Edward put in with a wink. "I will much prefer to enjoy my wife's company."

"Just so!" Fairbanks agreed. The men exchanged heartfelt courtesies, and Edward turned to survey the remaining faces. Bennet stood back, offering a pleased smirk which spoke as eloquently as any words could have. Fanny, however, started forward, hailing him with her hand when his eyes fell upon her.

He turned quickly. "Allow me to assist you, my dear!" Before Fanny could approach with her last-moment admonishments or advice, the new couple had mounted their carriage and the door closed. "Dodged a bullet there!" he exclaimed, settling back against the rear-facing squab as the carriage began to move. "We would have been here another hour!"

"She seems an affectionate mother and sister," Madeline answered slyly. "Is that a family trait?"

"Good heavens, no! Er…" he straightened the front of his waistcoat, grasping for words. "I mean, certainly affection is an estimable quality, but…."

"So, you are not an affectionate man? Oh, dear!" she lamented with a coy toss of her head. "I had so hoped otherwise!"

"Well, now, let us correct that misunderstanding," he smiled. As the carriage was by now out of the immediate view of onlookers, he switched seats. Somewhat bashfully, he slid his arm behind her shoulders—watching all the while for her pleasure. "Will this do, my dear?" he murmured.

"It is an improvement," she assured him.

"And what of this?" He touched her chin, so lightly she felt his warmth more than his touch. Her eyes answered for her approval, and his courage mounted. He tilted his head slightly, avoiding the brim of her bonnet, and lowered his mouth until it hovered near hers. "This?" he whispered.

Madeline gave the barest of nods, and as she smiled into his lips, he exhaled still lower until his mouth brushed hers. Their comfort grew steadily, each reciprocating more boldly with every new touch. She felt a shiver down her spine as Edward slid one hand up to cradle the back of her neck.

She trembled again when his mouth left hers to trail over her cheeks, then with a tickle and a slip of ribbon against her jaw, he had removed her bonnet and his breath shivered against her most sensitive skin. Somewhere, deep within her core, her maidenly habits rebelled against all that her heart yearned to accept. It was simply too exquisite for her! His touch was deliciously intoxicating, yet also a delicate sort of torment to one not accustomed to such intimacies. She drew a sharp breath, holding a hand to his chest.

"Madeline?" he whispered in concern. "Have I distressed you?"

"No!" she gasped. "Only let me catch my breath."

"Forgive me, my dear," he apologised. "I am afraid I was too eager."

"Edward," she touched a finger to his lips. "I beg you would not be troubled. I simply need to accustom myself to all of this. I am not displeased in any way, I assure you—quite the contrary!"

"I would not blame you," he smiled, daring a light kiss to her forehead. "Most couples come to know one another a little better before leaping into marriage."

"I knew what I needed to know," she answered firmly. "That you are a good and generous man, loyal to your family and tender with children."

"You forgot devilishly handsome and charming with the ladies," he grinned.

"Humble as well," she retorted with an arched brow.

"Naturally." He settled her against his shoulder with another kiss to her hair, then took her hand in that companionable, easy way of his which had first won her. They rode in peace for several minutes, their happy gazes largely on one another, but occasionally drifting to the scenery rolling by.

After a few moments, he cleared his throat uncomfortably. "Madeline... there is something I must tell you. I am afraid when we travel through London, I shall have to put off the rest of our trip by a day—perhaps two."

She looked up to him quizzically. "Some trouble with your business?"

"Far from it. Rather, an opportunity, as well as a chance to do another fellow a good turn." He grimaced, causing her to wonder whether he really liked performing the service, or did so only out of good character. "You remember that I was delayed in coming to you a few days ago?"

"Yes, but I was not surprised. I expected you would rather have all of your affairs in order so that you might not be concerned for your business while we were away."

"Indeed, I would have, but what delayed me was a matter which arose rather at the last moment. I stayed long enough to have the paperwork drawn up, and it remains for me to make the final approvals when we pass through London.

"You see, a... I suppose you might call him a former associate, though he never really was such—a Mr Ryan approached me last week regarding a loan. He imports tobacco, and his father-in-law imports silk. They had leveraged themselves rather too far, in the hope that the early risks of their new partnership would lead to greater profits in the future. Unfortunately, two of their ships encountered a dreadful storm last month around the Cape. It sounds as though the crew were spared, but the ships and cargo were lost."

"How frightful!" she exclaimed. After a breath's pause, she ventured, "Is this the same Mr Ryan who...?"

"The very one. He has lost some of his standing with his bank and with some other potential investors after this unfortunate affair. I and a handful of others believe that this setback will likely prove only a temporary difficulty—provided he can obtain the immediate funding he needs to continue paying his bank note."

"Is he not your competitor in a way?"

"Of course, though my trade in tobacco is but small."

"Quite naturally, then, you refused his request for a loan," she smiled knowingly.

"I did no such thing! The interest I will earn from this loan is not paltry, my dear."

"So, it was strictly a business decision? Your personal feelings did not enter at all? I admire that, Edward."

"They most certainly did. I could bear no grudge against the man who prevented me from making the worst mistake of my life. I shall gladly promote his efforts, knowing that it is I who now possess the greater treasure." He emphasised this statement by pressing a kiss to her nose.

"Edward," she whispered, sliding a hand bravely up his cheek and pulling him a little closer.

"Yes, my dear?"

"I love you, dear man." She spoke no further, and neither did he for some while.

Epilogue

Lambton

January 1815

MADELINE GARDINER LACED HER arm comfortably through her husband's as she alighted from the carriage. Edward tightened his elbow to his side and clasped her little gloved hand, smiling down at his wife. "Are you warm enough, my dear?" he inquired.

"Perfectly, my love," she beamed. "Edward, you mustn't keep troubling yourself over me."

"Well, it is only natural," he reasoned. "In your condition—"

"Please, Edward!" she hissed, darting a traumatised glance to the couple walking ahead of them. "I have not told Lizzy yet!"

"Come, my dear," he chuckled, "another Gardiner child will hardly be a surprise to anyone! I expect our Lizzy might *particularly* welcome the news just now."

"She has always been so fond of her cousins," Madeline smiled.

"Indeed, but it was not for that reason that I spoke," he teased, giving a little squeeze to her hand and a faint nudge to her side.

"Edward, *please!*" she begged in a whisper. "You will be overheard!"

"I think you needn't worry on that account." He leaned down near her bonnet. "Everyone in town is far more interested in Mr Darcy and his new bride than in their humble guests. No one is paying us any mind. Look there, my dear!" He flicked his chin toward a humble little residence at the corner.

Madeline drew in a deep breath and a wistful smile grew. "The old house still looks well! Papa would be so pleased. I believe he did miss it so when he sold it."

"I think he was more pleased to be with us those last years. Such a proud grandfather he was! My dear, did you wish to see the inside of the house? Remember, the Smiths said they would be happy to have you when we were here last summer. It is only a pity we were called away so soon and you had not the proper time to visit with all of your old acquaintances."

She pressed her smiling lips in thought. "No. No, I do not wish to see it again. I prefer to remember it as it was, with Papa's little things about." She turned her honey-kissed face up to her husband's, a gentle warmth lighting it which she reserved only for him. "My home has been with you for a long while now."

"And a lucky man I am for it!" he enthused. "My dear, whatever made you accept a man you barely knew, who intended to carry you away from this lovely little town?"

"I suppose he made me smile... or perhaps it was his nieces I enjoyed most," was the sly retort, delivered from below lowered lashes. "And only think how well it has all turned out! We may now stay at Pemberley whenever we wish to visit the Peaks district, rather than rumbling about draughty little inns."

"The Rose and Crown was far from draughty, my dear!" he laughed. "I thought it a very fine inn this summer when we stayed. As for the dear old Lion's Head, it has been so long since I set foot in it, and I was so diverted by other matters when I was there last, that I cannot say."

"Oh, it always had... shall I say 'character' ... I am told it still stands much as it did. Such a lucky thing that the Porters are here for a visit at the same time as we!"

"Indeed! Ah, here we are," he observed with satisfaction. They had caught up to Mr Darcy and Elizabeth at the door of the nearest principal establishment they had come to—which happened to be the Lion's Head. It was the proud young couple's first patronage to the town since their marriage, and this the first official stop on their little tour.

Fitzwilliam Darcy had dutifully paraded his young bride about London for a brief time after their marriage, and then whisked her to Pemberley as soon as the roads had become passable. Madeline understood that he had kept Lizzy sequestered away with him as much as possible for the entire fortnight of her new residence there.

It was not that he was a reclusive man, she reflected with a smile, admiring the shy looks he was exchanging with Lizzy. No, he was simply a deeply personal man, desiring depth rather than breadth in his intimacies. *With Lizzy as his wife, he will have to learn to accept both!* she chuckled to herself.

Darcy was performing the introductions now, and the current proprietor of the inn, a Mr Williams, had hastily brought forward his wife to pay their respects. "Mr and Mrs Darcy, it is such an honour!" he bowed enthusiastically.

"The honour is ours, I assure you," Darcy answered. "May I also present my wife's aunt and uncle, Mr and Mrs Gardiner from London," Darcy recited in that gallant, gracious way of his. "Mrs Gardiner originally hails from the area."

"Good sir, you needn't introduce Mrs Gardiner to me!" bubbled the innkeeper's wife. "Dear Madeline, it has been a long while!"

She started in some surprise. "Sarah Tuttle!" she gasped. "I'd no idea that you had married!"

"Five years ago," she blushed, casting a nervous gaze to Darcy, who had furrowed his brow at the name.

"Tuttle?" he asked hesitantly. "Why, you were not my sister Georgiana's nurse when she was very young?"

"Indeed, sir," she dipped a curtsey. "It was a right pleasure it was, sir. The young miss was the most enchanting child."

"She is enchanting still," asserted Elizabeth cheerfully. "She is to arrive tomorrow with her cousins, and I am greatly looking forward to her return. I shall be certain to bring her to see you, for I know she would like it."

"I would be most grateful to see the young miss again, Mrs Darcy," Mrs Williams thanked her bashfully. Turning her gaze back to Madeline, she spoke more freely. "I will send word up to Mrs Porter's room that you are here, Madeline. She told me that she was expecting you to call."

Edward led her to a seat—that familiar long table by the hearth—and Madeline took it in relief. The chill of the day and the demands of her growing babe had left her more fatigued than she would confess. Elizabeth, however, had begun to rove about the room with a slightly mystified look to her face. "Lizzy, dear?" she called as her niece passed. "Are you quite all right?"

Elizabeth paused, then looked quizzically to her husband. She continued to stare at him for another moment until he began to shift uneasily, then her eyes widened in astonishment and a great tide of laughter washed over her.

"Lizzy, what has you so amused?" Edward asked in confusion.

Elizabeth touched her fingers to her mouth, then spun about to gaze at the window—the seat, the drapes, the small table near it. Finally, her eyes fell upon the little chess table and she gasped aloud.

"Elizabeth?" Darcy came to her, curling his fingers about her elbow in concern. "I do not understand. Is something amiss?"

"Not at all!" she laughed. "William, I remember this place!"

"Remember it? That is not possible, for you stayed at the Rose and Crown this summer. When could you have been here?"

Her smile widened and she bit back a peal of laughter at his expense. "Did I never tell you, William? I was only seven and Jane was eight when Papa and Uncle first brought us to the Peaks district. Why, it was so long ago, I had nearly forgotten, but it was here that we stayed! I must say, you do have the most *dreadful* hailstorms here in Derbyshire from time to time."

His entire face frowned; from his lordly forehead and brooding dark eyes to his firm mouth—but it was not a frightening expression. One could almost see his thoughts stumbling over one another until his expression, too, underwent a transformation just as his wife's had done. "Little Lizzy!" he breathed. "How could I never have seen it!"

She laughed joyously, crooking her arm through his. "William, do you know what this means?"

"It means you were a tease and a scamp from the beginning, and I somehow powerless against you even then!" he replied.

"And you, Fitzwilliam Darcy, were never as stern or forbidding as you would have others believe." She leaned close and with her fingertips tugged his rigid lips into a smile. "Why, you were almost civil once in a while."

"You thought me civil? I was barely so, and only for a few moments, as I recall."

"You *did* surrender to me your king," she reminded him, at which the great Fitzwilliam Darcy's cheeks darkened.

"I may have won the round, but I lost the match," he protested—the faintest hint of a delighted crease at the corners of his mouth and eyes.

"Then I challenge you to another! Come, William, someone has already begun a game, I see. I shall play the light again."

At her teasing insistence, the Master of Pemberley followed sedately and poised himself behind the proper chair. "You would have me begin with the disadvantage this time?" he queried with feigned harshness.

His wife only smiled mischievously, then stood on her toes to whisper something into his ear. Any onlookers might have been treated to a fresh shadow over his cheeks and a start to his dark eyes. He took his seat promptly. "Your move, Madam."

Madeline and Edward had watched the newlyweds' little exchange with growing amusement. Both had rapidly solved the mystery of their cryptic conversation, and it only remained to chortle once more among themselves at the stately Darcy's utter helplessness before Lizzy's gaiety.

"Well, how do you fancy that?" a soft voice behind them chuckled.

The Gardiners turned to find Mr and Mrs Porter come down to them. Older and more frail now, the woman still possessed a snap to the eyes which gazed fondly now at the young couple across the room. "Mrs Porter," Madeline rose to embrace her friend. Edward happily greeted Mr Porter, and the two couples made themselves comfortable by the fire.

Madeline and her old friend exchanged niceties, but Mrs Porter's gaze was determined to drift back to the Darcys. "What a fine-looking pair they make," she sighed dreamily. "And to think, Madeline, that your little niece should have grown up to marry Mr Darcy! Why, I remember her as a wee thing—such a spry little lass she was."

Edward laughed. "She always was a handful! I did not know that she and Mr Darcy had met all of those years ago."

"Aye! The time I had trying to coax her to be nice to the young master and little Miss Darcy! Well, I see 'tis all right now," she assured herself comfortably. She smiled up at Sarah Williams as the new proprietress of the inn brought her a cup of tea. "Well, now, Madeline, you must tell me how the children are getting on. Is little Emily faring better after her illness last year?"

"She is quite strong now, but I think part of the credit goes to our Margaret for tormenting her until she began to mend," Madeline giggled. "She missed playing with her sister a great deal when she was ill."

"Much like their cousins, those two," Edward put in. "I tremble when I consider what the next few years may hold."

"Fear not, my love, for if they are indeed like their cousins, they shall grow in grace and accomplishments until such time that dashing young men will fall stricken with love, and after many trials and uncertainties carry them off to faraway lands," Madeline winked.

"That is precisely my fear!" he shuddered. "I have had enough of star-crossed lovers and all of their angst to satisfy me for a lifetime, thank you. I hope that the young men who come to claim my daughters are sensible and steady, and that matters may proceed in a reasonable fashion."

"Aye, not all young couples are so ready to love, nor so easily guided as you," laughed Mrs Porter. "All that was necessary in your case was a little proximity. Tell me, how has that dear Jane settled in? You wrote that she is married as well?"

"Yes, to a most agreeable man named Mr Bingley. He and Mr Darcy are particular friends."

"Ah, that is well. She was always such a sweet girl! I am certain that they suffered no such drama in their courtship as you describe."

Edward cleared his throat. "All roads are not perfectly smooth, as you say, Mrs Porter."

"Smooth or rocky, the scenery is worth the while, young man, though the destination be yet unknown."

"That is a maxim I will toast," answered Edward, lifting his fresh mug. "To beginnings and endings; to best-laid plans and pleasant surprises; from first impressions to intimate communion, may love ever be a noble cause, and directed by a wiser understanding than my own."

From across the room, Fitzwilliam Darcy heard the toast and turned his head to add, "And may we possess the humility to receive the gift."

"With the Gardiners, they were always on the most intimate terms. Darcy, as well as Elizabeth, really loved them; and they were both ever sensible of the warmest gratitude towards the persons who, by bringing her into Derbyshire, had been the means of uniting them."
—Jane Austen, Pride & Prejudice

K EEP READING MORE OF Darcy and Elizabeth's sweet romance! Pick up your copy of *Love and Other Machines* and find out what happens when Darcy and Elizabeth accidentally discover they share the same secret!

From Alix

THANK YOU FOR INDULGING with me and spending a little time with the Gardiners and Darcy and Elizabeth.

I hope you've had a delightful escape to Pemberley. I'd love it if you would share this family with your friends so they can experience a love to last for the ages. As with all my books, I have enabled lending to make it easier to share. If you leave a review for *The Courtship of Edward Gardiner* on Amazon, Goodreads, Book Bub or your own blog, I would love to read it! Email me the link at **Author@AlixJames.com.**

Would you like to read more of Darcy and Elizabeth's romance? I have a sweet romp for you to try next! Dive into *Love and Other Machines* and laugh along with our favorite couple as they find the love they were destined for!

And if you're hungry for more classic romance, allow me to introduce you to John and Margaret from Elizabeth Gaskell's *North and South*. Check out *No Such Thing as Luck*. If you like a tender slow burn love story with a swoon-worthy hero and a smart, determined lady, this is the series for you!

Stay up to date on upcoming releases and sales, and receive a free gift book! Join my newsletter: https://dashboard.mailerlite.com/fo rms/249660/73866370936211000/share

And now, keep reading for sneak previews of *Love and Other Machines* and *No Such Thing as Luck*.

No Such Thing as Luck

Hannah Thornton looked up from her needlework when she heard her son's quick step at the door. She did not smile, but her eyes acknowledged her affection in a slight crinkling around the corners; a miniscule softening of her expression which none but he would recognize. He did not look at her directly but passed by her chair in the dining parlor with a brief touch on her shoulder. Reaching for the pot of tea she had kept hot for him the last hour, he poured silently.

Mrs Thornton dropped her eyes back to her point work. She had made little progress today. The black stitching was wearing on her eyes, but that was not the real reason for her lack of success. For weeks now, her son had been laboring late hours, even for him, trying to singlehandedly make up for the disastrous blow to the mill caused by last year's strike. Mrs Thornton considered it a point of honour to never take her ease when he was in distress. As a consequence, they were both tired and worn.

She knew that business with the bank had called him out most of the afternoon. He had tried to make up for lost time all evening, poring over his ledgers. Over the rim of her sewing glasses, she arched an eyebrow- a silent invitation for him to reveal what he would of his latest conversation with Mr Dalton from the bank. He fingered the smooth rim of his teacup as he tried to form the words he must speak.

"Mother, we have few options left." She let go the breath she had been holding. She was as relieved to hear him finally speak as she was when she comprehended what he had *not* said- he did not say they had no options at all. She set her needlework aside and folded her hands in her lap, waiting for him to continue.

"The bank has extended the loan on the equipment I purchased last year. Twice, in fact. They will not do so again. I have little enough real property- all my assets are already leveraged and they do not like the risk. The banks are being very careful, as most of the mills are in a bad way. Cotton from the Americas is going up in price and our buyers are not paying for product on time. The weather has not warmed this summer as we had depended upon, and we have little hope of a good season at this point. It is a time of bad trade in general.

"That speculation of Watson's paid off handsomely last week. Most of the other mill owners invested in it, and will now have ample capital to ride out the lean times. Marlborough Mills will be seen as a liability in comparison, so it will be difficult for us to attract new orders." He took a long, pensive swallow of his tea. The lukewarm liquid swirled tastelessly in his mouth. He set it down impatiently and went to the sideboard to pour himself a drink.

Mrs Thornton watched him silently, waiting for him to continue. "We had so much bad product from the Irish workers all those months ago that we had to discard much of our material and got even further behind on the orders. We never have caught up, and I have no idea how we ever shall. We are going to exhaust our supplies before our buyers finally pay up. By summer's end, I will either not be able to purchase more cotton, not be able to pay the hands, or the bank will collect on the equipment."

He finished the contents of his glass and dropped it with a loud *clink* on the table. Mrs Thornton cringed as much at the abuse of her furniture as the words he had said. All of these things she knew already. John was clearly trying to persuade himself to something radical.

"But," probed she cautiously, "you believe we do have options? Do you mean selling and giving up the lease on Marlborough Mills?"

"Possibly," he murmured. Steepling his fingers, he continued, "However, there may be an alternative. An investor.... A partner, really," he amended.

Her surprise was evident. John had gotten his start in the mill through the aid of a partner, who had been a trusted business associate of his father's. Since then, however, he had assiduously avoided such entanglements. He preferred to do business according to the strictest moral standards, and no one was ever deemed trustworthy enough.

"There *was* another alternative, you know, Mother," he went on. "Watson, he's been gloating all week about how that scheme of his paid out. He was right, and now he has proof that I was wrong. Despite all, Mother, I cannot bring myself to regret not joining him in the venture. I would have had to invest all the capital I have left, much of it not rightfully mine. Still, it is true, all of our worries would now be at an end." John bit his lip and blinked rapidly as his mind again reviewed the week's events.

"John, you must not look back with regrets. You were right to refuse. What if it had failed?"

"I would not be able to pay my debts, leaving my creditors without hope of recovery. The mill would fail, and all the men would be out of work immediately. I would have injured others for my own selfish gain."

"I would not have you compromise your honour and dignity. I will stand proud knowing my son is a man who would not yield to the temptation of an easy fix at the price of his integrity." Mrs Thornton's eyes flashed, her square chin raised emphatically.

Despite himself, he could not help a small smile. He clasped her wrinkled fingers in grateful recognition of her unswerving support. "Mr Dalton knows of a fellow in Spain who has been making inquiries, a Señor Barbour. Apparently, he owns a large shipping business, having contacts throughout the Continent as well as Africa and South America.

"In addition, he appears to have recently acquired an interest in an estate which grows cotton in the Andalucía province. The province does not grow the quantity of cotton there that the Americas or Egypt do, but they do have the right climate and have become a reckonable source on the Continent. Apparently, his estate is rather large- exceedingly so- and he claims the soil is excellent.

"He has taken on a young English partner, a Mr Marshall, who is by all accounts resident in the country now. He speaks glowingly to this Señor Barbour of the opportunities for industry here in the North. It seems this partner had an occasion recently to see what we have built here, and Barbour wishes to forge an alliance. He believes there is money to be made in eliminating a few middlemen and dealing directly with the mill owners. He proposes a partnership with an English mill to refine his product which he will then sell at a better margin."

Mrs Thornton considered. "What about your profits? Would you be losing a great deal?"

"I believe not, no." Agitated, he poured himself another cup of the tasteless tea, wisely deciding not to return to the sideboard for another drink. "Dalton had a financial proposal drawn up from the fellow. Interestingly enough, Señor Barbour contracts to supply me exclusively at a fixed price. I may buy elsewhere, of course, since he will not be able to meet all of our demands, but he proposes to ship all of his raw product to me. The contract dictates that he will place orders of his own for a fixed percentage of the finished product. The rest I would sell to other buyers for cash up front.

"In effect, I would be paying for my raw material with finished orders, rather than ready cash. The tradeoff is favorable for me, in terms of our usual profit margin. If the cotton is the quality he claims it is, the proposal has merit. It solves our immediate supply problem, at any rate, and might buy us the time we need.

"There is the additional advantage of having a steady supply outside of the American cotton. I fear for the political instability there. However..." he looked up from his cup, "I will have to go myself."

"Go? To Spain?" She tried to conceal her distress, but was only partially successful.

"It is the only way to work out the details of what he proposes, as it is a rather radical shift from the way we usually do business. Also, I need to see for myself what manner of man he is. I would rather sell out this minute than become irrevocably involved with an unscrupulous partner, no matter how deep his pockets or intriguing his ideas. Yes, I will have to go to Spain- to Cádiz. And I will have to leave soon if I am to make a go of it."

She slowly blew air through her clenched teeth, seeking control of her words. "How soon?"

"I hope to leave in three days. There is a steamer, the *Esperanza,* to set sail from London on Monday. I just missed the Liverpool packet. The next ships are not until much later in the week. I asked Mr Dalton to send word to his contact in Cádiz to expect me."

"How long will you be away?"

"I am not sure, exactly. It should take three or four days to sail each way, and of course I will have to spend some days viewing this

Barbour's operation. I hope I should return inside a fortnight, but it may well take longer to settle matters. I hate to leave with things the way they are here, but I believe I must. You will not be worried to stay alone?"

"Nay, John, I shall manage. You will do as you must, as you always do." Her firm conviction reassured him. He had spent many years caring for his mother's every need and concern. He felt derelict in his duty leaving her to her own devices. Of course, she would be cared for in every physical comfort and certainly would be safe, but he knew her days would be consumed with lonely worry while he was gone.

"Thank you, Mother," he replied with sincere feeling, truly appreciating the brave sacrifices she made to support him. "Perhaps you may wish to stay some days with Fanny and Watson while I am away?"

She made a derisive noise. "I should be much more comfortable here."

He scrubbed his face roughly with his hands, raking his fingers through his hair. He blew out an exhausted sigh. "I must begin making preparations. Do not wait up for me, Mother."

She nodded, and he rose to go. No more words were needed between mother and son. Their conversations had always been concise and to the point, but lately they spoke even less. He had become withdrawn from the one person to whom he had always gone for advice. He was always gentle when he spoke with her, but never revealed his deeper feelings.

Never, since... since *her*. Mrs Thornton pursed her lips in irritation as the image of a queenly young woman with a proud demeanor came to memory. Margaret Hale had left Milton over four months ago, bereft of family and destitute in grief, but a mother's sense knew that the young woman could still count her brave son's heart among her few possessions.

With a rush of anger she did not understand, she picked up her work and stabbed her needle through. She blamed Margaret for the distance between herself and her favorite child. She had seen him often, when he thought she wasn't looking, slip into a state of anguished loneliness. His haunted eyes spoke of the great yawning chasm of emptiness slowly devouring him.

In sudden mortification, the widow admonished herself for ever believing she could satisfy all of her son's needs. A heart as generous as his needed the love of a woman and the hope of a future. None had ever caught his eye, much less held his interest, until the displaced beauty from the southern countryside. *The one woman*, she reflected grimly, *who failed to see all that he was.*

At the time, Mrs Thornton had been well pleased to discover that her son had escaped the grasp of such a headstrong woman. She did not deserve him. For his part, he ought to have a wife who could honour and respect him, not a foolish lass who subverted his authority at every turn. Miss Hale had too much fire and spirit to ever make a respectable wife for one such as her son.

Despite all the very sound reasons he should put her out of his mind, it was clear that thus far, at least, he had been unsuccessful at banishing her from his heart. Mrs Thornton could almost find it within her to regret that Miss Hale had failed to see her son's finer qualities. Margaret had salt and pluck- Mrs Thornton wished she could have liked her. Particularly now, when John most needed a staunch supporter, she would have been comforted to know that he at least had the woman he loved by his side.

Would pampered Miss Hale have remained loyal through his struggles? Inwardly she doubted. The girl was a puzzle of discrepancies she did not understand. At once so regally distant, and yet so warmly caring for those she loved, Margaret Hale was an enigma. Could the young woman have ever renounced her Southern prejudices in favor of the virtuous and tender-hearted man who loved her?

No, she decided, *that is not likely. She does not even realize what she rejected.* She had her fashionable airs and graces and, Mrs Thornton admitted, a lovely face, yet with all of that Margaret would never find a truer heart than her own son's. *Let her be happy in London*, she thought sourly. *Where she can torment him no longer.*

She sighed heavily. *I suppose it is too late for that.* She could not reasonably blame Margaret Hale for John's business troubles, but his state of mind could most certainly be laid at her door. *At least she is gone to London for good,* Mrs Thornton thought. *Back with her own kind in Harley Street, wherever that is. He never has to see her again.*

M R THORNTON ROSE EARLY the next morning to set into motion everything he must do before his departure. His overseer, Williams, arrived soon after, and Mr Thornton pulled him aside for an hour's conference on the status of the mill. Williams would be stretched to the full during his absence, trying to cover the tasks of two men, but Thornton had no doubt of his competence. Though he ought to be nearing retirement, Williams had always been loyal and honest, as well as keen work master. The mill would be in good hands.

Behind two stacks of papers, they reviewed the next week's orders. The Brighton order was complete, but the New York order was behind schedule. Biting back whatever scalding remarks he would once have made to his overseer, he resolved to speak to some of the hands. A few of the older machines had proven difficult to adjust to the finer cotton fibers they had been receiving of late. He knew specifically the man to ask about that.

A quarter hour later found Thornton buried behind a stack of invoices. The fingers of his left hand drummed out a quick staccato on the pile of papers as his right hastily recorded figures into his ledger. His mind consumed with accomplishing his task as quickly as possible, he was taken by surprise at Higgins' knock. "Come in," his authoritative voice summoned.

Higgins stepped inside, doffing his cap out of respect for the mill master's domain. "Yo' wanted to speak wi' me, sir?" he reminded the younger man.

Thornton rose, both annoyed at the interruption to his work and grateful for a brief respite. He had come to see this plucky fellow as something of an ally, if he was not quite willing to call him a friend.

"Yes, thank you for coming, Higgins. I have something I would like to ask of you. I will be leaving the country on Monday and I shan't be back for perhaps a couple of weeks. I have to go to Spain to see about a source of raw cotton. I would like you to give Williams a hand supervising the men while I am gone. Will you do it?"

Higgins looked surprised. "Me, sir?"

Thornton came round the massive desk to face him. "You, indeed. You know the equipment, you know the workings of the mill, the men respect you, and I trust you. Williams will have his hands full. You're to be under his complete authority and assist him with whatever he requires. Your pay will, of course, be adjusted to suit your extra responsibilities. Agreed?"

Higgins was flattered beyond measure, but his old pride would not allow him to show it. He nodded smartly, his hands twisting his cap. "Aye, Master." Then the idea of Mr Thornton's destination struck him. Thornton was about to step away when Higgins boldly stopped him. "Master, ha' yo' heard aught of Miss Marget lately?"

"Miss –who?" replied Thornton. His mind was already returning to his ledgers.

"Miss Marget- Miss Hale- th'oud parson's daughter? Me and my Mary, and the children, you know we're right fond o' her. I was wond'ring, were she doing well?"

"Oh, yes!" and suddenly the deep melancholy etched into Mr Thornton's face had been replaced by a warmer expression. "Yes," here a long pause, "Sadly, I cannot satisfy you. I have heard nothing since her maid left Milton some three or four months ago, after the last of the family's affairs were settled."

His voice was so soft, his eyes smiling distantly, that the suspicion which had already taken seed bloomed in the old weaver's mind. Higgins decided to follow to where it might lead. "And she's na' go' married, Master?"

"Not yet, I believe." Thornton's face closed once more into his customary mask. "There was some talk of it, I heard once, with some connection to the family- some attorney."

"Then she'll na' be for coming to Milton again, I reckon."

"No!" Thornton shook his head, and the astute Higgins caught a glimmer in the younger man's eye.

Higgins leaned closer and whispered confidentially, "Is the young gentleman cleared?" He enforced the depth of his intelligence by a wink, which only made things more mysterious to Thornton. The Master narrowed his eyes curiously.

Higgins was about to clarify his question when an altercation broke out between an angry drayer and two of the dock hands unloading cotton bales. Rough shouting and coarse epithets ensued until Thornton, his expression stormy, opened the window of his office and bellowed commands for the lead workers to secure order once more among their inferiors.

He turned back and sank down heavily in his chair. The clawed feet of the furniture clattered against the floor as he adjusted his seat to resume his work. His mind weighed ponderously with other matters. He seemed to have forgotten that Higgins was even there.

"Master," he began slowly.

Thornton looked up, surprised. He had come to value the man too highly to snap at him, but he was impatient at finding him still there and demanding his attention. "Yes?"

Higgins looked down, fingering his cap. He wasn't entirely sure what he wished to say. Something jogged his memory. "If yo'd forgive me sir, I was jest thinkin' tha' I wish our ou'd friend Hale were here. Jest Master, tha' you seem a knot o' worry. Th' ou'd parson, 'e knew how to ease a man's soul."

Though Higgins had no business speaking to his employer thus, Thornton's eyes grew misty as he stilled for a moment. "He was a good friend to me," he sighed softly.

"When my Bessie passed, it was th'ou'd parson wha' brought me comfort." Higgins decided to carefully avoid mentioning the man's daughter again. "'E was a man wha' knew sorrow." Higgins chuckled ruefully to himself. "E'en go' me to pray with him once. I 'adn' done that since 'fore my dear Jenny passed."

Thornton smiled wistfully, trying to picture the scene. "I would imagine it was not he who suggested it."

Higgins did not reply, but his face confessed the truth. It was Margaret who had brought him to her father after Bessie's death, keeping a promise to her departed friend to drag him away from the bottle. In her sweet determination she had insisted they offer him whatever comfort they could. With a dying wife and a crumbling future, the gentle old man had done as his daughter asked.

"They were kind folk, the Hales. Bro' me a deal o' good, though they was suffering theyselves."

Thornton glanced away, suddenly blinking rapidly. "Thank you, Higgins," he murmured in a low, lingering tone. His face schooled carefully back into that of the Master, he nodded curtly to dismiss his worker. Whatever pain the man was feeling was ruthlessly bottled back up.

Pity for his wealthy employer filled him as Higgins confirmed in his mind that he was quite certain now of the source of that pain. "'Tis a sorrow," he murmured to himself. Still, 'Miss Marget' had embodied to Higgins everything that a lady ought to be. She was as lovely as the most beautiful of her class Higgins had ever laid eyes on, but her tender compassion and genuine kindness won his old heart. There could be none finer, and knowing that his employer had cared for her, even in vain, elevated that man in his estimation. It made him seem almost human.

He closed the door and shook his head, wishing once again that matters had settled differently for the young lass. Whistling tunelessly, the old weaver shoved his hands in his pockets and walked slowly back to his post.

Thornton struggled valiantly to return to his task, but Higgins' words had effectively disrupted any coherent train of thought. Sighing deeply, he sat back and tugged open his desk drawer. Inside was a musty old book with a worn leather cover.

Gently caressing the gold leaf lettering, he let the book fall open in his hands. Plato. He treasured the book as his old friend's possession, but he cherished the note inside even more. It was brief, written in a graceful feminine hand which his heart had memorized. The edges of the note were frayed with reverent caresses, but the writing was still crisp and clear as the day it had been penned some months ago. The words were thoughtful, but carefully chosen to convey no real feeling from the author. His fingers stroked the edges of the paper as he once again tried to imagine what she was doing, far away.

"MARGARET, DARLING, YOU HAVE scarcely touched your dinner!" Edith Lennox's blonde curls bounced perfectly as she shook her head in mock consternation. "You know Mamma will be calling the doctor again if you do not eat more."

Margaret Hale drew her gaze back to the young woman sitting across from her. Mentally she chided herself. It was not like her to be so distracted. "I am sorry, Edith. I was just… thinking about Mr Bell in his travels." Margaret's eyes dropped to her plate as she tried to quell her emotions. The excellent braised poultry could not spark her interest any more than last night's delicious veal had.

His note had spoken of dealing with urgent business affairs, requiring his personal attention, so she knew better than to think she could do other than be in his way. Still… she worried about him traveling alone. He had seemed more frail on his last visit. He was several years older than her father, and his usual boundless energy had seemed somewhat subdued. He had looked to her quite worn, although Edith, who did not know him as well, claimed to notice no difference.

Making an effort to eat a little of her meal, Margaret focused her attention back on the dinner conversation between her aunt Shaw and her cousin. They were discussing tomorrow night's dinner party at the Whites,' which interested Margaret not a whit. Pleading a headache, Margaret excused herself and withdrew to her room. She had never liked London society with all the swirling events, and found its demands to be exhausting to her quieter disposition. Her heart longed for deep, sincere connection with dear friends, not endless chatter among bare acquaintances.

Edith, on the other hand, had blossomed into the ideal young London wife during the last two years. After her marriage to Captain Lennox, she had spent well over a year stationed with him in Corfu. She had easily become the leading officer's wife in social circles. Now that she was returned home, her popularity as a London socialite was firmly fixed.

Margaret had grown up with Edith, shared her lessons and her confidences, but was not a sharer in the wealth and status to which Edith had been born. Though never treated as such, Margaret was the poor relation and had always sensed her differences. Their connection had brought Margaret many material advantages, but at her heart Margaret had always craved the peace of Helstone over the finery of London. Since her visit with Mr Bell, however, her feelings had undergone a remarkable change.

Margaret knew that her time in Milton had changed her in her cousin's eyes as well. She had eschewed the traditional socially correct topics, and could not stop herself from speaking out of the cares of her heart. She knew she had raised a few eyebrows among Edith's friends, but she could not help herself. Her concerns were deeper now. She spent hours in thought and prayer, unable to forget the people she would probably never see again.

Margaret heaved a sigh as she thought of Mr Thornton. Too late she had realized how greatly she had misjudged him. Margaret covered her face with her hands. The feelings of shame *would* come whenever she thought of him. She had treated him with disdain and scorn, but when given the opportunity to treat her in kind, he had instead shielded her.

She had wanted for so long to tell him about Frederick, to explain some part, only, of her actions to him, even if her reasons could not justify her falsehood. She felt like he deserved the entire truth- she trusted him with the entire truth. She wanted for him at least to know of her gratitude, but she would never force her communication on him.

He had lost all respect for her; he had told her as much. Any attempt at explanation now would seem only like a vain attempt to justify her wrongdoing and he would be well within his rights to refuse to hear her out. She would never again have a chance to right her wrongs.

She swallowed hard. At least she did have that comfort; she would never have to face him again. Time, though, had done little to ease the familiar ache whenever she thought of him.

"**I** DON'T KNOW WHAT'S to be done with her, Mamma," Edith pouted after Margaret hastily left the table. "She is still wearing black and she barely eats."

Mrs Shaw thoughtfully sipped her port, pondering the problem of her niece. "Well, if you want my opinion, she needs to be getting out in Society more. It would do her good; she only sees us and Sholto. Has Henry Lennox called lately?"

"He was here last week, but he did not stay long. Mamma, I really think he does fancy her. Do you think he could lift her spirits?"

"I do not see why not. They always got on well enough, and he is family now. We ought to be inviting him more to be in her company.
"

"It would be so wonderful if they were to marry! Then she would never have to leave us. Why, I know Henry has little enough of his own money, but he is sure to do well in his profession in time. And Mamma, I do so dote on Margaret, and she is so helpful with Sholto, that I would wish them to remain with us after they marry!"

"Then, my dear, you must try to create opportunities for them to see more of each other. If Margaret will not go to dinner parties with you, you must have more here and invite Henry. Having him here will also give you the advantage of arranging the seating as you like." Mrs Shaw smiled into her glass as she finished the last of her port.

"Excuse me Ma'am," Nancy, the housemaid, bobbed a curtsy as she entered the dining parlor. "The post has arrived."

"It is so late today!" Edith exclaimed. She took the tray and her eyes scanned her invitations. Indeed, it was about time for another dinner party of her own, and after her meal she would sit down directly to issue invitations. "Oh, Nancy," she called to the retreating maid. "Here is one addressed to Miss Hale. Would you take it to her, please?"

"Yes, Ma'am," Nancy retrieved the tray with the remaining letter and went to find Margaret.

Edith and her mother withdrew to the downstairs sitting room. With much enjoyment, she thumbed through the rest of her correspondence and decided which to answer first. She looked up in surprise when Margaret appeared suddenly in the doorway, holding a letter in trembling hands, her face white as a sheet.

"Why, dear Margaret, what is wrong?" Edith did not rise, but anticipated that Margaret would come to sit near her. She did not.

Margaret was clearly fighting back tears. "It is a letter from Frederick. He writes me about Mr Bell! Oh!" She covered her face with a sob and could not continue.

Edith did go to her then, draping an arm around her cousin's shoulders and drawing her to the sofa. As girls the two had shared many confidences, many heartaches, and Edith instinctively knew there was nothing she could say until Margaret was ready to speak.

Margaret wiped at her eyes with a handkerchief, her free hand kneading her skirt. Mrs Shaw wanted to chide her about making her eyes puffy or wrinkling her gown, but she decided in favor of silence.

Margaret sniffled a little as she composed herself. "Frederick says that Mr Bell did indeed come to stay with him, and that he's fallen deathly ill. He does not expect him to live long!" Margaret hid her sobs in her handkerchief. Her initial reaction of shock and dismay that Mr Bell had gone to see Frederick without her had worn off, to be replaced with overwhelming grief. Mr Bell was the last remaining friend of her father's- with whom she was on good terms- and she had come to care a great deal for the old codger. If she never saw him again, was never able to say goodbye to him as she had not been able with her father... her heart rebelled violently at the probability.

"There, there, Dearest," Edith crooned, drawing Margaret's head onto her own shoulder. She stroked her cousin's arm soothingly. Edith had never known what to make of Mr Bell. He was far too sardonic for her taste, and she did not understand him. She knew, however, that Margaret would be plunged back into grief at his passing, and for that she was very sorry. Her mother was quite silent.

"Does Frederick say what the matter is?" asked Edith gently.

Margaret drew away and attempted to calm her shattered nerves. "He thinks it is an illness that has been coming on for some time. The doctor's been, and he thinks the heart is weak. Frederick says they have no hope he will live more than a few more days, a week or two at most!"

Edith clucked comfortingly over Margaret, but knew there was little she could do to console the young woman who was more like a sister than a cousin. With a plaintive look, she begged her mother to ring for Dixon, Margaret's loyal ladies' maid.

Dixon eventually hobbled into the room. Her gout was acting up again, but she would not relinquish her care of Margaret to one of the younger maids. Miss Beresford's daughter held a special place in the older woman's heart. Her face red and puffy, she shooed her young Miss upstairs. It would not do for Margaret to be seen so by her aunt and cousin, but once safely upstairs she would comfort the girl as if she were her very own.

Dixon firmly but gently escorted Margaret to her room. Thinking it would be helpful to soothe her worries, Dixon ordered hot water to be sent up for a bath. Margaret meekly submitted. She was too preoccupied with the contents of Frederick's letter to make much objection. She sobbingly wiped her eyes before allowing her servant and friend to lift her gown over her head.

Once her young charge was settled for a good long soak, Dixon betook herself to her own quarters, a comfortable little nook off Margaret's dressing room. About time, too. Her toe felt like it was on fire! Gritting her teeth, she prepared her own soaking solution and eased her foot into the salt bath. Her aging bones sighed in relief as she lowered her ponderous weight into a battered old chair.

There was much Margaret hadn't told her aunt and cousin about Frederick's letter. Languishing in the bath, she re-read the letter, careful to protect it from the water.

8 July, 1856

My dearest Margaret,

I am sorry to have to write you thus. I have sad news. Our Mr Bell is currently staying in my house. He did not want you to know of his visit right away, but now he begs me to write and tell something of his circumstances.

He told me he was settling some affairs, and has indeed been visiting quite a number of local agents. I do not know all of the details of his transactions, but during one such visit with a broker he collapsed. He was brought back here, and has not been able to rise from his bed.

We summoned the doctor, a friend of Dolores' family who studied medicine abroad. He is the very best in the city. He believes Mr Bell has been suffering for some time from water on the heart. He has done all that he can, but I am sorry to report that he does not expect our dear friend will live more than a fortnight, more probably less.

Now, dear sister, I know you will want to see him, but I fear the journey may be impossible. Mr Bell has been asking for you, saying I must tell you something as soon as may be, but he has yet to tell me what that is. At times he is not quite reasonable, I think due to the remedies employed by the doctor.

He mentioned that he would like to have brought you with him but that he had feared his health may fail for some time now, and did not

*want to trouble you with an ailing companion. That was the most we
have been able to coax out of him.*

*Dearest, you know how Dolores and I would love for you to come to us.
I know Edith's husband is a retired captain, perhaps you can persuade
him to accompany you here. If not he, perhaps his brother Henry could see
to your safety. He seems very fond of you, little Sister. I trust the Lennoxes,
and I know you would be in good care if one of them can ensure your
safety.*

*I would not wish you to travel without an escort, so please, dear Mar-
garet, do not attempt to travel alone. You see, I know you, my little sister!
The voyage is not arduous, but the company aboard ship is not something
a lady should face alone.*

*I am eager to see you again, and I truly hope it possible that you may
be able to come before Mr Bell is no longer with us, but I beg you to only
travel if you can do it safely. Give Dixon my love, and please send your
reply soon.*

Yours,

Frederick

Margaret again wiped the tears from her face. The letter was dated
five days ago. She may already be too late! Still, if there was a chance....
She set the letter down on a little desk near the tub and got out without
calling for Dixon. She dressed herself and lay on the bed, deep in
thought.

K EEP READING *No Such Thing as Luck* to find out what happens when lost lovers stumble into each other, and dare to set
sail on the dream they'd once given up.

Love and Other Machines

I T WAS NOT MY fault.

Not entirely, anyway. The explosion might have been, and perhaps I might share the blame for the flooding, but not the fire... that was all *his* doing—Mr. Darcy. The proudest, most conceited, most maddeningly self-assured and quite possibly the most frustratingly *right* man in all of England. And he was my partner.

I T ALL STARTED WITH Jane. It would mortify her if she knew I said that, but it is true. Jane is always proper, never causing so much as a raised eyebrow or a sniff of condescension from anyone, save Mr. Bingley's sisters. I do not count them.

My favorite sister had achieved our mother's dearest wish and got herself betrothed. Mr. Bingley, the new tenant of the neighboring estate and an exceedingly genial man, had tumbled head over ears for her the moment they met. I could see it from the beginning—they fit, like cogs in a wheel. It was such a promising attachment from the start that in my own head, I began calling her "Jane Bingley" within a fortnight of their first meeting.

It made sense. He was handsome and affable and conveniently well-off; she was handsome and modest and unfortunately impoverished. What remained to be answered in such a serendipitous pairing?

His sisters were violently displeased, and they made certain to inform me of it whenever they got the chance. At first, I amused myself by agreeing with them that Mr. Bingley and Jane could never suit, and Miss Bingley almost started to like me for it. However, I could never keep a sober face for long, and she at last saw through my ruse and declared me pernicious, deceitful, ill-favored, and... well, I forgot the rest. Her final threat was to invoke the name of Mr. Bingley's absent friend, Mr. Darcy, and announce that *he* would call Mr. Bingley off "this sham of an entanglement."

I had not, at that time, met Mr. Darcy, and merely shrugged it off as Miss Bingley's irrational denial of the inevitable. Had I been acquainted with the gentleman's temperament or the weight of his persuasive abilities, I might have been more nervous. However, with little to concern me, I looked forward to the day when Jane could truly take the name I had been calling her in secret for the past two months.

As it happened, Mr. Bingley was not merely a nouveau gentleman, but also something of an elevated tradesman. His father had made a fortune selling buttons to the army, enough so that his daughters could boast dowries to make my mother swoon and Mr. Bingley could afford to purchase an estate that would make five of my father's inheritance. Any average man would have cut his involvement in the industry and departed for the gentle countryside, never to show his face in Birmingham again, but Mr. Bingley was rather... odd, as my aunt Philips once described him. He kept close ties to his factory and was not ashamed of his background in trade.

Consequently, he and my uncle Gardiner became fast friends. It was this happenstance which thrust me into the ill-conceived decision that might well have ended my life—or, at least, my life as I knew it.

Uncle Gardiner had got his start as an apprentice to a carriage maker, and then somehow found his way into the ironworks and crafting machine parts, such as gears and spindles, and later large machining tools. He was too clever to be left at the smelting pot, and so his employer elevated him to a mechanical designer, but to be truthful, he was terrible with drawings and even worse with his figures. He was far better at talking to buyers and solving problems with machines that were already built—a family trait, we found. By the time he was five-and-thirty, he had done so well in sales that he moved to London and began purchasing more and more interest in his company until he owned it outright. And, as luck would have it, he had sold Mr. Bingley some equipment that was now malfunctioning.

Mama had taken Jane to London to purchase her trousseau, and she insisted that I come along as well—to keep me out of mischief, she claimed, but my sort of mischief was, sadly, the more readily found when my uncle was near to abet my questionable interests.

On only the second day of our visit, Mama twisted her ankle quite badly on the step, requiring her to put it up in a most un-ladylike fashion and remain in her room. It could not be helped. Jane needed her wedding clothes, and Mama could not abide for Jane not to take advantage of the very best warehouses when they were just down the street. Jane and I went out with our aunt every day until poor Jane was pink in the face at the thought of another night rail or mob cap.

Mr. Bingley himself met us on our return one afternoon. He was just coming out of our uncle's study, and he glowed quite as much as Jane when they greeted one another. They instantly fell to silly lover's chatter, talking about the weather and the day's events and such inconsequences as would make any other two acquaintances think their conversation partner the dullest in the world.

"My dear Miss Bennet," he said at length, "I have been very much longing to have you and your family to my townhouse some evening for dinner. What do you say?"

"Oh! My mother would be delighted, Mr. Bingley, but she cannot stir at present. Perhaps in a few days she might be well enough."

My uncle came just behind. "I am afraid there is no point in making such plans, Jane. Mr. Bingley and I are bound for Birmingham tomorrow to look over some issues with his lathes and punches."

Mr. Bingley's face fell. "Goodness, I had already forgot. I certainly hope we shall not be long—not more than a week, perhaps two. You will not have gone back to Longbourn by then, will you?"

"I do not know." Jane glanced at me with a helpless shrug. "It depends upon how well Mama recovers."

"Dear me! Then I shall not see you until nearly the day of our wedding." The poor man nearly pouted, but in such a good-natured way, I could not help but wish he might not be disappointed.

"I may be able to suggest a solution to our dilemma," my uncle offered. He, too, sent me a sly look, then grinned like a Cheshire cat as he thought over his words before uttering them. "Yes, I believe it will do nicely. Mrs. Gardiner and Mrs. Bennet may remain here in London, but if Jane and Lizzy would like to accompany us to Birmingham, I would be proud to escort them. I am certain we could find suitable rooms in the inn for the ladies and their maid. What do you think?"

Mr. Bingley brightened at once and reached for Jane's hand. "My dear, it is a perfect idea! I had hoped you might be inclined to come north with me after we are wed, to see my factory and so on. Would you come?"

Thus, we were all bound for Birmingham the following morning.

T HE MOMENT I SET eyes upon him, I knew I had a problem. A broad-shouldered, unhappy, and accursedly clever one.

Mr. Bingley had told us much of his good friend, Mr. Darcy, for that gentleman had been supposed to join him at Netherfield in October. An unfortunate situation—Mr. Bingley never clarified what that situation was—had prevented the gentleman's coming to Hertfordshire, but Birmingham was a deal nearer to Mr. Darcy's estate in Derbyshire. Mr. Bingley claimed his friend only met us there out of his own goodwill and desire to be helpful, but I suspected that the gentleman's primary concern was to approve, or disapprove, of Jane.

We were taking our morning tea at the inn with my uncle when the gentleman arrived, darkening the doorway with his impressive height and then the room with his equally impressive scowl. Mr. Bingley had his back turned at first, but I noted the gentleman because... well, because any woman with two eyes and half a wit could not do otherwise. His gaze fell directly on our party—flitting between all of us until they settled with finality on me.

Mr. Bingley jumped from his chair when he discovered his friend's arrival. "Darcy! I cannot tell you how delighted I am that you have come. Miss Bennet, may I present to you my friend? Fitzwilliam Darcy of Pemberley in Derbyshire. Darcy, this is Miss Jane Bennet of Longbourn, and these are her sister Miss Elizabeth Bennet and her uncle Mr. Edward Gardiner."

Mr. Darcy appraised Jane in some surprise. I expect he had thought *I* was Mr. Bingley's betrothed, and the more open, friendly manner he adopted when he greeted Jane irritated me more than I liked to confess. He was respectful yet reserved with my uncle and hardly spoke a word to me. I decided to return the favor.

"I asked Darcy to come—" Mr. Bingley was explaining to Uncle Gardiner—"because you will seldom find a cleverer fellow. He was a true Classic at University, but his real interest was Mathematical and Engineering pursuits. Why, only last year, he was invited to give a guest lecture at Cambridge on the many advancements by the Arkwright style mills—you know, there is that famous mill in Wirksworth, not far from Matlock, and Darcy has studied it extensively."

I sat up straighter. Truly? A gentleman interested in mechanical pursuits? This, I had to hear.

"As an academic exercise only," Mr. Darcy was careful to remind his friend.

"Of course, of course," Mr. Bingley agreed. "But I find your advice to be invaluable, nonetheless."

"Well, then, Mr. Darcy," Uncle Gardiner said, "I trust between all of us, we will soon discover the problem and put Mr. Bingley's lathes and punches to rights."

"Oh, it is not just those," Mr. Bingley sighed. "I had word when we arrived last evening that the shaker machine is not operating smoothly. We use it to shake the dust and debris from the finished buttons, and it has been shaking a deal more than it is designed to do. Oh! Do forgive me, my dear," he apologized to Jane. "I know our business can be of no interest to you. Shall you find it very dull to pass the day here while we determine the problem?"

"Mr. Bingley, if you do not mind," my uncle interrupted, "I was hoping to satisfy my niece's curiosity by permitting her a tour."

Mr. Bingley and Mr. Darcy both turned their eyes to Jane—one in near exultation, the other in clear dismay. "But of course, my dear Miss Bennet! I had not thought of it, but how very fitting that you should see my family's factory just once. Now that I think of it, I cannot think of anything that would please me more than for you to know where I come from."

I hesitantly lifted my hand. "I beg your pardon, but it is I who wished to see the factory."

Mr. Bingley's face lost some of its enthusiasm, but the most marked change came over Mr. Darcy. His countenance bore a poorly concealed pique that I could only presume was visceral disapproval. "Bingley," objected he, "are you certain it is a suitable environment for the ladies?"

"Why..." He frowned and looked thoughtful. "Why, to be sure, they will be safe enough, while we escort them. It is not thought of as seemly for a lady. In fact, I would never expect a lady to tour a factory at all, unless she has some particular reason."

"Is curiosity not a compelling enough reason?" This I asked not of Mr. Bingley, but of Mr. Darcy, who was still looking askance at me.

"Certainly not," he answered flatly. "But I shall leave that decision to your guardian."

My uncle appeared somewhat uneasy. I knew very well why he had arranged matters as he did, but equally clear was his desire to avoid any unpleasantness with the gentlemen. I relieved him of his dilemma by smiling sweetly at Mr. Bingley.

"Sir, if you are certain of our safety, my sister and I would count it a memorable experience to see with our own eyes what your father built."

His brow cleared. "Then that settles it. I shall call for the carriage."

R EADY TO FIND OUT how these two learn to work together and accidentally fall in love? Pick up your copy of *Love and Other Machines* today!

Acknowledgments

This book would not have been possible without the brilliant JAFF community. I have lately come to know some of the most remarkable people in the world—people who love gentility and goodness, who delight in seeing love prevail and wrongs set right. You have restored my faith in literature and inspired me to keep tapping away at the keyboard.

Blessings to you all!

www.ingramcontent.com/pod-product-compliance
Lightning Source LLC
Chambersburg PA
CBHW032209190626
46810CB00019B/2393